It was a dread... ease between t... though she was sitting with a stranger.

Dick talked, justifying, reasoning, as unhappy in his way as she was, Liz supposed.

He understood that she felt cheated by not having a child of her own . . . he had given it a lot of thought, he realised that it might seem unfair to her, but he was bound to say that at their ages, with their responsibilities, they were better off as they were . . . and this was as much in her interests as his . . . a first pregnancy, night feedings, nurses, their whole way of life turned upside down.

Frankly, and he had to say this, the time for her to consider motherhood had come — and gone . . .

Choices

SUSAN GOODMAN

SPHERE BOOKS LIMITED
London and Sydney

First published in Great Britain by
Century Publishing Co, Ltd 1984
Copyright © 1984 Susan Goodman
Published by Sphere Books Ltd, 1985
30–32 Gray's Inn Road, London WC1X 8JL

Set in 9½ on 10½pt English Times

Printed and bound in Great Britain by
Cox & Wyman Ltd, Reading

To Lawrence and Jeremy, my sons

CHAPTER 1

Waking in her Manhattan apartment one bright May morning, Liz Conrad's first thought was of her approaching birthday. Her thirty-seventh. Her second — and happier — conscious thought was, *Jessica's here from London. I'm going to see her today* . . .

Eyes closed, she moved her arm across the bed. Dick must have left already; crept out for his ritual morning run in Central Park. For a few blissful moments she allowed herself the luxury of a slow awakening. Far below — the apartment was on the thirtieth floor — she could hear the muted roar of the city gearing itself for another working day.

Still half asleep, Liz's mind wandered pleasurably. Dinner with friends the night before at a new French restaurant and the soufflé grand marnier . . . not the office, not yet, although it was going well, circulation up for the third straight month . . . the interview in *The New York Times* recently when she had read of herself, flattered and astonished, as 'one of the most influential women in publishing . . . classic good looks and a down-to-earth approach to fashion . . . a prototype of the successful woman of the eighties . . .'

Well. You could have fooled me, Liz had thought, wryly, agreeably surprised. Dick had, literally, glowed with pride and come home from the office that day with a sheaf of photocopies. She mustn't forget to tell Jessica. She had already sent her a copy. She smiled against the beige and white striped pillows, drifting briefly back into oblivion.

The previous year, Liz had married for the second time. Her present husband, Dick Conrad, was fifty, a prominent

1

corporate financier, divorced, with a six-year-old son called Jason. Liz's first, brief marriage had been to a reporter whose by-lines in newspapers and magazines she still tended to avoid. The marriage had never worked and they were divorced after three years.

She was childless.

The alarm buzzed softly. Awake and out of bed, Liz strode into her gleaming white bathroom. She threw off her towelling robe and stepped on the scales. One hundred and forty pounds. Not bad for a woman close to six feet tall. 'Big and beautiful' was how people described her. She knew this and it amused her. 'Built like a treetrunk,' she said to herself. 'When I put on a few pounds I just expand all over, like a tree . . .' And cramped in the back of a New York cab, knees up to her chin, she would say of her long and lovely legs, 'God definitely intended me to be a giraffe.'

People liked Liz. She had warmth as well as intelligence; she was fun, she could laugh at herself. Even shop assistants put themselves out to find shoes half a size larger or a belt that fastened in the way she wanted. When she smiled, which was often, her brown eyes wrinkled at the corners. All her features were good – short, straight nose, a pretty mouth, well defined brows. Although inclined to freckles, her skin tanned easily. After two weeks at the shore, superb neck and shoulders set off by a pale dress, Liz Conrad would shine at New York's most sophisticated gathering. And frequently did.

But beneath the good looks and the affability, she had learnt to be tough; an uncompromising professional. The publishing world of New York was a hard school. Power achieved, Liz had no hesitation in dismissing a writer or an illustrator; or in killing a story which failed her specifications. As the new editor-in-chief, she had taken on one of the country's top women's magazines, one that had been a household word for almost a century. But dull and almost defunct – failing – before she took it over, changed the format, revamped the content, gave it verve and style.

'And I don't know how they found me, how they even knew about me,' she told the interviewer from *The Times*, smiling confidently. Her previous jobs were grinding

2

editorial positions on topical, up-market magazines; hard work, long hours, not much glamour. And poorly paid. But she had learnt her craft and learnt it thoroughly. And she had been noticed — watched, talked about. Her looks and her personality did the rest. Two brief interviews had secured her present job. She had been amazed at how easily, even casually, it had been agreed. A plum; and all hers. New York open before her.

And it had been a success, a stunning success, even by New York's most extravagant standards. Month after month, now, the striking covers stared up at her from her desk; from the corner news-stand as she walked to the bus stop. People came up to her at parties; waved to her at press receptions and across crowded restaurants.

'Liz . . . Liz Conrad . . . of *Gibsons*' . . . do you two know each other? terrific job you're doing, Liz . . . you're looking *great*.'

And very sweet the recognition was, too. Compensation, she sometimes thought, for early tragedy. Liz and her sister Caroline, one year older, were orphaned at six and seven when both their parents died in the crash of a private plane. An unmarried relative of their mother's, Cousin May, brought the dazed and bewildered little girls into her well-ordered house in Connecticut — where, to the unspoken relief of other relatives, they remained. Although past fifty and quite unused to children, Cousin May took charge, firmly and pleasantly, and raised the girls from that day on. The somewhat unusual household, which also included Cousin May's many cats, was a close and happy one. As Caroline said simply, 'She loved us, we became her life — and we loved her back.'

At his death, the girls' father was a junior partner in a large New York law firm. (Liz and Caroline had only the vaguest memories of their parents. Recently, Liz had realised with astonishment that her father had been five years younger than she was now when he died . . .) There was not much money, but Cousin May had seen to it that after high school, the girls went on to college at Vassar, as their mother had. Summers were spent at the family cottage on the Cape, off the coast of Massachusetts. Since Cousin May's death

3

last year, it belonged to Liz and Caroline. They had always thought it a special place — remembered the hours spent on the worn, wooden verandah overlooking the sea — and had agreed, amicably, to keep it. Caroline, married to a doctor, would spend July there with her four children. Liz and Dick would go up towards the end of August, with Jason.

I shall be thirty-seven, then, Liz thought as she reached for the shower cap. Thirty-seven and three months. Almost.

She showered and scrubbed her teeth. In the mirror, she saw that the thick brown hair which sprang back from her forehead was definitely, and not unattractively, streaked with grey. She grimaced.

'I may be earning a hell of a lot of money, but it's aged me by ten years . . .' she murmured to her reflection. 'Even Caroline thinks so . . .'

Thirty-seven in two weeks. A good job — yes, she allowed, a fabulous job. Running one of the most famous women's magazines in the world. A challenge which she met, and conquered, daily.

'No, no children,' Liz had told *The Times*' reporter, chin on hand, facing her directly. 'But my step-son, Jason, is such a cute kid and he spends as much time with us as possible.'

Childless. An unpleasant word that. Like 'spinster' it implied some innate and depressing failure of womanhood. 'Barren' in Biblical terms; unfulfilled. Absurd that these connotations still lingered.

And thirty-seven in two weeks. The panic points, with which she was now so familiar, started. Moistness in her palms, along her upper lip, scalp tingling; tightness in her stomach; a slight nausea.

Remember. Jessica. She's here. The lovely surprise of hearing her on the 'phone last night saying, 'No, you idiot, I'm *not* in London . . . I'm *here*, in New York . . . just got in, leaving on Friday night . . . business, or so I hope.'

Could she tell her, Jessica, she wondered; unload some of this — inner agony? Destroy the image she projected of total and serene success?

Not to Caroline, she couldn't. In any case, she rarely saw her these days without a stationwagon full of tumbling kids and dogs in tow; dashing, breathless, through

4

Westchester — from school to scouts to her volunteer job in the hospital.

No, not to Caroline, for all her kindness. Her other women friends either had children and were now struggling with schools and adolescence; or, she assumed, had never wanted them in the first place. Or had they? Now that was a thought . . .

But Jessica? There was a closeness in their friendship which she had with no one else, surviving distance, dissimilar backgrounds, odd accents, hurried meetings, shouted transatlantic telephone conversations.

Jessica was different.

And also childless.

She flicked on the radio. 'And this is Thursday, the twentieth of May', a voice soothed. 'Good morning, New York . . . and yes, it surely *is* a good morning.'

May the twentieth. Her birthday was on the thirtieth; in ten days, not two weeks. The panic — dammit — intensified. Opening the bathroom cupboard, she took out a packet of pills. They were neatly, artfully, wrapped in blue and silver. Turning the plastic dial to the appropriate day, she shook one out and swallowed it. After so many years, it was almost a reflex action. 'No side effects that I'm aware of and — well — it solves all the problems, doesn't it?' she had said to her doctor after every check-up, folding the prescription and putting it in her handbag.

She didn't feel that any longer; hadn't for some time, certainly not since she and Dick had married . . .

Dick. *He* was the problem. Next year, Liz, he said, procrastinating, changing the subject, flying off to Tokyo, buying a new picture, suggesting a week in the Bahamas.

And last week, seeing a baby sitting up in a pram she had almost burst into tears. She, Liz Conrad; right on 72nd Street.

What in God's name was she going to do?

CHAPTER 2

'Liz? Hi, I'm back.' Through the open bathroom door, she heard Dick in the hall.

'Coming,' she called, knotting the sash of her robe, pushing her feet into slippers. She went to meet him.

'Gorgeous day. It's going to be hot, hot.' Panting hard from the exercise, Dick rubbed a towel vigorously over his arms. He was very tall — well over six feet — and very thin. He had a clever, nervy face. 'Distinguished', Liz had thought when she first met him; and thought so still. His grey hair had begun to recede, about which he was highly sensitive.

Dick Conrad headed the mergers and acquisitions department of a Wall Street investment house. It was a risky, competitive business played for high stakes. There were deals that went off at the last minute after weeks of negotiations; overnight flights to Europe or Tokyo — anywhere at all — to try to get them on the rails again; and the occasional brilliant corporate strategy that worked, worked superbly, like a row of falling dominoes. That alone made it worthwhile.

But despite the constant travel and the business tensions, Dick Conrad lived moderately. It was always Perrier or Tab for lunch and runs in the Park every morning, wet or fine. Off on a trip — to London or California or the Far East — his jogging gear went into his suitcase automatically.

Privately, Liz thought this exercise mania childish and decidedly boring. She also thought: it beats the hell out of a middle-aged man's face and neck, all this running. If only they could see it.

6

But she knew, from her own magazine research, how strongly the narcissistic winds were blowing through the country. New diets, regimes, face lifts, revolutionary skin care, hormone therapy. Anything with a new slant that was apparently youth-prolonging — for *me*, *me*, *me*.

What was wrong with a few wrinkles anyhow?

Which brought her back to her approaching birthday and her clammy hands . . .

With a quick wave in Dick's direction, she went into the kitchen. Her chest felt tight but she managed a deep breath.

'The Park must have looked just beautiful this morning. A few more weeks of this weather and it will be a burnt out Gobi desert. Plus trash and muggers. Croissant?' she called out.

Dick was in the hall cloakroom, sloshing his face with cold water.

'Sure.'

Deliberately, Liz turned on the stove and put in the croissants to warm. Now where on earth was the butter knife? On the rare occasions she tried, mostly at breakfast or on weekends, she would never find anything in this damned kitchen. Lilly, the daily housekeeper, put away literally everything that could be picked up, neatly stacked in drawers and cabinets. But which drawer? Which cabinet?

Compounding her irritation, she felt tears stinging her eyelids. Coming to stand behind her, Dick was extolling the beauty of Central Park early on a fine spring morning. 'The blossom, Liz, the greenness, the sheer exhilaration . . .'

Liz poured two mugs of coffee — coffee he had freshly ground and put on to percolate before leaving the apartment — and handed one to Dick.

'All the same, I'd still rather spend an extra hour in bed,' she said unsteadily.

He saw her face.

'Hey, what's the problem' He put down his coffee and caught her arm.

'Liz, what is it?'

She had controlled her tears; she wasn't so sure about her voice.

7

In any case he knew what it was.

In any case this was not the time or place.

In any case she could not help herself.

'*You promised*,' she accused, emotion flooding to the surface. 'You said: when we're married. A baby . . .'

'Liz, I said we would *think* about it, discuss it.'

'Well — let's.' Defiant; glaring at him; beautiful with her head thrown back.

Dick grinned. He said, as she knew he would, 'You do pick the darndest times and places to bring these things up.' He spoke kindly, gently. He touched her cheek with his fingertips. She moved, half fell, against him.

'It's so bad,' she said, her voice muffled in his chest. 'Like being hungry or thirsty. Continually. And time running out . . . it makes me dread — a birthday. Sometimes I'm afraid, really afraid . . .'

'Liz, Liz.' He held her away from him. 'If it's that important to you, we can — we can try.'

'When?'

'Soon.' He shrugged. 'Any time. But you know what I think?' He took a long drink from his coffee.

'What?' She pushed her hair out of her eyes.

'I think you are obsessed with the idea of a baby. *Of having a baby*. Not with a child, a child to raise.'

'What's the difference?'

'The difference,' he said quietly, 'is our life.'

Silence. He lifted her coffee mug and put it to her lips.

'Here,' he said. She drank.

'A child would change everything, Liz. We both work damned hard for the kind of life we have. I'm afraid of change. I don't want to lose what we have, the way we are.' Liz put the mug down on the counter. Her emotions still ran high.

'But what about me, my feelings? *I want a child*. The most natural instinct in the world. You *know* that. You always have.'

'You don't just want a child, Liz. Be honest. You want everything. A good life, a top job, clothes, vacations.'

'Better,' she interrupted. 'It could all be better. I could make it work. I know I could. We've got the money for

8

help, private schools . . .'

'If you'd let me finish.' His voice was suddenly cold. 'You do, as I say, want everything – *this* job, *this* life-style, a child. The fact of the matter is that if you had genuinely wanted a child, you would have had one by now. You would have, Liz. The relationship with the father may or may not have lasted. But you would have put a child before a bigger job, a promotion, the way upwards.'

'That's not fair, Dick. The timing. It was never right. Not until now.' Dick shook his head.

'I don't buy that. It's a question of priorities. For women today – women of your calibre – there are choices to be made. Consciously or not, I believe you made your choice, Liz, made it right along.'

Choices. And what was her choice?

As she had expected, she had struck the underlying hardness of his nature. The toughness which got him out of the Boston tenement in which he was born; put him through college with no help from anyone; through Harvard Business School and into a high-flying career in the top echelons of Wall Street. Capable; a good mixer; highly paid. He had 'made it'. But not really big, not in the way he had wanted since he was eighteen – and wanted still. And could still. Especially with her, Liz, as his wife.

They were silent. Liz saw the line between his jaw and cheekbone was taut, his mouth unyielding. She thought, this is how he must face people across his desk when the bargaining and the jockeying – for huge stakes – came down to the final crunch.

In a way, that was what he was doing with her – bargaining, jockeying.

'Another thing, Liz. We're not kids. Let's face it, I'm fifty. And I don't know that I'd even want you to go through a first pregnancy at thirty-six.'

'Thirty-seven,' she corrected automatically.

'Well – thirty-seven.' He was sincere in that, Liz knew. Though plenty of other women were managing it, she thought angrily. With or without live-in husbands.

'I realise that it's not fair to you – and I mean that truly – but I do have Jason.' He loved Jason. Liz did, too. A freckled six-year-old with lots of cheek and charm and a great sense of humour. But it was not, for her, the same. He did understand that. And besides, Jason lived with his mother, Linda, in Boston. Ironically, it was after Dick's successes, moving up the ladder from one investment house to another, after Jason's birth, that the marriage had collapsed. Quite simply, they had nothing much in common any more. So Linda, who had never liked New York or seen much sense in their life there, took Jason and moved back to Boston where Dick had bought a house. Soon after, they were quietly and amicably divorced.

A couple of years later, at a large party, Dick found himself seated next to Liz at dinner. She was looking wonderful in a slinky black dress; she was amusing. To Liz, life in New York made a lot of sense. It was a power game which she knew how to play – and play well. She was on the verge of outstanding success in publishing, since achieved. She had just ended a lengthy and bruising affair, semi-public, with one of the most glamorous political figures of the time. She found Dick bright, ambitious and available. He was also, clearly, virile; an attribute no unattached woman in New York could take for granted in a dinner partner. From their first casual exchange of names – each peering at the others' placements – Dick admired her looks, her style, her breezy self-confidence. To him, even her recent attachment, openly discussed in sophisticated circles, only added to her appeal.

That night, he took her home to her apartment in the Village. By the end of the week, they were more-or-less living together.

In Boston, happy in the small, suburban house, Linda became a school-teacher again. She had not remarried. For most of the year, she had Jason.

And now Liz, of the stunning black dress and the super career wanted – was desperate for – a child.

Choices?

'The croissants. They'll be ruined' Liz opened the oven door. They weren't – quite; and they ate them standing up, forgetting the butter, oblivious of crumbs.

'Look,' Dick said through a mouthful. 'If you still feel the

10

same at the end of the summer, we'll go see Pete. Talk the thing through together. Very honestly.' Peter was an old friend from his early Boston days, now a doctor in lucrative private practice on Park Avenue. Liz liked him.

'OK?'

Liz nodded. She *was* feeling better. The panic, at least, had gone. She might − she *might* − move him. She and Pete together.

At least they could talk.

She believed their relationship was sound.

That was something.

That was a lot.

Dick gave her a kiss on the cheek, his mouth flaky. 'Hey, I still love you − even if you are the worst croissant warmer in town.' Liz smiled wanly. Dick picked up his towel.

'I'm heading for the shower.'

'Don't forget,' Liz called after him. 'Jessica Vane's in town. Just for a couple of days. She's coming here for dinner. So will you try and get out of that meeting? She's my best friend and you've never even met her.'

'I'll try.' Dick's voice was muffled by the shirt he was pulling over his head. 'I'll give you a call at the office when I know.'

Liz heard the sound of the shower running. She took her coffee and went into the living-room. It was after eight. She must get going. She was usually in her office by 8.30. There was some interesting copy on her desk which she wanted to go over carefully. Somehow, today, she would evade the endless detail, the administration, involved in putting out the magazine. She would concentrate, instead, on scrupulous editing.

The early sunlight dazzled the hard whiteness of the room − walls, furniture, rugs. It silvered the glass and steel of lamps and tables. Gashes of colour from the bold abstract paintings became electric.

'Stunning,' people always said when they first walked into the room, 'just stunning.'

'All Dick's,' Liz would reply − nonchalantly, ambi-valently. He had a good eye and the courage and the means to indulge it. All the same, Liz often yearned for the cosiness

11

and clutter of her old apartment in the Village.

Heaven knows what Jessica will make of all this, she thought, amused, remembering Fontwell, her parents' old home in the Cotswolds. The heavy, faded silk curtains; the family portraits; the crest on the silver almost worn away.

Glancing at her watch, still smiling, she took a pad from beside the 'phone and started to write a note to Lilly about dinner that night.

CHAPTER 3

It was close to midday in the New York offices of *Gibsons'
Magazine*. Like the magazine itself, they were very sleek,
very glossy. Floor-to-ceiling windows were banked with
shiny green plants. An elegant receptionist greeted visitors.

The place was teeming. Calls from the Coast, from
Chicago, were coming in thick and fast. Advertising;
circulation; production. There was an editorial crisis — the
first of the day — on the lead piece for the issue which was
being put to bed at that moment. It was too long, difficult to
cut. Should they hold over? Substitute something shorter?

Printing deadline was approaching for the magazine
which, within days, would be available throughout the world
— on news-stands, in homes, in waiting-rooms. Casually
leafed through, a particular article or short story enjoyed, a
recipe or a fashion noted; or perhaps devoured, word for
word, on some endless flight between continents.

Gibsons'. Known, bought and admired by generations of
American women. An influence in the land.

'I remember my grandmother reading it when I was a
child,' a friend told Liz recently. 'She would gasp if she
could see the way you've taken it apart and put it back
together again . . . that article on palimony last month, the
'tell-it-alls' . . . after all those years of boy-meets-girl,
happy-ending stories and deep-dish apple pie recipes.'

Liz and Caroline remembered it from their own
childhood, too. Summer after summer they had seen Cousin
May's — lying on the verandah at the Cape, sand embedded
between pages which curled with damp.

'You always were the clever one, the one who was going to

13

succeed. But who would have imagined, then, little girls with braids, that one day you would edit *Gibsons*'?' Caroline had exclaimed, admiringly, as they stuffed the turkey in the kitchen last Christmas.

And Liz, then, was doing just that — editing. Isolated in air-conditioned stillness, guarded by her secretary, she sat calmly at her desk, head bent, pencil in hand.

Even for New York, the views from her office were amazing — mighty towers and canyons stretching down to the water. Usually, these watery expanses were muddy grey; but today, touched by brilliant May sunshine, they sparkled and danced, alive with craft.

Absorbed, Liz read on, marking each page, re-reading, making notes. A new lead paragraph, ideas for illustrations, a question mark in the margin, a sentence struck. Although quite aware of the frantic activity in the outer offices — the telephone calls, the cajoling, the clacking telex, yet another layout problem — Liz gave her full concentration to the article in front of her.

'That's Liz,' everyone in the organisation said, resigned, admiring. Fending the 'phone calls, postponing decisions only she could make. For somehow, by whatever sixth sense, Liz seemed to know just what it was that women wanted to read about, to be told or told again, to discuss with their men, their children, other women. She picked up trends and ideas, apparently out of the air. Usually, she was right. The increased circulation, the advertisers, the readers' letters, told her that. And she did not spare herself or her time. She worked with the copy, with her writers, until she got the ideas, the presentation, exactly the way she wanted. As she was doing now.

Finishing the piece, she clipped the pages together and looked at her watch. After 12.00 already. She must fly . . . She couldn't keep Jessica waiting, not when the time they spent together was always too short. They had met ten years ago when she, too, was living in London, trapped in a deteriorating marriage to an American newspaperman and a boring job. The marriage had ended; she had given up the job and returned to New York. But her friendship with Jessica — and her family — had remained.

14

No, she couldn't keep Jessica waiting.

Grabbing her shoulder bag and linen blazer, she opened her office door.

'Here.' She handed her notes to her secretary. 'Pam, if you could get these corrections typed as soon as ever . . .'

'Sure. Liz, calls from Chicago . . . the article on second marriages is too long. They're holding it over. OK? I didn't want to disturb you when Ben called.'

'Too bad.' Liz frowned. 'I guess that's that and we'll have to do some quick thinking. Look, tell them not to do anything until I've thought it through. Call Ben now and tell him that. I'll get back to him later in the afternoon . . .' Pam handed her a list. 'More calls. Nothing too urgent. I told everyone you were in a meeting and couldn't be disturbed.'

'Good girl,' Liz responded automatically. She glanced at the paper.

'Dick 'phoned?'

'Right. He said to call after lunch if you've a minute. He will definitely be home for dinner — about 6.00, he said.'

'Great.' Liz handed the paper back to Pam. 'I must rush. I'm meeting an English friend for lunch and I'm late already.'

She was shrugging into the blazer when an assistant editor put her head round the door, waving a long sheaf of proofs.

'Liz, can I have a word? The piece on inter-racial adoption.'

'Sure, Jane. But not now. Later. I promise. We may need it sooner than I thought. I've got a lunch date and I'll never make it.'

In the cloakroom, she looked at herself in the mirror as she washed her hands. Pale, she thought. And too many pounds on the hips. Too much sitting at a desk; too little exercise. She put a comb quickly through her hair; fluffed a bit of colour onto her cheeks, gloss on her lips. Long ago, at Vassar, when everyone else was experimenting with eyeliners and purple shadow, she had decided that make-up wasn't for her. And she had stuck to it.

Lines, too, she noticed as she rubbed off most of the colour she had just put on. All the pressure, the worry, the constant responsibility to the advertisers, the circulation

15

manager. Weeks when ideas didn't come or didn't work.

She straightened her skirt, which matched the blazer, was a bit creased, she noticed. So much for 'pure' fabrics. But the shirt looked good, cream silk, beautifully cut. A few gold chains and Gucci belt and loafers. She'd do.

The panic of early morning seemed a long way away.

'Choices,' Dick had said. 'There are choices you must make.' To hell with choices. She made a face at herself in the mirror.

'I'll be back by 2.30. Latest,' she called out to Pam. 'Keep everyone at bay until then. *And 'phone Ben.*'

'Will do. Have a good lunch.'

'Thanks, Pam.' And she was gone . . . Into the elevator and the swooping descent.

'Lovely morning, Miss,' said Jack, the elevator operator, eyeing her appreciatively.

Either I'm looking better than I think or no one has told him that I've been respectably married for a year, Liz thought, amused.

Across the lobby, through the revolving doors and out into the bright rush of the street. God, but the day was beautiful. One of those few perfect days that fall upon New York in the spring; blessing after winter; a pause before the real heat and humidity descended. Brilliant sunlight, cloudless blue sky. Even the spindly New York trees had blossomed into drifts of green.

Liz swerved, narrowly missing the swinging arms and briefcases of two men, walking together, talking, oblivious of the fast-moving crowds around them. Up to the corner. The lights were with her and she surged over the rough street, part of the herd making for Fifth. She would be late but it couldn't be helped. Jessica would understand. She last saw her a year ago, making a quick stop in London en route to Paris to meet Dick. And it was a funny thing with Jessica. Whenever they met, they carried on − as though they were merely continuing a conversation begun last night.

Surprising that Jessica had never married. She was exactly a year younger than Liz. That would make her thirty-five, almost thirty-six, Liz thought, remembering with the familiar sickening lurch . . .

When she came down from Oxford, Jessica had begun a series of jobs — all tackled with initial enthusiasm but somehow unfulfilling. (They both had jobs with London publishers at the same time and met at a party to launch a book.) At last, Jessica had stumbled on the right thing. Now, she was the owner of one of the most unusual small shops in London, selling individual sportswear and specialising in superb handmade sweaters. A cottage industry, in fact. And the shop, although Liz had not yet seen it, was said to be delightful. Clever Jessica.

But she had never married, despite numerous boy friends and lovers. Last year, Hugo had been the one. She remembered they had all had drinks together in the tiny garden of Jessica's house in London. She had thought Hugo, a barrister, loud and rather full of himself. But good-looking all right. And married. Jessica at the time clearly besotted.

Brakes screeching, a cab drew up beside her. A crosstown bus lumbered by. Liz ducked between an elegantly dressed woman with an armful of Saks Fifth Avenue boxes and a bell-ringing Hare Krishna. Almost there now. Beneath the fumes and dust of New York she could smell — she was sure of it — the sweet, salty smell of the sea. But what a day!

Her mind still on Jessica, she remembered another spring, ten years ago now. It was soon after they met. Alone in the tiny flat in Chelsea much of the time — Jake away tracking down stories all over Europe — Jessica had taken her under her wing. One weekend, she had invited her down to her family's place in the Cotswolds. Even now, Liz could remember clearly her first sight of Fontwell, the old stone house nestling at the bottom of a magically green valley. The walls, she remembered, were softened by sweet-smelling mauve wisteria.

Katherine Vane, Jessica's mother, had made her feel instantly at home. 'We've always loved Americans,' she greeted her. 'Tommy met so many during the war. We've kept in touch with several — and now their children and grandchildren pop in on us here. Usually with those awful packs on their backs . . .'

That weekend, as on so many others, there had been picnics and walks and tennis parties. Christopher, Jessica's brother, a gangling youth of twenty – awkward, shy, fair hair falling perpetually over his forehead. But beating everyone at tennis, partnered by Vanessa, the small girl, dark as a gypsy, whose parents farmed the land that marched by the Vanes'.

To Liz, the Vanes and their house formed a perfect family background.

'You're so lucky, Jessica,' she would say, half amused, half cross. 'You take it all so for granted. You don't realise . . .' And yet, Liz reflected, not everything could have gone their way these past ten years. Although Jessica seemed to be thriving in her business, the Vanes must, secretly, have hoped differently for her; must have envisaged Jessica with a home and children, married into the same sort of background from which she came.

And Christopher. Tragedy there that hardly bore thinking of. He and Vanessa had married in their early twenties, childhood friends, then lovers, who had scarcely known, or sought, any companionship but each others'. It had seemed, as Jessica wrote not very long ago, 'such a perfect, promising match. The most natural thing in the world. With Christopher more or less taking over the farm from Daddy, Vanessa almost a part of the family from when she was small.'

During the early part of a first pregnancy, Vanessa was diagnosed as having leukaemia. She lost the baby. 'After that, everything was done,' Jessica wrote sadly. 'She did have periods of remission as you know. Often, she looked amazingly well. There were times when we all dared to hope – at least for a little while.'

She died two years ago. She was twenty-five.

That poor, dear Christopher . . .

A screeching siren brought Liz back to the present. One more block. It was warm, too. She wished she had left her blazer at the office. She felt the cloth rub uncomfortably between her shoulders. The temperature must be well up in the eighties.

This was it. She pushed open the door and the noise of the restaurant engulfed her. Yes, she had booked, she told the headwaiter who recognised her immediately. Yes, yes, he beckoned – nodding, smiling, obsequious. And her guest had already arrived, was waiting, he whispered beneath the conversational hum.

They walked past the banked greenery, the modish bamboo chairs, the crowded bar. And there was Jessica. Liz saw her instantly. Fair hair pulled back from her face; fresh blue and white dress; lots of beads. Her back very straight.

'*Jessica*!'

She hugged her and slid into the seat opposite. Jessica grinned. And Liz registered two things: one that Jessica looked radiantly beautiful; and two, that she was pregnant.

CHAPTER 4

'*Jessica*!' Liz gasped.

Jessica sat there, grinning; face glowing, brown eyes steady.

'I didn't know. I mean *when* . . .?'

'I'm not,' Jessica said at last, flushed, laughing in pure delight at Liz's discomfiture. 'Married, if that's what you mean. Just pregnant. Due on August 27th.'

Liz gulped. She was genuinely shaken − half pleased, half dismayed. She found she didn't know how to react. *Jessica*?

'Look, just order me a Bloody Mary while I collect my wits and marshall a few questions.' In her crisp English voice, Jessica ordered the drink for Liz, Perrier for herself and two chicken salads.

'I thought you might be a bit surprised. *Had* thought of breaking it to you on the 'phone last night. But I couldn't resist seeing your face. It was worth it,' she added. Typical Jessica − sardonic, direct, a law unto herself for all her quiet good manners. And steely, in getting what she wanted. Stubborn; fiercely loyal.

The drinks arrived. Liz raised hers towards Jessica.

'I needed this.' She drank and settled back, eyeing the pregnant Jessica with a mixture of amusement and incredulity. Then,

'OK. First question. Hugo?'

'Right.'

'But why, Jessica? I mean − you're not exactly making life easier for yourself, are you?'

Jessica faced her steadily.

'Perhaps not. I don't know yet, do I? I've thought it

20

through, obviously, and I can't see too many problems. Not yet, at least. But to answer your other question, I really did want a child — do want one — very badly indeed. I mean, I can't see much point in *not* having one, put it that way if you like. And *every* reason *for* having one. I'm not married and may never be . . . I feel I can cope with the problems, one always has those, no matter what — but I couldn't have coped without having a child. It seemed like — lacking a whole dimension in one's life.'

'And Hugo?' Liz asked quietly.

'Hugo, as you know, went on for years . . . three, four . . . it was like a virus, something I simply had to go through, to get out of my system.'

'I met him in London last year. Very briefly. But what's he really like?'

'Hugo? Oh — very English, public school and Cambridge. Clever. A bit of an actor. Doing terribly well at the Bar. But he drinks far too much. He really wants every kind of cake to eat at the same time. He is, in fact, quite irresponsible. A sort of rather super, very good-looking sixteen-year-old who happens to be grown-up.'

'Married, of course?'

'Not half. Three kids in private schools. Ambitious wife. Actually, it was when he started threatening to leave his wife that I began to see the light. I thought: God, no, I can't have *this*!'

Liz grinned. 'And the baby?'

'I told you. I wanted one. With Hugo. Simple as that. It wasn't even an accident.'

'Presumably Hugo *knows*. How does he feel about it?'

Jessica shrugged. 'When it happened and he realised, after the initial shock, that I wanted nothing from him — certainly not money — it was fine.'

'Do you still see him?'

'Sometimes. But it's over. The intensity. It sounds dreadful, but — he has become — irrelevant.' The waiter arrived with their food. Liz was curiously relieved at the brief interruption. Her thoughts were still in some confusion. Jessica began to eat.

'I'm ravenous,' she said through a mouthful. 'Now

21

enough about me and this baby. We can go back to that later. I want to know about you — Ms. prototype female of the eighties . . . or whatever the hell they call you.'

'Didn't you love it? I had to send you a copy. No one else would have seen the funny side.'

Jessica reached for the pepper. 'Splendid salad. Always one of the nicest things about New York. Where were we? Oh — I confess, when you arrived on my doorstep at eight o'clock one morning ten years ago, looking terrified, saying you'd left your husband and what should you do next, nobody would have actually predicted such dizzy heights of success.'

They started to laugh and found they couldn't stop.

'You were at your most — *crisp*,' Liz gasped, reaching for a glass of Perrier. 'Told me I could stay with you but that I should nip back smartly and collect my clothes because it didn't look as though I'd be getting any new ones for a while.'

'My God, was I that much of a cow?'

'You were great. A pal. Over that — the clothes — you were right, too. Listen, one more thing. Your parents — how have they taken it?' Jessica's expression sobered.

'It *is* hard on them. I do see that. All those questions in the village and snide remarks from so-called friends . . . But they have both been terribly supportive. Mother particularly. Dad's a bit bemused by it all.'

'And where are you having the baby?'

'The Royal Free. All splendidly up-to-date. I'm having it on the Health which has been OK so far apart from quite a lot of hanging about waiting to be seen. Oh — and the amniocentesis went wrong the first time and had to be done over again. Waiting for the results was a bit scary, I can tell you. But all was well. And I'm attending antenatal classes religiously.'

'Breathing? Exercises?'

Jessica grinned. 'Quite right. The house, as you know, is tiny. But at least it's mine. And there are three bedrooms, so in due course I'll get an au pair to help with the baby. The two girls in the shop have been super, rallying round collecting gear like carrycots and a high chair . . . but you know,' Jessica finished, suddenly serious, 'I think it was Vanessa — her death — which made up my mind finally. About having a baby. It was all so terrible' — she closed her eyes briefly — 'I felt I had to have something to hold on to. Can you understand?'

Choices. Jessica's choice.

'I think so. Yes, I can. Is Chris — recovering?'

'Don't know really. He's totally introverted. You just can't get him to open up. He's working for our uncle in the City. He couldn't stay on at Fontwell — in the cottage — after Vanessa . . . And he was so amazing with her, Liz, so strong and caring. They were planning a holiday driving through France the day before she died. Of course, *we* knew it would never happen but I don't think Vanessa did.'

'Can your father manage the estate, the farm, without Chris?'

'Another problem. This worries Mother a lot. His heart's a bit dicey. But so far, he's coping. By the way, our Christopher is now amazingly good looking. All the shyness disappeared. He's much pursued.'

The waiter arrived and Jessica firmly ordered coffee and cheesecake; Liz only coffee.

'Something to get me through the afternoon,' she grinned. 'Wait until I tell you my schedule. But honestly, Liz, I feel marvellous. Terribly well. And I have all along.'

Liz thought: her skin literally glows. There's not a line on her face. She said, 'I know you do, Jessica. I could tell at once. You look absolutely fabulous.'

'And you, Liz?' She met Jessica's direct, rather quizzical gaze.

'Well — OK.'

'Can't fool Jessica.'

'No?'

'No. I've been sitting here, thinking, all the time we've been talking. There's something. It's not that high-powered job which is exactly what you've always wanted — and obviously do superbly. Let's see, what about that new husband of yours?'

'Dick?'

'Yes. Dick.'

23

Liz sat back and waited as their coffee was poured.

'No, not exactly . . .' She took a deep breath. 'What would you say if I told you that what I want more than anything else in the world is a baby?' The words came out in a rush.

'I'd say: now it's my turn to sit and gasp. True?'

'Yes.'

'Well, what's stopping you? Time is not on our side, you know . . .'

'You're telling me . . .'

'And you say *not exactly Dick*. What is that supposed to mean?'

'This.' Liz again took a deep breath. 'That he doesn't want one. Jason is enough. He promised that we would discuss it at least after we were married. *He promised*. He knew how I felt − still do feel. But he won't even talk about it. Not seriously. Awful scene this morning.'

'I think that's rotten. On you.' Her jaw was set firmly.

'Yes. I thought you would.' Liz sighed. 'Dick says a child would change our lives, complicate everything. I suppose it would. But I know I could manage. Thousands of women do, even with demanding jobs like mine. We certainly have the money to provide all the back-up. She looked at Jessica appealingly. 'Jessica, I'm desperate. *What can I do*?'

'Go ahead and have one anyway. See what happens then.'

'I couldn't Jessica. Don't think I haven't thought about it. But . . . I like Dick too much to do that to him. Does that sound crazy? And I think if it's to have a chance, in our situation, the feeling must be mutual. We must *both* want a child, even if I'm more passionate about it.'

'I don't think,' Jessica said slowly after more coffee was poured. 'I don't think Dick is being very fair − or very considerate − towards you.'

'I don't either. But he does say − did this morning in fact − that he wouldn't want to put me through a first pregnancy *at my age*!'

'Rubbish! Look at me!' They both laughed. 'And I haven't yet told you my plans for this afternoon.' She looked at her watch. 'Blimey, I must be off.'

'Where to, exactly?'

24

'When you see the bulging sort of sack I've checked in the cloaks you'll know. I'm here, complete with samples, to show my wares.'

'The sweaters?'

Jessica nodded.

'Two dozen of the very best. Handmade, individual colours, smashing designs. I've raided the shop. Two buyers, one from Bloomingdales, one from a buying agency, came in last week — and loved them. So I thought I'd strike while the iron's hot and set up this trip on the spur of the moment. God knows when I'll be up to it again.'

'Jessica, that's great! Look, I may be able to get you some publicity if they take them.'

'I *hope* it's great. It could be. The trouble is, once I get the orders I have to start worrying about filling them. It's a cottage industry, not a factory, remember.'

'But going well?'

Jessica crossed her fingers.

'For the moment. Lots of nice write-ups recently — in *Vogue*, the evening paper, a couple of mags. And we've got one of our best and most reliable knitters to do exclusive patterns now. Look, it's a battle. But I enjoy it.'

'I must come over and see it. Soon. The baby will be a good excuse. Pretty beads, Jessica,' Liz said absently, admiring the mix of blues and whites which somehow made the simple cotton smock special. Jessica always looked good in her individual, off-beat way, Liz reflected. Aloud she said,

'You always did have style. I mean it.' Jessica smiled awkwardly, pushing back the strands of soft blonde hair which had escaped the casual chignon.

'Flatterer,' she teased, suddenly shy, reminding Liz of the young Christopher.

'No. I told you. I mean it.' Liz waved at the waiter and asked for the bill.

'Can't we be American, go Dutch?' Jessica asked.

'No chance.'

Waiting for change, Liz said, 'Tonight we'll eat in the apartment. I've got a great daily housekeeper who is cooking us a nice meal. And Dick will be there. You will finally meet him.'

'Lovely. I warn you, I'll be a wreck after all those grinding appointments, bearding the buyers of New York. It's hot, too. What a day to show sweaters!'

They stood up, and Liz saw for the first time the full ballooning effect of Jessica's expanding stomach. But her athletic arms and legs were as slim as ever. From behind, Liz thought, following her out of the dining-room, she hardly looks pregnant at all.

They collected the sportsac from the cloakroom.

'All stuffed with my loveliest sweaters,' Jessica grinned, shouldering it easily. 'I warned you.'

'But you're not going to lug that thing all over town?'

'Of course I am, you idiot. What do you think I'm here for?'

On the sidewalk, the full glare of the sun hit them.

'Whew! It's like the South of France in August,' Jessica said, squinting. 'How do you stand it?'

'This is nothing. August *here* is like a steambath.' Liz patted Jessica's rounded stomach. 'It looks nice. Honestly – when I first saw you . . .' And they were off again, laughing helplessly.

'It's amazing, the whole thing,' Jessica gasped when she had recovered. 'The disappearing waist . . . you just *feel* so different . . . and then starting to feel him or her move.'

'Now you're depressing me,' Liz said lightly.

'You mustn't miss it. Not wanting it so much. Look.' Jessica was suddenly serious. 'I haven't forgotten what you said. And I'm going to give it thought.'

'Don't. My problem. I'll work it out. Talking has helped. But only to you.'

'Well,' Jessica said doubtfully, 'I'm a bit worried about you actually.'

Liz laughed. 'We'll worry about *you* first. Unmarried mum. I've got to get back to work. Now go sell those sweaters before you melt.'

She flagged down a cab and bundled Jessica and her sportsac into it.

'Good luck. See you tonight. Any time after six.'

She stood – watching, waving – until the cab was lost in the surging traffic. Then she turned and started to make her way back to the office.

Half way there she thought: God! I mustn't forget to 'phone Dick and warn him.

Enjoying the warm spring sunshine, remembering the emotional confrontation of that morning, the irony of Jessica's pregnancy struck her forcibly. She smiled to herself.

There *might* be a way after all . . .

CHAPTER 5

Exhausted by the heat and rush of the day, Jessica sat in the corner of the long, white sofa. She was trying hard not to look at a large abstract painting, slashes of vibrant reds and orange. It would, she knew, shortly give her a headache. How on earth could Liz live with the thing?

Her fair skin was flushed by the warmth; her long hair, naturally blonde, was coiled neatly and rather elegantly, on top of her head. But the blue cotton dress, so fresh that morning, was crumpled. Her legs were bare and she wore sandals.

Liz, Dick and Jessica had arrived at the apartment within minutes of each other, all agreeing, a little too heartily on the exceptional heat of the day, the bliss of air-conditioning and their need for a drink.

When she was introduced by Liz, Jessica held out her hand to Dick with her characteristic mixture of awkwardness and confidence. She smiled her nicest, her most direct smile.

'Hullo,' she had said, shoulders straight, head erect. '*So* good to meet you — at last!' And Dick had laughed and agreed and said, 'Well, gee, yes,' and 'I feel I know you already,' and 'Liz really misses you and your family,' shepherding her into the glare of the living-room and the corner of the white sofa.

Following them, Liz had thought, irritated: I do wish Dick wouldn't drag his hair over his head like that. It looks terrible. I must tell him. Immediately, she noticed Jessica's stern look around the room and partially lowered the light blinds. At the end of the day, the sun always seemed particularly strong in this corner of the room.

For a few minutes, they sat talking, politely, a little restrained. They spoke of Jessica's parents; of Dick's brief trips to London — always hectic, via Concorde, seeing nothing but the inside of fancy hotels and a restaurant or two, he said smoothly.

They spoke of Fontwell.

'I've heard so much about it from Liz,' Dick said enthusiastically. Only Liz noticed his long fingers nervously drumming the arm of his chair. 'I have been to Gloucestershire a couple of times. The house must have — great charm.'

'The bits that aren't falling down,' Jessica said, rather too abruptly.

Dick got up and walked over to an elaborate bar in the corner.

'Now, Jessica,' he said. 'What can I get you to drink?'

About time, Jessica thought. Her feet and her back had been aching all afternoon. She was tired and thirsty.

'Oh — something long and light, please. Vermouth with lots of ice and soda would be lovely. No gin.'

'Gin for me,' Liz called out. 'A martini. Strong as possible. This afternoon was a killer.' She had taken off her shoes and rolled up the sleeves of her pale shirt and was sitting, curled up, on an identical sofa opposite Jessica.

'Coming right up.' Dick started pouring, measuring, mixing, shaking. What a performance for a couple of drinks, Jessica thought, watching him. To Liz, she said,

'What was so ghastly about this afternoon?'

'The usual sort of panic. A piece was too long and another had to be subbed at the last minute. Threw out all my careful planning. Anyhow, it's done now.' She unfurled herself from the sofa, offering Jessica a bowl of nuts and taking a fistful herself.

'Have some.'

Ceremoniously, Dick handed the carefully prepared drinks, each with a paper coaster.

'I hope that's all right for you, Jessica.' He was looking at her quite anxiously. She had a strong desire — quickly suppressed — to giggle. She sipped.

'Splendid. Thanks.'

29

Settled with their drinks, Liz said, smiling, 'Now Jessica. We're dying to know how you got on with the sweaters. Aren't we, Dick?'

'The sweaters?' Dick looked puzzled.

'Dick. I told you. The ones from Jessica's shop in London. Buyers from New York were in last week and liked them. That's why she's *here*.'

'Oh sure, sure. You had me confused there for a moment. How did it go, Jessica?' he enquired politely. He was sitting in a straight backed chair, one knee thrown over the other, trousers perfectly creased.

He could at least pretend to be a bit more interested, Liz thought. Maddening.

'Actually, rather well,' Jessica was saying. The drink had cheered her up. Her back felt less strained. Obviously, pregnant ladies had no business lugging heavy sacks round Manhattan selling sweaters. Particularly on boiling days. Well, she had survived.

'Meaning?' Liz asked.

'Meaning orders. From Bloomingdales and Bendels, at least. Two others, buying agencies, will let me know tomorrow.'

'Jessica! That's great!'

'Not bad,' Jessica agreed. 'Bloomingdales is thinking of featuring them in their Christmas catalogue.'

'Better and better,' Liz cried.

'Well, yes. If I can get the orders filled. That's the question. I'm dealing with a temperamental band of lady knitters, not a factory, you realise.'

'You use only outworkers?' Dick asked sharply.

'That's right.'

'On an hourly basis? Or by the piece?'

'The arrangements are individual,' Jessica answered, coolly.

'I see. But you have other clothes in the shop? Not only the sweaters?'

'Yes. Some.'

'All more or less individual, like the sweaters?'

'More or less.'

'Do you buy any particular designer's line?'

30

'Yes.'

'The shop's leasehold?'

'Yes.'

'A long one?'

'Reasonably.' Jessica was becoming redder in the face as her answers became more monosyllabic.

Liz knew that Dick would have calculated, more or less correctly, the yearly turnover, profit (if any) and growth potential. She intervened. 'The right stores could give you a good outlet here, Jessica,' she said. 'Have you thought of your own catalogue?'

'We're working on one now. I'm hoping to do one twice a year — depending on how the next six months or so go.'

'Sales over here could help you a lot, surely?'

'True. The numbers are so small — minute to a shop like Bloomingdales . . . but it helps getting the shop known . . . getting the tourists in when they come to London. And it's quite attractive,' she said, looking pleased.

'I'm dying to see it,' Liz said, polishing off her martini.

'You must. We've done it well. You can sit and have a coffee while you're looking at everything — or trying on. And the girls are super, endlessly patient. We're selling embroidery canvases now, all one-offs. Plus the silks and yarns. That's been going rather well.'

'Good old Jessica,' Liz got up. 'Look, Dick why don't you catch the news while Jessica and I do one or two things in the kitchen? But another drink for both of us before you go.'

Jessica looked round the kitchen.

'But where *is* everything?' she asked.

'Good question. I'm so horribly undomesticated these days. Lilly does everything. This morning, I couldn't even find the butter knife, for God's sake!'

'Well, I hope you manage to find the dinner. I'm absolutely starving after lugging that bloody sack the length and breadth of Manhattan.' She sniffed. 'Smells good, I must say.' She began to open the faceless banks of cupboards and peer inside.

'I really have never seen a kitchen like this,' she said,

31

mystified. 'Except for ads. in *Homes & Gardens* . . . it looks so *virginal*.'

Liz laughed. After much searching, she had found heatproof gloves and was checking inside the oven.

'I suppose you think that applies to the entire apartment — white walls and so forth . . .'

'Well,' Jessica began cautiously, 'the word I was going to use was — clinical. Can't say I care for all the paintings.'

Tactful, for Jessica, Liz thought.

'Dick's taste,' she said briefly, removing the lid from the casserole. Jessica looked over her shoulder.

'That looks absolutely marvellous. What a cook!'

One oven warmed duck cooked with oranges, the other a heatproof dish of rice.

'Salad in the refrigerator, cheeses and fresh fruit salad in the dining-room. Any complaints?'

'Certainly not. Anything useful I can do like laying the table?'

'All done.'

Shutting the oven door, Liz turned and faced Jessica, arms folded.

'Well,' she enquired, 'and what do you think?'

'Of the apartment? I told you. A bit clinical. But smashing.'

'Not the *apartment*. Dick. As you expected?'

'More or less.' She paused. 'He looks clever.'

'He is.'

'And you wanted to marry him and you did.'

'Yes. I liked him. We're good friends. It's important.'

'Very.'

'And Jessica . . . I couldn't go on living alone in New York . . . I couldn't take one more of those long hot Saturday afternoons alone in the city . . . waiting for you-know-who, our friend the Senator, to call . . . afraid to go out in case he did, knowing, really, that he was stuck with the family somewhere and couldn't get away . . . knowing that even when we were together, towards the end, we were miserable . . . afraid to break it off because, because it seemed better than the void, the nothing, without him in my life.'

'You were mad about him,' Jessica said briefly. She had been with them on several occasions in London; once, in Paris. 'He treated you abominably. He's a bastard.'

'And a superb politician. And magnetically attractive, as the mags, like mine, describe him. By the way, he has, apparently, left his wife at last. He could still be President, you know.'

'Poor old America.'

After a moment Liz said, 'Anyhow, it's all past history. For me. A nice, quiet life. That's the thing.'

'It wouldn't be with one of these,' Jessica said, grinning, and indicating her stomach. They laughed.

'True. We'll mention the subject, delicately, at dinner . . . here, now do something useful.' She thrust a bottle of wine and a corkscrew into Jessica's hands. 'Ask Dick to open this . . .

Putting her head round the kitchen door, she called, 'À table everyone.'

They sat at a round table in an alcove off the living-room. The table was charmingly laid with an organdie cloth and napkins, fresh flowers in the centre.

'Lilly insists on all the props of gracious living,' Liz said, lighting tapered candles. Around them, the lights of New York winked and glimmered. The sky, suddenly darkened, was dramatically streaked with reds and purples. In the street, far below, a siren screamed.

As it happened, it was Dick who first mentioned Jessica's pregnancy.

'This must be rather a rough trip for you, Jessica,' he said seriously, pouring the wine. 'Two transatlantic trips in three days, appointments with buyers, in and out of taxis . . . when's the baby due?'

'The end of August. In three months. I must say, I did feel a bit shattered towards the end of this afternoon.'

'I'll bet you did,' Liz said feelingly. 'You know you could have stayed here – can any time. We hardly use the second bedroom except for books and clothes.'

'I know. But I didn't want to turn up on such short notice.

Besides, two nights at the Westbury are an unusual bit of luxury.'

In the softly lit alcove, enjoying the meal and the company, all three relaxed after the individual pressures of their days.

'. . . and we're spending the weekend with friends in Easthampton,' Dick was saying. 'I hope the weather holds . . . it's marvellous out there now, before the crowds, isn't it, Liz?'

Through the hazy candlelight, as he looked at Liz across the table, Dick's features seemed less severe, his expression gentler. And he does adore her, Jessica thought, watching him. He's shy – and not terribly sure of himself, either, they should have a child. He should let her try, at least. He promised, Liz said. And now he won't. It's unfair, treacherous.

'This time tomorrow, Jessica will be on her way back to London.'

'That's right,' Jessica said, toying with her glass and stifling a yawn. 'Christopher is meeting me and we're driving straight down to Fontwell. I'm going to collapse there for a few days while Mother pumps me full of good food and vitamins.'

Dick looked at his watch.

'Girls, I'm going to play the heavy.' He pushed back his chair and stood up, putting his hands on Jessica's shoulders. 'It's time Jessica was in bed. I'm going to order a cab and take her back to her hotel.'

'No, really, there's no need.' But she was exhausted – and grateful.

'I insist.'

While Dick was 'phoning down to the doorman, Jessica said, 'I must visit your lavatory before I go. One of the less attractive aspects of the pregnant state.'

Standing with Liz in her bedroom, pushing up escaping strands of hair with pins, Jessica said, 'I really am on my knees. Thank God I haven't got any early appointments tomorrow.'

'Thank God you haven't. I wish you didn't have to go back so soon. You've cheered me up.' Liz was sitting on the bottom of the cast-iron double bed, skirt hitched up over her knees, long legs stretched before her.

'I needed it.'

Jessica turned from the mirror towards Liz, removing the last pin from her mouth.

'I know you did. Look — I like Dick. I think he's right for you.'

'Good. I thought you would. Rum life, isn't it?'

'Meaning?'

'Well — here you are, look at you, due in three months, no husband. And look at me. Two husbands — current one most respectable, you'd agree — dying to get pregnant — the years flashing by — and I can't get anyone, *get Dick*, to listen alone do anything about it.' She was smiling wryly.

'I think you should — have a baby. Try to, at least. Keep working on him.'

'You think so?'

'Yes.'

'OK. Will do.'

Alarmed, Jessica clutched the door handle as the cab lurched over potholes and swerved round corners. The night was very warm and the sidewalks were jammed. Bars, cafes, shops and galleries were all still open. More like parts of the continent than London, Jessica thought.

'Look,' Dick was saying, 'if you need any financial help or advice in the business, you've only to let me know. I'll do whatever I can. You know that.'

'Yes. I do. Thanks, Dick.'

'Don't forget, now.'

'I won't.'

The taxi screeched to a stop outside the hotel. Dick walked into the lobby with Jessica, a protective arm round her shoulders.

'I don't like leaving you here alone. I wish you'd stay with us as Liz said . . .'

'Next time. Don't worry. I'm fine.'

35

'Well — good luck with everything. The business and the baby.' He kissed her on the cheek. 'It was great getting to meet you. I mean it. See you in England — and look after yourself.'

'I will. And Liz.' Jessica gave him her most piercing stare. 'Look after Liz, won't you?'

———————

Liz was already in bed, surrounded by newspapers and magazines, when Dick returned.

'All right?' she asked, as he walked into the bedroom, loosening his tie.

'Sure.' He took off his jacket. 'I like your Jessica. A little stiff at first — she sure doesn't waste words. But she's a gutsy lady. She's cute, too. The way she looks — it kind of grows on you.'

'I'm glad. She liked you, too,' Liz said, taking off her glasses and putting aside the paper she had been reading. She yawned and raised her arms above her head. She stayed like that, expressionless, staring straight ahead, until Dick came out of the bathroom, buttoning his pyjama top. He turned out the lights and climbed into bed, pulling her close with his arm. For a few moments they were quiet. Then,

'What did you think, at lunch, when you first saw that she was pregnant?' he asked.

'As Jessica would say — *shattered*.'

'Does she still see the guy?'

'Sometimes. But it's over, she says.'

'What the hell can her parents think?'

Liz sighed. 'They are supportive, of course. But they're very conventional . . . It's hard for them, must be.'

'The shop can't produce much income. The Vane money is probably tied up in the land. My guess is that she's working to keep the overdraft going.'

CHAPTER 6

On Saturday afternoon, in Easthampton, Liz and Dick headed for the beach. The fine weather held, but in the Hamptons there was a fresh breeze – more redolent of spring than summer. Now, before the Memorial Day weekend, the place was quiet and green and beautiful, many of the white clapboard houses still shuttered.

At the end of the lane, near the house in which they were staying with friends, the wide, clean sweep of sand and sea stretched ahead of them. Taking off their sneakers, jeans rolled up, they began to walk along the waterline, white foam licking deliciously about their ankles.

They walked companionably; clasped hands swinging; talking only if they felt like it.

The relief, Liz had thought at the beginning of knowing Dick, the sheer heavenly relief of an open relationship; of reliability; of being sure of times and dates and places. Those lost years as mistress – the only word for it – of the country's most notorious, most eloquent politican. Not, she could admit to herself now, that he was very eloquent or even very bright, away from the political arena . . . But she, Liz, had been taken in by the glamour of it all. What woman, given the chance, wouldn't have been? His family name; his physical authority; even the odd, rather grating, voice.

'*You were mad about him*,' Jessica had said that week, coldly, disapprovingly.

And madness it was. Muffled 'phone calls at all hours, no names ever mentioned, blank-faced aides to whisk her about the country in planes and limousines. It made her laugh, now, to think that a serious consideration of her life had been locating hotels with elevators which led directly from underground garage to bedroom floors; into the suite itself if possible.

The risk and the danger — the ever-present spectre of screaming tabloid headlines — heightened the intense sexual excitement. Which was what it was all about, of course.

He drove her, one summer night, in his convertible. He drove very fast, barefoot, a cassette blaring. One hand on the wheel, the other on her. Everywhere on her. She moved, abandoned to the thrill of it all, the excitement, the most — ever. The ending and her scream lost in the warm, dark, rushing air.

And back at her desk on Monday morning; cool, with her clean-cut Vassar educated good looks.

Madness. Irresponsible madness. When she thought, after, of the thousand disasters so narrowly missed, she felt like falling on her knees in gratitude.

The soft salt wind on their faces, Liz and Dick walked for miles.

'Let's sit,' Liz said, suddenly. So they climbed up onto the dunes, the spiky grasses pricking the soles of their feet. Nearby, two children were flying a red kite, shrieking happily as the wind lifted it. Liz lay back and closed her eyes against the sun. Fine, silvery sand trickled through her fingers.

'When we get back I said I'd go over to the yard with Jim and have a look at the boat,' Dick was saying. 'They want to get it in the water soon . . .'

'Mmm . . . OK . . . and I must give Martha a hand with the dinner . . .'

'We could get a house out here, Liz. Did you ever think of that? Closer than the Cape.'

'We could . . . I guess.'

———

Later, soaking in the bath before dinner, Liz remembered that Jessica would be back at Fontwell by now. She thought, with genuine nostalgia, of Gloucestershire in late May, the sweet tumbling blossoms, the emerald grass of the hill which rose so steeply behind the house. The peace of the place, the settled calm.

Actually, as Jessica, dear Jessica, would say, *actually*, it's probably raining there — in Gloucestershire — now. Liz smiled, pulling out the bath plug with her toe. And they're all huddled round that huge fire saying things like, 'A *fire* and it's almost June . . .' and 'We've had *no* spring, I never remember a worse one . . .'

She laughed aloud and, dripping, reached for a towel. Of the three years she had lived in England, the Vanes and Fontwell were her happiest, most enduring, association.

———————

Although the day had been warm, the evening was chilly with the beginnings of a damp sea-mist. Liz dressed in a long woollen skirt and light sweater, both in the neutral shades of beige and oatmeal which suited her so well. The afternoon in the sun had warmed her skin; her hair fell, heavy, to her shoulders.

She found Martha, an old friend from Vassar days, in the kitchen.

'Liz. Hi. The sea air must suit you. You're looking great. And I thought you looked bushed when you arrived.'

'I was. That job, Martha. You can't imagine . . .'

'Sure I can. But you always were a career gal. And look at the success you've made of it! I mean, that's right, isn't it? Your choice, Liz . . .'

A career.

Choices. Liz's choice.

Martha handed Liz a lettuce and a knife.

'Can you make the salad while I see to the casserole? Even at college, Liz, we knew you'd get to the top. Just as I knew that for all my fancy education I'd never do anything, really, except be a housewife and mother.'

Choices. Martha's choice.

But it's not that simple, Liz thought to herself as she cut into the lettuce. It's not that simple at all . . .

The month they graduated, Martha, blonder and plumper than now, married James Harrington Cooper III, of Harvard and Harvard Law School. A big wedding, which

39

Liz attended, on a sunny June day in Greenwich, Connecticut. A marquee on the lawn, bridesmaids, dancing and a many-tiered wedding cake. Two years later, a son was born, another James Harrington but always known as Harry; Lisa, even blonder than her mother as a child, arrived when Harry was three. Jim was made a partner in his law firm; they bought an apartment on Park Avenue and then, with an inheritance from Martha's father, the house in Easthampton.

'It's worked out fine for you, Martha,' Liz said, running the cold water tap. 'You and Jim have a good marriage, the kids, and your painting . . .' Now that the children were older, Martha, who had always had an artistic bent, attended art school three mornings a week.

'Right. But we're terribly lucky, Liz. First of all, we're happy. Jim earns a lot of money. We have this house which we all adore. I guess I could get a job as an illustrator – I would if I *had* to – but I think of myself as – well – a homemaker for Jim and the kids.'

'And the kids are great. I can't believe it, but Harry's a teenager now.'

'Don't remind me. God! How time flies . . .'

'Doesn't it though . . . and having kids is a bit like getting on an escalator. You've got to do it at the right time.'

'Liz! You sound broody . . .'

'Perhaps,' Liz answered lightly, starting to dry the lettuce.

'Why not? There's still time. Dick only has Jason and you two get on so well together. Half our class have managed to juggle jobs, kids, careers.'

Choices. Mixed and matched. The modern way.

I want a child.

Why can't Dick understand?

'We'll go see Pete . . . talk it through . . .'

Why did they have to talk?

'And speaking of Dick,' Martha was saying, looking out of the window. 'Here come the guys. I thought they had deserted us in favour of that crummy boat. Come on, Liz, let's have a drink while they clean themselves up.'

———————

After dinner, clearing up, Liz asked, 'Martha, do you

remember my English friend, Jessica Vane?'

'Sure do. When Jim and I were travelling in England a few years ago, you gave us their address. Her parents'. We dropped in on them in the country. Lovely people. Why?'

'Well, Jessica was in town last week and we saw her and guess what? She's pregnant.'

'She is? I didn't know she was married.'

'She's not.'

'No kidding,' Martha said thoughtfully. 'There must be a story behind that.' Then, 'I'll bet *that* made you think.'

'Come here,' Dick said in bed that night. 'Where are you?'

'Here,' Liz giggled. They had all drunk a good deal of wine over dinner.

'Where's here?'

'*Here*!'

'*There*!'

After, blissfully, warm, Liz murmured against Dick's shoulder, 'Martha thinks I'm broody . . .'

He was asleep.

There's hope, Liz thought, drowsily. Jessica . . .

CHAPTER 7

Jessica's baby, a girl, was born late in August. Liz got the letter – barely legible, written by Jessica in the hospital – at the Cape, where she and Dick were spending some time with Jason.

'All well, present and correct,' Jessica had scrawled. 'She's a bit odd looking, but they tell me this will go. Seven pounds – just over. I'm being kept in hospital for ten days – probably on account of my advanced age. The whole business of birth was fairly shattering, although I was assured that I had *an easy time* . . . God help anyone who doesn't, thought I . . . Anyhow, *she* is called Katherine Elizabeth after you and Mother, but will be known as Kate. Short and nice, I think. You must be godmother, I wanted to ask you when I was in New York but felt suddenly overcome with superstition. Christopher is doing the honours for the male side. He came in yesterday and seemed quite chuffed about her (Mother and Dad are, too). Nurses all agog at Chris's appearance – my stock round here rose instantly. I had some gloomy moments, after he had gone, thinking: it should have been his and Vanessa's baby, a child to grow up in the heaven of Fontwell like we did. Nothing in this life seems to work quite as it should, does it? The girls from the shop and a couple of pals have kept me well supplied with gin and truffles. Both strictly forbidden. I know you're at the Cape and will send this there. Time to feed Kate. It's messy and not going well but I'll persevere. All love to you and Dick.' It was unsigned.

Still holding the letter, Liz raced out into the sunshine.

'Dick, Dick,' she shouted to where Dick and Jason were

on the beach — immediately beyond the sloping stretch of garden. 'Jessica had a little girl.'

Dick waved back. 'That's good news. We'll be right up.'

Back in the kitchen, Liz found she was tremendously happy, almost elated. And, yes, thrilled to be godmother, to have the baby at least partly named after her. Kate. Pleasing. And so like Jessica, somehow, to choose a name that was short and definite. She looked again at the pencilled letter. The baby was born on the 21st; today was — the 28th. A week old. Jessica had been a mother for exactly one week. Jessica, a mother. She could imagine her, easily, with older children, playing, reasoning with them. But with an infant?

Liz opened the fridge and surveyed the contents for lunch. She took out two lagers, bread, ham, mustard and pickles. A visit to the supermarket was needed this afternoon. Jason would enjoy that. With a soupy milkshake thrown in, it made a pleasant change from the beach.

'What's this about babies? Who's had a baby?' Jason demanded, bursting into the kitchen, scattering sand from his damp bathing trunks.

'A friend of mine in England. Jessica Vane. She had a little girl. Isn't that nice?'

'Boys are better,' Jason grinned. He was a thin child, tall for his age, with his father's long, slim extremities. His rather angular features were quite unchildlike, Liz always thought. His hair was bleached the colour of straw from the long, sunny days on the beach, racing in and out of the water.

'What's her name?' he asked curiously. 'The baby's?'

'Kate. Like it?'

'I don't know.' He considered, head on one side. 'I don't know about names.'

Liz laughed. 'Well, what do you know about? Lunch?'

'Peanut butter and . . .'

'Jason Conrad! Every single day we've been here you have had the same lunch. How about a nice ham sandwich for a change?'

They faced each other, laughing. Liz had her hands on her hips. She was wearing jeans and a bikini top, her hair pulled back by an elastic band. She was very tanned, a line of freckles along her shoulders.

'Tomorrow maybe. The same today. OK Liz?'

'OK.'

Liz reached in the cupboard for the jar of peanut butter saying, 'Go back outside and get all that sand off you . . . and put on your flipflops. They're on the verandah . . .'

She thought, as she scooped out the almost empty jar; Shades of Cousin May . . . She remembered her imploring Caroline and her not to track sand into the house, to put on sandals, to bring toys up from the beach. And here she was with Jason, saying just the same things . . . I suppose you do with children, bring them up more or less as you were brought up yourself. It's the only way you know.

Jessica will do that with Kate.

And if I have a child, I will, too. Spooning the jelly, she smiled to herself.

She heard Dick walking over the verandah, dumping the battered selection of balls and lilos, used from year to year by Caroline's children, which he and Jason had lugged down to the beach that morning. He came into the kitchen, a towel draped round his shoulders. He looked lean and fit, years younger than his New York, Wall Street self. He came up to Liz, put his arms round her, and kissed her cheek.

'Wonderful news about Jessica. Should we call, do you think?' Taking out two glasses, he began to pour the lager.

'It's only been just over a week. And she says she won't be coming home for a day or two . . . here, here's the letter.' She went on making the sandwiches while Dick read.

'I really like the name, Kate. And I'm even pleased to be her godmother!' Dick finished reading and took a long gulp of beer. Although the summer was drawing to an end, middays on the beach were still scorching.

'Good for Jessica. A daughter may be easier for her — under the circumstances. Looks like her mother is coming through . . .'

'She will. Jessica will manage. And well. You'll see.' She piled the sandwiches onto a plate. 'Let's eat lunch outside. Can you bring the lagers, Dick?' She pushed through the screen door onto the verandah, calling for Jason who was

44

inspecting a crab which he had caught that morning.

———————

When they drove to the supermarket that afternoon, Jason, in the back of the car, was uncharacteristically silent.

'We'll get a milkshake on the way home,' Liz said. 'OK?'

'OK.' A pause, then, 'Liz?'

'What?' Liz glanced in the driving mirror and saw Jason sitting thoughtfully, almost frowning.

'That friend of yours, the one who had the baby . . .'

'Jessica?'

'That's right. Well – is she old? I mean, like you and Dad?' Liz laughed, reading his thoughts.

'She's my age, Jason. Almost exactly. And we're really not so very old, you know . . . why do you ask?'

She knew, of course, perfectly well. But he said it himself which pleased Liz.

'So could you and Dad have a baby like her?'

'We *could*, Jason . . .'

'Will you, Liz?'

'I don't know, Jason. I truly don't know. I would like to . . . so *maybe*. It might be rather nice, don't you think?' Liz watched the intelligent, sharp little face – so like his father's at that moment – carefully, in the driving mirror.

'It would be different,' he said.

Liz almost laughed aloud. Like father, like son. But she said, gently,

'The way we feel about you wouldn't be any different, Jason. We'd love you, all of us, just the same. And it might be rather fun – for you – to have a little brother or sister . . .'

'They cry a lot. Babies,' Jason said, sagely. 'But when it got older I suppose it wouldn't be so bad,' he added, brightening. Liz turned into the supermarket.

'Here we are. Hop out.'

As they walked across the parking lot, Liz found Jason's hand in hers.

———————

Over Labour Day weekend, they took Jason back to Boston.

School started the following week. Before they left, Liz found him gazing thoughtfully at the sea.

'It will be here next year, Jason. Just the same. Caroline and I always felt a bit sad when it was time to go . . .'

'Why does Boston have to be so far from New York?' Jason replied.

Linda and Jason lived in a small house on a tree-lined suburban street. As the three adults, Liz, Dick and Linda, stood chatting awkwardly by the car, children on bikes wobbled and raced past them – shouting, noisy.

Jason stood to one side, hugging his cat, apparently totally absorbed in the warm, purring ball of fur. Hating the fuss; longing for it all to be over. Tuning out us grown-ups and our crazy world, Liz thought, watching him with affection. She came over and gave him, and the cat, a quick hug. Moments later, waving goodbye to him through the car window, she felt the sharp tug of loss.

As they had arranged, they drove back to the Cape for another week. After Labour Day, the change about the place was dramatic. Almost overnight, the hordes of impossibly beautiful youngsters with their burnished hair and golden bodies disappeared – from the beach, the lanes, the drugstores, the boats, the bars. Gone – until next summer; back to jobs, families, colleges.

Tranquillity settled. And the cottage seemed, to Liz, almost eerily quiet without Jason. There was no sand between the rugs or in small piles on the verandah. She found a couple of Dinky toys, socks, a broken kite. Nothing worth sending. The jar of peanut butter was empty and she threw it out. She imagined Jason ready for school, the first day, still sunburnt, with his hair cut and new shoes and neatly pressed shirt and trousers.

'I really miss Jason,' she said to Dick that night as they were having a drink before dinner. 'This house needs children.'

'You're good with him, Liz. I'm often distracted, I'm afraid, absent-minded.'

'Not here,' Liz said quickly, 'not here you're not. And he does adore you, Dick. He can't leave you alone. He's all over you like a puppy.'

There was a violent storm that night. The following morning, the air was crisp and the waves still foamed close to the garden wall. Dick got up early for a long run.

'I feel like it — energetic,' he said, kissing her as she lay in the warm bed, half asleep.

In the kitchen, waiting for him to return, watching the coffee percolating, Liz shivered. A chilly morning. Summer was almost over. She sat at the old pine table, idly thumbing through yesterday's paper. She paused. Despite the smudgy newsprint, the familiar face, handsome, rather florid, was unmistakeable. The Senator, her previous lover, vacationing with his children. And he was a good father; no faking that. Despite his much publicised preoccupation with the under-privileged — the poor, the sick, the black — Liz had found him, in a personal relationship, rather cool. An added challenge, perhaps. Only with his children was he completely at ease. The paper also mentioned that his wife was 'with friends in Europe. Divorce is not contemplated at this time.'

But it will be, Liz thought cynically, carefully scripted at just the right time. He's off and running. The Presidency, no less.

Nursing her warm mug of coffee, watching for Dick out of the window, Liz felt no stir. Nothing. She folded the paper neatly. It was four years since she had found herself saying over the 'phone, 'No, I can't have dinner. Not tonight. Not ever again.' Using his name; breaking that most basic ground rule of their relationship.

And she hadn't had dinner, not that night — nor ever again.

Three months later she had met Dick.

No regrets there.

'I simply can't picture my life without you, Liz,' Dick had said last night, late, as they lay in bed listening to the storm howling outside. He sounded humble, unlike his usual self. She had turned towards him, comforting, reassuring.

And she had, now, what she wanted. A quiet emotional life; solidity; a partnership.

Everything except a child . . .

———————

The golden days, honed by the sharp touch of Fall, stretched easily from one to the next. They went for long walks, read, swam. One evening, they gorged themselves at a famous local restaurant on daiquiris and seafood. The place was almost empty; only a week before, a table had to be booked days ahead. A sure sign that the summer people had gone.

Liz wondered, often, about Jessica and Kate. She would give them a few days at home and then 'phone. From New York. She banished all thoughts of the office; daily, it receded further and further from her mind. The circulation, those magic, earthshaking figures: up or down? She didn't, for the moment, care. Later − next week − she would face it all. For the present, her only real considerations were whether to grill fish or steak for dinner that evening; and whether the roof would survive another winter's battering of storms.

Two nights before they were to return to New York, at about five in the afternoon, the 'phone rang. They were sitting on the verandah, watching the softly rolling sea, reading. Dick got up to get it. No shout, so it's for him, Liz thought, returning to her book. But her attention soon wandered. Watching Dick's face carefully, noting his marked lack of tension, Liz had waited, daily, for just the right moment to say, casually:

'Summer's over now. It's time, Dick, time we thought about a child. Seriously. We'll see Pete . . . when we get back to the City. Like you suggested, *promised*.'

Something like that. However the words suggested themselves. But the meaning plain. A child.

The moment, somehow, had never come. Tonight, perhaps?

After half an hour, chilled by the breeze, Liz went inside to fetch a sweater. Dick was sitting on the arm of the sofa, receiver cradled between neck and shoulder, furiously taking notes. Every few seconds, he barked a question. His body was coiled like a spring. Whoever he was speaking to had, Liz knew, his full attention.

It must be the office − and it must be important.

As she went outside again, pulling on her sweater, Dick

did not even look up.

He came out finally, nearly half an hour later. Liz knew this because she had, by then, almost finished her book.

'Some 'phone call,' she said, looking at him, smiling. 'What's up?'

But she already knew.

He pulled up his chair beside hers and took her hand. She had never seen him look so determined, so full of suppressed energy. And excitement

'Liz, it's going to happen. The biggest deal I've ever had wind of. We're talking in billions. Names that are known in every corner of the world. And it's mine.'

Liz put her arms round his neck and pulled his face down to hers.

'I'm thrilled for you, Dick. Really. You deserve it − and you'll do it.'

'And Liz . . .'

'What?'

Still holding her, he said into her hair, 'We'll go see Pete. Soon. When we get back. OK?'

'You mean that?' Excitement and joy welled up in her. 'Really?'

'Yes.'

All evening, Dick could speak of nothing except the deal − the personalities involved, the lawyers, the difficulties, the alternatives . . . Later, there was another long 'phone call. And the following morning, the day before they had planned, they packed the car and shut the house and set off back to New York.

CHAPTER 8

In the event, it was Liz, not Dick, who 'phoned Pete. She called him from the office one day the following week, catching him, handily, between patients. Recognising the name, the nurse put her through immediately.

'Liz? — hi, what's up?'

'Pete. I need to see you. I wouldn't have 'phoned like this otherwise.'

Attuned to recognising distress he said, 'Can it wait until the weekend — or not?' He glanced at his watch. There were several patients still to be seen.

'Yes — yes, it can.'

'Sure?'

'Yes.'

'Look, I'll come round to the apartment about noon on Sunday. OK?'

'That's fine.' The tremor in her voice came over the wires.

'And Liz if you need me before, just call. Here or at home. I'll tell my nurse to put you through at any time. Understand?'

'Thanks, Pete.'

Liz put down the 'phone, closed her eyes and took a deep breath. Thank God for Pete. She was better now. The attack, or whatever the hell it was, was over. She had just lived through one of the worst, the most frightening hours of her life. Was she dying — or just a little mad?

It began when she came out of Saks. An autumnal gale was blowing over New York that day. Rain bucketed down in torrents, turning the gutters into gushing streams. The lunchtime crowd battled over street crossings, umbrellas bent or turned inside out; eyes half shut against the stinging, slanting rain. In Saks, Liz had bought a smocked dress and coat with matching bonnet. All palest pink, pretty, frothy — totally impractical. But it had looked so enchanting in the shop that she had thought: perfect, for Kate, she must have it.

'Charge it,' she had told the salesgirl, writing out the card. 'And send it, please. By airmail. To London.'

She thought, even at that moment, that it was ridiculous. Something pretty *and* practical would have been the answer. Down-to-earth Jessica would have preferred dungarees or stretchsuits . . . who on earth was going to look after hand-smocked dresses for her? Not Jessica, certainly. Anyhow, everyone knew that the best baby clothes came from England. America had the edge on wearability. OK. A mistake. But made with the best of intentions. Jessica would know that . . .

Quite suddenly, outside Saks, buffetted by the searing wind and rain, she began to feel ill. Her whole body tingled painfully. She was faint — black shadows rose and fell in front of her; she was finding it acutely difficult to breathe.

Careful, she told herself, careful. Don't panic. Try to breathe normally. You need food. Willing her legs to move forward, she fought her way across the street. She would grab something to eat before going back to the office. Thankfully, she turned into a coffee shop on the next block. Rain was trickling down her neck inside her raincoat. She collapsed in a booth and ordered a hamburger and coffee.

Inside, it was crowded, hot and steamy. A juke box blared. The smells of cooking sickened her.

'A glass of water, please,' she said to the waitress. She opened her raincoat and took off her headscarf. She took a sip of water — with difficulty. Swallowing was unaccountably hard. When the coffee and hamburger were put on the table in front of her she knew at once that she could not touch them. It was a moment of pure horror. She opened her mouth, touched her throat. She thought, afterwards, that she had tried to scream, to say something.

Nothing happened.

She could not breathe.

Fumbling in her purse, she put a five dollar bill on the table. She got up and fled, blundering towards the door, scarf in hand, raincoat open.

Outside, the cold, wet rain was a relief. Gulping air, she began to run in the direction of the office. She was panting — at least she could do that.

She had left her umbrella in the coffee shop. Her knees felt like rubber. Was it sweat or rain — or tears — pouring down her face? Her hands clutching bag and scarf felt clammy; there was a screaming noise inside her head.

At last, she reached the office building. She pushed her way into an elevator. Thank God for the weather. Everyone would think her damp cheeks, flying hair and general disarray were the result of the wild wind and rain . . . not some freakish emotional manifestation . . . of what?

Or perhaps she really was ill — physically?

She went straight to the cloakroom, calmer now, breathing slowly and with care. She washed her hands and face and combed her hair. Her knees still felt shaky. She had only been back in the office for a couple of days. 'You're looking so good, Liz,' everyone had said. 'Great tan . . .'

She had felt well, too. And confident. And rested. Now why this? Ashen beneath the tan and the freckles, she went into her office.

'Liz,' Pam called through the door. 'Can you 'phone Dick? And the meeting has been postponed until 3. Herb and Ben got involved in a heavy lunch.'

Liz looked at her watch. A quarter to two. That gave her over an hour to pull herself together. And the meeting was one she was dreading and had been, secretly, for weeks . . . circulation had taken a sudden nose-dive, grumbling from the advertisers . . . all the changes she had made when she first took over, given it style and a fresh personality, all that had worked. Worked superbly. But keeping it up — constantly ahead, coming up with new looks, new ideas — *that* was the difficulty.

Her mouth felt dry. And her hands, she noticed, were still trembling. She had brought a paper cup of water back into the office. She sipped it now. Her breathing was still tight.

It was then she 'phoned Pete. After talking to him, she felt calmer. But cold. She put a sweater round her shoulders and dialled Dick's private number. He answered at once.

'Hi,' he greeted her. 'What a day . . . Listen, I wanted you to know that I've ordered a car for tonight. Picking us up at 7. Remember, there's a reception first . . .'

She hadn't remembered. The Metropolitan Opera. Opening night. Black tie. Dick's firm had a box. Tightness gripped her throat again. She swallowed painfully.

'Sure. Sure, that's fine . . . I'll try and leave early.'

But how? Pam came in with some fashion layouts, placing them carefully on her desk.

Oh God! Her dress. The black Halston. She had found it in a heap at the bottom of the closet yesterday morning. Lilly had taken it to be cleaned. Was it back? She buzzed Pam.

'Pam, be an angel and phone Lilly and ask her about that black evening dress. I need it for tonight, tell her.' She took a pencil from the drawer. 'I've got to get on with this layout before that meeting . . .'

'Will do. Liz — are you feeling all right?'

'Why?'

'You look — pale. Not like yourself.'

'I'm all right.'

Around noon the following Sunday, Peter McEwen, MD, settled himself on the white sofa in the Conrad's sunny living-room. He was a big, rather shambling man with wild hair which was still more red than grey. He looked around, quizzically, holding a glass of beer.

'What do you do with a glass in this joint?' he asked. 'I can't handle so much perfection.'

Liz laughed, producing a coaster and a bowl of nuts. She always felt at ease with Pete. He had the knack of inducing confidence. One leg balanced on his knee, he regarded Liz shrewdly.

'Well, Mrs Conrad,' he said at last. 'You're looking very attractive, very svelt this morning.'

And so she was. Walking and swimming on the Cape, she had lost a few pounds. She was wearing well cut trousers — and her good figure was apparent. Her hair had been newly trimmed; her skin was still golden; she was clear-eyed.

'So I'm just wondering,' Pete went on slowly, 'why that

phone call the other day.' He took a drink of beer, placing the glass carefully on the coaster.

'I sensed extreme stress,' he finished crisply, professionally. 'Was I wrong?'

Liz shook her head. Her expression was serious.

'No, Pete, not wrong at all. I was in − the most awful state. I wouldn't have 'phoned otherwise.'

'Tell me.'

As truthfully as possible, she relived those agonising minutes when she couldn't swallow − *couldn't breathe* − when all she could think of was getting back to the office − alive . . . the noise in her head, the clammy palms. *The fear.*

Pete listened carefully.

'Go on,' he said, nodding.

'Well − then I 'phoned you, started to feel a bit better. Still chilled and rather shaky . . . even Pam, my secretary, asked if I was feeling all right. Somehow, I got through the meeting. We even went to the opera that night. By then, I was OK. But honestly, Pete, I can't understand it. *I could not control myself.* I've been feeling so well recently. The vacation on the Cape was great, very relaxing.'

'So you haven't had these kinds of anxiety attacks before?'

'Never so bad − so acute.' Liz thought back to the spring, to the near terror she experienced before her last birthday, before seeing Jessica. 'These past three months I've been fine. And at the Cape, Dick was very gentle, very affectionate, and Jason was with us which I always love . . .'

Her voice trailed off. They sat silently in the big, bright room. Through the walls, very faintly, came the sound of Dick's voice. He was closeted in the den next door, working. And Pete had announced quite firmly, on his arrival, that he wanted to see Liz alone . . .

Now, he leaned forward, hands clasped between his knees.

'The job all right? Going well? Nothing you can't handle?'

Liz shook her head: 'Always problems, but nothing dramatic.'

'Look, Liz. I've got a few suggestions . . .'

'Go ahead.'

'First of all, I'm going to give you a prescription for one of those little tranquilliser pills . . . and before you start on their well publicised dangers, let me say that I *don't* expect you to become addicted to them, Liz. I do think that on occasions you feel anxiety building up, you would be wise to take one.'

Liz grinned. 'With discretion. No pill popping.'

'Exactly. I believe the episode you describe to be one of acute anxiety, and we must identify its cause. But I'd still like to see you in my office for a checkup. OK?'

Liz nodded. 'I'll make an appointment next week.'

'Good. Now let me ask you a question, Liz.' He leaned back, his long arms stretched along the top of the white sofa. 'It's a personal one — and may seem unrelated. Tell me, have you and Dick ever thought about starting a family?'

Colour flooded Liz's face. She laughed, pushing her hair back from her forehead.

'Right on target. Anxiety detected. To be honest, Pete, for the last year or so — since we were married, really — it's never been far from my mind.'

'You want a child, Liz?'

'Yes. Desperately.' She shrugged. 'Unfortunately, your friend Dick doesn't feel the same. At least, he didn't . . . he may be weakening now. Before we were married, he promised we would. *Promised*. To be absolutely frank, the idea of having a child was one of my reasons for marrying. I want a child — I always have — but somehow the timing was never right . . . jobs, men, husbands. Now, I felt, with a stable, caring relationship, the job fairly well worked into . . .'

'And Dick?'

'As I say. He really doesn't want one. He doesn't want anything — our life, our relationship — to change, he says. Full stop. For months, I couldn't even get him to discuss it . . . then, last spring, we had it out . . . he just couldn't ignore my feelings any longer. And he said — we both agreed — that we would have a chat with you, both of us, and take it from there.'

'So?'

'So — here we are. And Dick in the next room. Working.

The deal's on. The biggest he's ever handled.'

Pete shrugged. 'I don't see you need *me* to tell you what to do.'

'I don't either.'

'At the risk of sticking my neck out, if a child is that important to you, Liz, I think you should see Mattson — he's your gynaecologist, isn't he? — and get on with it.'

'Jessica does, too.'

'Jessica?'

'An English friend,' Liz said quickly. 'You've not met her.'

'So — do you want me to tell your old man what I've just said?'

'Please, Pete.'

'OK. Somewhat unethical. Only for you, Liz . . .'

Liz smiled at him. 'Thanks, Pete.'

'Any time.' He looked at his watch. 'I've got to be on my way. I must drop in on a patient in hospital. Don't forget to make that appointment — or to see Mattson. That's important.'

'I won't.'

'Good girl.' They stood up. Pete put an arm round her shoulders. 'I'll write out that prescription now. And never worry about 'phoning.'

'I won't.'

'Look — I hope you know what you may be letting yourself in for. Our private family zoo now houses three teenagers. Marj and I went out for dinner last night and seriously discussed checking into a hotel rather than go back and face that lot . . . *the goddamned noise*!'

Liz laughed. 'But how would you feel without them? That's the question.'

'As Lyndon Johnson would put it, there are times when it would hurt real good.'

'You don't really mean that, Pete. Marj certainly doesn't.'

'Maybe not. And you, Liz. You want a child. I believe you. But when you say that, what image comes to your mind?' He spoke with genuine interest.

After a few moments, Liz, said quickly, 'I know exactly.

56

I want to see my child – our child – at the Cape – run
down the beach to the sea.'

'*Tell Dick that.*'

'I will.'

CHAPTER 9

Sitting in Dr Mattson's waiting-room, Liz realised that she was nervous. Her stomach was a hard knot as she turned the pages of magazines, unseeing. When the nurse came out saying, 'Mrs Conrad? This way, please', with a bright, professional smile, Liz got up quickly and awkwardly, dropping her bag on the floor.

Still in a state of confusion, she faced the doctor across his desk. She was never sure that she liked him very much. Perhaps his immaculate white coat de-humanised him; but she also sensed he was cool, rather sardonic. She had been coming to him for check-ups since Pete recommended him a couple of years ago. 'He's the best, Liz,' Pete had said. 'Absolutely sound.'

Now, glancing at her chart in front of him, he looked up with a smile.

'I see you were in for a check-up three months ago, Mrs Conrad. Everything fine. No problems. What can I do for you?'

Liz hesitated. Ridiculous to feel shy but she did.

'That's right, but I wanted to talk about – to consider . . .'

'In that case, can I guess why you're here, do you think?' He was smiling at her quite warmly now. Liz relaxed, sitting back in her chair.

'Guess ahead, Doctor?'

'Are you perhaps thinking of a pregnancy?'

'Yes. Yes, I am.'

Dr Mattson had known at once. Like Pete. It must be written all over her. But how?

'I couldn't be sure, of course. But I am seeing – as are my

colleagues – many patients, like yourself, who have successfully established careers and, getting along in their thirties, feel that having a baby is now or never. It's certainly a phenomenon of our time.'

'And for which the reasons are obvious.'

Dr Mattson shrugged. 'Exactly.'

'And they are, of course, my own reasons. The first job out of college, an early marriage that didn't work out. Then I was really on my own . . . into publishing. Nothing very ambitious to start with, but terrified of another marriage failure and somehow all the energy went into the jobs – and the jobs got better and more demanding . . .'

'And birth control methods more efficient,' Dr Mattson interjected, picking up her chart.

'Well – yes. And unlike a woman twenty, or even ten, years younger, I was never made to feel that I was missing out on something very important.'

'But you feel so now?'

'Yes,' Liz said quietly, 'yes, I do.'

'And you would like to have a child?'

'Yes.'

Dr Mattson leant forward, looking at the notes on his desk. 'Let's see, you are thirty-seven now, married . . .' He looked up. 'And your husband? How does he feel about this?'

Liz smiled ruefully. 'I wish I could say – the same. But the fact is that Dick really doesn't want us to have a child. He already has a son by his previous marriage, who is almost seven . . .' Liz paused.

'Go on.'

'It's mostly negative on his side. Apart from having Jason, who lives with his mother except for vacations, he says he doesn't want, at fifty – he's quite a lot older than I am – to go back to bottles and diapers and nurses and babysitters. He likes our life the way it is and doesn't want it to change. He's tremendously involved in his job. Ambitious. And he says he also feels I'm too old to go through a first pregnancy and everything it entails.'

'So your attitudes – over this – are really very different?'

'Very.'

'You've spoken of your husband's negative attitudes. Any positive ones you can think of?'

'Me. That's all. If having a child is so tremendously important to me, he's willing to consider it. Or so he said. That's why I'm here.'

'And *is* it that important?'

'Yes. I think it is. Now. Desperately. Call it femaleness . . .'

'Fair enough.'

'Yes?'

'I think so.'

'Of course a child would change our lives enormously. I accept that. But I could manage my job, I'm sure of it. Lots of women, women I know, cope in similar situations. I feel it would all be worth it. And I can truly say that this is the first time I've had a relationship in which I feel − safe enough to raise a family.'

'You have already told your husband what you're telling me, presumably?'

'Yes. Yes, I have.'

'And does he know you're here − today?'

'No. I wanted to see you first − and then discuss it with him again.'

'I see.' Dr Mattson picked up his pen. 'Have you ever, for any reason had a pregnancy terminated?'

'No.' Liz shook her head.

'Have you ever, to your knowledge, been pregnant?'

'Never.'

He made a couple of brief notes and leaned back.

'Look, there are two distinct sides to this situation. One is purely medical − your medical history and your husband's, risks involved in late pregnancies and so on. I can't, of course, be sure, but nothing gives me reason to suppose you couldn't successfully bear a child. Now the other side, as you're very well aware, is wanting to start a family in the context of your present life, both your lives. I think you want to be very sure of your ground here. In view of your husband's misgivings, I'm going to make a suggestion. Talk it over with him again, tell him you've seen me, get to grips with the attitudes, feelings − and fears − you both have. Then come back and see me and we can talk it through. I'd be glad to see your husband alone, if he wishes, but I would prefer to see you together. Make another appointment today if you like. Give yourself a month or two — and then come back. This gives you a focus, a framework. How does that sound?'

'Sensible. I'll do it.'

'And if you do decide to go ahead, there are some tests I'll be needing.'

'That's fine.' Liz looked at her watch and they both stood. Dr Mattson shook her hand.

'Whatever you decide is, of course, entirely between you and your husband. But I'd like to mention that there is, in my opinion, a good deal to be said in favour of, well, mature parenthood. I am seeing it, increasingly, work out very happily indeed. Good luck.'

———————————

Outside, crossing Park Avenue, Liz turned up the collar of her coat against the chilly wind. Dry leaves blew through the gutters. 4 o'clock already. Turning into a crosstown street, she saw a coffee shop and went inside. Ordering a coffee, she made a note of the appointment she had made — for early in the new year — in her diary.

I liked Mattson today, Liz thought. And he seemed reassuring enough. She drank the hot coffee, watching the people hurrying by through the window. She felt pleased and hopeful. Dr Mattson could see no reason why she should not have a child, he had said . . . And he was right about Dick, the importance of his attitude. But after her outburst last spring (by astonishing coincidence, the same day she had lunched with the then pregnant Jessica) he had been gentle and affectionate. He had been happy that summer at the Cape, too, playing on the beach with Jason; more relaxed than she had ever known him. She felt that he was beginning to understand her longing for a child of her own.

And that was what it was. Since talking to Pete, defining the hunger, she had had no more paralysing anxiety attacks.

Pete understood.

Dr Mattson understood.

Jessica understood.

61

Surely Dick had relented by now. She would pick her moment; tell him about Dr Mattson; suggest that they talked to him together — show him the actual date and time of the appointment she had made. He would not refuse.

But the merger, the all-important deal, was a consideration. If only it hadn't blown up at that particular time, concentrating all his mind, all his energies. Liz had been uneasily aware during the past week that the initial euphoria had worn off. Problems he had foreseen from the beginning loomed. She knew all the signs so well — the tension, the irritation.

Which reminded her of the office. In sudden panic, she looked round for a 'phone. 'No crisis. A few calls. Nothing that can't wait until Monday,' Pam soothed. Her weekly hair appointment was at five. She decided not to go back. *Gibsons'* would survive without her for an hour or two on a Friday afternoon. Instead, she would stroll along Fifth. Working long hours, always under pressure, the odd times she found to window-shop or browse through Bloomingdales had become a luxury.

As the daylight faded, the bold and brilliantly designed shop windows dazzled. The crowds moved quickly up and down the sidewalks. There was a crisp tang of Fall in the air. A vendor roasted chestnuts over a brazier. Liz walked briskly on down Fifth Avenue and pushed her way through heavy doors into Saks. The ground floor was like a brilliant modern bazaar, luxurious and crowded. Making quick decisions, she bought two shirts and a pale lipstick. Clutching her gold-and-white striped packages, she darted up and down the aisles, her eye irresistibly caught by goods on display — a bag here, that belt, a jewelled sweater.

She grabbed a cab just as a shopper was disgorged.

'Hi, Mrs Conrad. You're a little early. Barry will take you in a few minutes.' Cocooned in a pink cotton wrapper and slushy music, isolated from the real world, Liz waited, leafing through a rival magazine. It was pleasant not to have the pile of work she usually brought with her. Looking up at the mirror in front of her, she saw the colour wizard of the salon standing behind her chair.

'I'm dying to get my hands on this,' he murmured, lifting

strands of her springy hair. 'It's too grey, darling. Not pretty.' He pulled it, tousled, round her neck and stared at the mirror. 'And such a marvellous face.'

Liz smiled back at him, her nose wrinkling. 'And what, exactly, do you have in mind?'

'Highlights. Just a few. Here — and here. Lighter round the face.' Liz considered. Today, for once, she had the time. A flippant gaiety caught her.

'Why not?' she asked their mirrored faces.

'Trust me.'

Back in the apartment, she switched on the lights. She was surprised to have got home, after the lengthy hairdressing session, before Dick. His day must have been busier than he expected. She caught sight of herself in the mirror — the front of her hair decidedly tawny blonde — and went straight to the 'phone.

'Caroline? Hi, it's me. I've got something very exciting to impart.'

'*Liz* . . .'

Liz laughed. 'No. Not that. Not yet, at least.' Although it was rarely mentioned between them, Liz knew Caroline hoped she and Dick would have a child.

'Oh,' Caroline sounded genuinely disappointed, 'I thought Jessica's example might have encouraged you.'

'It did. Nevertheless, there are other excitements. I am now a brand new streaked blonde me . . . tell the girls.'

'Hell of a day,' Dick said, coming in and throwing his coat in the direction of a chair. 'I'm really bushed.'

'What went wrong?' Liz kissed his cheek and put the ice bucket she was carrying on the bar.

'Every goddamned thing.'

He loosened his tie, poured them both scotches and collapsed with his feet up on the sofa.

'Honestly? Try and forget it. You're home. It's Friday. Notice anything?'

He pushed up his glasses, gave her a long look and

63

grinned. 'Hey, Blondie . . . come over here.'

She knelt beside him. 'Like it?'

Dick considered, head on one side. 'Not sure. I'll have to think about it.' He took a long drink of scotch. 'What else have you been up to today?'

She so nearly told him then. His closeness, the warming drink, the lights in the blackness outside shining through the gauzy curtains. The safeness; the familiarity. Something stopped her.

'Same old day in the *Gibsons'* saltmine. What about you?'

'I told you. It was all bad. I'm taking your advice and forgetting.' As Liz moved away, Dick put his hand on her arm. 'Don't go. I think I'm going to like a blonde wife for a change.'

'*Blondish.*'

'However you like.'

He bent towards her and kissed her. After a while, Liz said,

'I thought you were bushed.'

'Mmmmm . . . I'm reviving . . . I could be persuaded to at any rate . . .' Lights were dimmed, the cushions on the sofa rearranged. 'It's the hair,' he said against her bare shoulder, 'definitely aphrodisiacal . . .'

Much later, Liz said,

'I thought we were going out for dinner?'

'Change of plan. Why don't we just call out for a pizza — and have another of those nice, smooth scotches?'

CHAPTER 10

'Why don't we go out for lunch — or brunch?' Dick asked next Sunday morning. At eleven, they were still ploughing through a mound of newsprint; exchanging sections of *The New York Times*.

'Great idea. I'll get ready.' Liz was still in her robe and slippers. Sunday mornings were the most relaxed time of her week. Dick, after his morning run, sacrosanct even on Sundays, had changed into corduroy trousers and polo necked sweater. He looked trim and youthful.

'Is it cold? Hard to tell in here.' Liz looked down onto the quiet street far below.

'Nippy. But sunny. Some air will do us good. I'll book at O'Reilly's.' Dick leaned forward and picked up the phone. He had been sitting in the apartment long enough; he needed movement, action, a change of scene.

The meal was pleasant and leisurely. The restaurant, newly opened and popular, was crowded with couples like themselves — immaculately groomed, casually and expensively dressed. All the waiters, goodlooking young men, were out-of-work actors, waiting for a break.

Whatever the recent problems with the deal, they couldn't be too serious, Liz decided, relieved. Across the table, drinking a Bloody Mary, Dick appeared relaxed. There was no sign of the intense nervous irritation he exhibited when a deal went sour or an assistant displeased him.

They discussed friends, an impending political scandal in Washington, an article Liz was considering for *Gibsons'*. 'Hi,' Dick waved and smiled to an acquaintance seated at the other end of the bright, noisy room; across trailing greenery and bentwood chairs; across the tables of successful New Yorkers lunching, at ease, on a Sunday morning in November.

Dick leant towards her and touched her hand when the waiter had brought their coffee.

'I like the hair – now that I'm used to it. Very becoming...'

Liz smiled back at him.

They walked home through Central Park. Despite the sunshine, the wind had a glacial touch of the winter ahead. Soon, it would be Thanksgiving.

'And last week was the anniversary of President Kennedy's death,' Liz said. 'Remember?' She had been at Vassar. She remembered walking out from the library with an armful of books, coming upon a group of friends, their stricken faces. The disbelief. Dick had been living in Boston, then, married to Linda. Both Dick and Liz – they discovered this accidentally, years later – had been invited to the Yale/Harvard football game in Newhaven that Saturday, quite separately. It was cancelled, of course, as the world slowed in grief; the lights of Broadway dimmed; the streets emptied.

'Who could ever forget?' Dick replied.

They walked on against a background of outcropping boulders, greyish earth, and stark trees. Central Park played out its usual Sunday scene. Earphoned rollerskaters, colourfully and outrageously dressed, skimmed paths and thoroughfares like exotic birds. Transistors blared. The exhibitionists paraded. The elderly sat quietly on benches, grateful for the last faint warmth of the year's sun. Children, cheeks whipped pink by the wind, clutched balloons and ran, delighted, shrieking, through piles of rustling leaves. New snowsuits, bought several sizes too big, obscured small hands and faces. One little boy, in particular, caught Liz's eye. He was pedalling his tricycle furiously, shoulders bent over the handlebars. Liz laughed.

'He reminds me of Jason,' she said, 'such fierce determination.'

She shivered and pressed closer to Dick. It was then that

she said, spontaneously: 'I saw Dr Mattson this week . . .'

'You did?'

'Mmm – on Friday afternoon.'

'You didn't say – didn't tell me you were going.'

'No. I wanted to go first – get it over with. And then tell you.'

Dick did not reply. Liz glanced at him sideways. He was looking straight ahead, his expression set. Shafts of sunshine fell symmetrically across the buildings bordering the park. Ignoring his lack of response, Liz continued, 'I've talked to Pete, too.'

'You've *seen* Pete. He came to the apartment. That I know . . . I was there. After, you went to his office for a check-up.' He spoke sharply.

Reckless, open, ignoring the warning signals, Liz repeated, 'Yes, but I've *talked* to Pete, too. About us. About my having a child. In fact, he guessed, asked me straight out . . . he thought we should go ahead. If it was that important to me. He didn't know what we were waiting for. I said I didn't either.'

After a moment Dick said, 'Thanks for consulting me – at this late stage.' His voice was as icy as the wind which stung their faces and blew Liz's hair into a halo.

They stopped. Roughly, Dick shook off her arm, turned and faced her.

'*Dick* – but I thought – you said – I thought you knew, you understood . . .'

'*I will not be manipulated in this way.*'

'*Dick* . . .'

Liz's hand reached out towards his arm, pleading, conciliatory.

'But we agreed, you said . . .'

'Anything I said or agreed was between us. You and me. Not – other people. *Any* other people. Our life planned, discussed, behind my back . . . What kind of conspiracy is this, anyway?'

'*Conspiracy*? Dick . . .'

Liz was stunned; totally disbelieving of his brutal change of attitude; they had been so happy together, so content. Her hand was still on his arm when he said – she knew because she heard the words exactly, never to forget them.

'*You want a stud? Go find one. With your record and your looks it shouldn't be difficult. But not me, lady.*'

When Liz saw him disappearing into the strolling crowd ahead, she thought: I must look crazy — quite mad — standing here like a statue, tears pouring down my cheeks. (Indeed, strangers passing were giving her odd looks even there, in Central Park, New York City, where nothing was very remarkable on a Sunday afternoon, not even a well-dressed woman, standing alone, crying silently.)

But Dick has the keys, she remembered miserably, a few minutes later, as she started to walk in the direction he had disappeared. She was numbed, lifeless. At the entrance to the park she turned right, onto Fifth Avenue; waited to cross at the traffic lights; started walking south, then, automatically, left across town. Through her tears, everything was blurred. She felt nothing — absolutely nothing. Sam, the doorman, had a set of keys, and would let her in.

In fact, going straight to the apartment, she found Dick was there before her.

Abject, he warmed her cold hands in his. He made tea, slicing a lemon, the way she liked it best. He brought her cashmere stole from their bedroom and put it round her shoulders.

'Forgive me, Liz,' he said. 'Please.'

She nodded and even tried to smile.

Why not? Gratefully, she sipped the hot tea. 'Won't you have some?' she asked politely. 'It's so good. China. From Bloomingdales.' She wondered why he went on staring at her like that, doing nothing, looking helpless.

Someone had told her once — it must have been Cousin May, years and years ago, when she and Caroline were quarrelling — remember, there are things that can be said which can never be *un*said. Never.

She was right. Sitting quite calmly on the white sofa, holding the delicate cup and saucer she had known since childhood, Dick's words, those dreadful words, came back to her.

One in particular. *Stud* . . .

Feeling returned; she felt the first stirrings of anger.

Rejected.

It was a dreadful evening, one of the worst, Liz thought afterwards, that she had ever spent – certainly with Dick. The naturalness and ease between them had vanished. Liz felt as though she was sitting with a stranger.

The light went early and the empty hours stretched ahead.

Dick droned on interminably, justifying, reasoning; as unhappy in his way as she was, Liz supposed.

The deal was proving tougher than even he could have guessed. Last week, one of the parties had been on the verge of calling it off. He had patched it up, for the moment. But would it hold? If this went off, he would never, he knew, have such an opportunity again. It was a fluke – a sheer accident, a particular contact – that it had come his way in the first place. His nerves were in shreds.

He understood that she felt cheated by not having a child of her own . . . he had given it a lot of thought . . . he realised that it might seem unfair to her . . . but he was bound to say that at their ages, with their responsibilities, they were better off as they were . . . and this was quite as much in her interests as his . . . a first pregnancy, night feedings, nurses . . . their whole way of life turned upside down.

Frankly, and he had to say this, the time for her to consider motherhood had come – and gone. He believed this sincerely. That he should have expressed himself in such terms, to her, was unforgivable.

Yes, Liz thought, suddenly alert, that was what it was. Unforgivable.

Impatiently, she stood up, excruciatingly bored by his self-justification, by the jargon, by the flat tone of his voice. She was feeling slightly sick. She switched on some lights. They had been sitting in half darkness.

'Look. Let's forget it. Over. Finished.' She picked up the *New York Times Sunday Magazine* and began turning the pages. She felt overwhelmingly tired.

Later, no she didn't want a drink, thanks. No, she wasn't hungry. She tried to settle to reading an article, but she found she wasn't concentrating.

Dick put on some music – Mozart, one of their favourite pieces. The enchanted sound filled the room, lightening the atmosphere. Liz curled up in a corner of the sofa and relaxed a little. Dick appeared absorbed in the papers. Putting her head back, eyes closed, Liz gave herself up to the music.

I pushed and pushed and pushed. I knew Dick never wanted us to have a child. I deceived myself – willingly – over that. I thought he was relenting, changing. I was wrong. And eventually, today, I pushed him too far.

She thought back along the years. With Jake, there had been no possibility of children; their short time together had been no more than a series of good and bad times in between Jake's globe-trotting assignments. Returning to the States from London, she had landed her first decent job on a respectable current affairs magazine. The job, not the men she went out with, absorbed most of her attention then. She was uneasy when Caroline married Alex, not long out of medical school; watched her floating up the aisle in blissful confidence. How can she be so sure? Liz had wondered. How can she possibly know?

But the marriage had worked. Four children arrived in five years; Alex working long hours as a busy young surgeon, often on weekends and holidays. Exhausted, Caroline had coped with tantrums, runny noses, first steps and playgroups. The twins were now delightful eleven-year-olds who wanted Laura Ashley skirts for their birthday, and the boys both sports mad. They were all healthy, marvellous children and she couldn't imagine life without them, Caroline had told Liz recently, wondering why she and Dick . . .?

And now that the family was growing up, Caroline was considering getting a master's in French and perhaps teaching.

Like Martha, taking up her art again.

But Liz had worked professionally, worked hard; been noticed; achieved; and been admired for it. She couldn't, honestly, regret that. In fact, she had often wondered how on earth Caroline would get through another winter of croups and colds, been grateful that she didn't have to wrestle with finding a child the right school or worry about a particular behavioural problem.

And in her early thirties, already into a bigger job, she had met the Senator. A current boyfriend had brought her along to dinner with a group of media acquaintances one sweltering July evening in New York. The Senator was present and had noticed her at once. 'Hi there, haven't we met somewhere before?' A drink in one hand; the other, almost immediately, round her shoulders. They had sat together during dinner. And so began, for Liz, three years of emotional slavery; a silent telephone and lonely weekends balanced by encounters of almost hysterical excitement.

Jessica, her one confidante in this relationship, had disapproved from the first. 'He's a bastard,' she had commented soon after meeting him. 'You do know this, of course?'

She did; but it hadn't mattered – enough.

No trust, no safety, there. A wife, children; callously, casually, other women. Through it all, she had held onto her job; that, at least, had never suffered. It had been the one thing that kept her sane.

Soon after it was over she had met Dick.

Before, she had never felt safe with a man.

Did she now?

She sighed. The irony of her situation struck Liz forcibly. And it must apply to so many women of about her age today – in London, Paris, New York, capital cities where bright, ambitious women got on in life these days, in the liberated '80s. Women who, only decades before, would have been prisoners of their own bodies. Frequently pregnant, whatever their social status; debilitated; facing dangerous childbirth. Barred from most professional opportunities, in any case.

And yet for all the pills and all the options, nature still retained the upper hand. Was there, yet, a pill to banish femaleness – or whatever it was that made her, Liz, weak at the knees when she saw a baby sitting up in a pram on East 72nd St?

71

True, a motivated woman could have children young and still manage to hang onto a career. Her life hadn't worked out like that. Now, no matter how much she achieved, was lunched, fêted, appeared on chat shows – the magic number forty flashed ahead. If she wanted to have a child, it was now or never.

She had an older husband who already had a child; a settled and expensive life-style; tough professional responsibilities.

It seemed that it was to be – never.

They had been, she and Dick, such good friends; known deep affection, sexual fulfilment, perhaps love. In one stroke, standing in Central Park that afternoon, he had both damaged her pride and destroyed her hopes, high hopes, of motherhood. Rejected her femininity.

The music ended. Liz opened her eyes. Dick had put on another record, instantly recognisable, Rubinstein playing Chopin.

Choices, Dick had said last year, there are choices which women like herself must make. But had she ever chosen, consciously, not to have a child; to put her career ahead of motherhood? She honestly believed not. It was a choice she felt she had never had until now.

Jessica had made a choice; made it differently and courageously. She had wanted a child – desperately. And now there was Kate.

The 'phone rang in Dick's study and he dashed to answer it, taking his glass of scotch with him.

Alone in the room, desolate amid the glorious music, Liz realised there was nothing for it but a hot bath, a sleeping pill and an early night. And another round at the office tomorrow.

CHAPTER 11

Jason came to New York for Thanksgiving. He arrived the evening before the big day. Liz hardly recognised him when he walked into the apartment with Dick, who had brought him down from Boston on the shuttle. He had grown taller and seemed even thinner. His small, angular face was all eyes. Winter pale, he seemed quite different to the bronzed child they had returned from the Cape last summer.

He chattered excitedly as Liz removed anorak, gloves, scarf and assorted comics. He had a nasty cough. He had had a cold, he explained, and on the way down, in the plane, one of his ears was hurting.

Mention of the plane set him off. As Dick confirmed, the journey had been a rough one. They had flown through a severe storm and for a few seconds the 'plane had lost height dramatically. Racing from room to room, nervous, excitable, Jason could talk of nothing else.

'We dropped, Liz. Right down. Look . . . like this.' He stood up on a chair in her bedroom and dive-bombed to the floor, landing in a small, crumpled heap at her feet.

'Never mind. It was only a storm and you came down safely,' Liz said, soothing, helping him up. 'Lilly is cooking fried chicken for dinner. Let's go and see how she's getting on. Then we can unpack your bag.'

Dick had gone into his study. He had a few papers he wanted to look through, he said. And only the office had called, was that right? No other messages?

'None,' Liz replied briefly.

Jason went ahead of her towards the kitchen — hopping, half running — talking breathlessly all the while. Liz noticed

73

that his shoulder-blades were so thin that they stuck out beneath his navy jersey. He was blinking a lot, too, and almost stuttering he spoke so fast.

It's bad for him, Liz worried, shuttling between homes like this. He's too intense a child, too highly strung, to take the change of cast, change of backgrounds, in his stride.

But he lived with his mother, with Linda; which was doubtless correct. Liz knew so little about her from their brief, careful conversations concerning Jason's visits. Dick rarely mentioned her, although Liz surmised that it was Linda's salary as a teacher which had helped Dick get started, made Harvard Business School a possibility. 'Quiet,' was how he described her. A quiet woman who liked a quiet life. A small suburban house. A few friends.

They were married for years before Jason was born; Dick totally dedicated to his work. Soon afterwards, they separated. Liz doubted that Jason could have any clear memories of them living together as a family. She fancied that Jason mentioned his mother less than she would have expected; but perhaps this was out of innate deference to her – his step-mother. Liz found it hard to suppress all feelings of possessiveness. As a personality, Jason appealed to her; they laughed together; her fondness for him was quite apart from the fact that he was Dick's son.

In the kitchen, they found Lilly moving about in her calm, deft way. As usual, her white uniform was immaculate. I should have changed, Liz thought guiltily, looking down at her old grey flannel slacks. She had been working at home that day. Lilly rarely stayed on to serve a meal unless they had a dinner-party.

'Lemon meringue pie!' Jason shouted, rubbing his stomach. 'Yummee . . .'

'Wash your hands and go and tell Dad that dinner is almost ready,' Liz told him, taking a covered vegetable dish from Lilly.

Jason came into the dining-room a few minutes later, plonking himself down at the table.

'Hands washed. Look.' He held them up for inspection. 'Dad says he has to make a 'phone call. To abroad. And it may take a while. He says we're to begin.'

He drooped visibly.

Lilly handed him his plate and asked him what he would have to drink.

'Milk — or coke, Jason?'

Jason glanced quickly across at Liz who said, 'Coke's fine, Lilly. Oh — and could you keep the chicken warm for Mr Conrad, please? He's making a business call. And I'll have a glass of wine. We'll have a feast, Jason. Together.'

Lilly had lit the green candles and put small bowls of candy at each place. The table had a festive air.

Dick should be here tonight. Liz felt her anger growing. He should have made the effort to eat with us this first night. Jason, who adored him, minded, Liz knew. He had gone suddenly quiet.

One day — one day soon — she would rip that damn telephone right out of its socket. Is there no way of getting his priorities straight? she thought helplessly.

'What shall we do tomorrow, Jason?' Liz asked, watching him tucking into his chicken, cutting it awkwardly. Then, 'Let's eat it with our fingers . . . it's easier and tastes better that way.'

'Will Dad always be so busy, Liz? I mean his whole, whole life?' Jason asked through a mouthful of chicken.

Liz smiled across at him. His hair is badly cut and much too short, she noticed irrelevantly. She said, 'No. Not always, Jason. He has something specially big on at the office now. It will be finished soon. By spring, anyhow.'

Towards the end of the meal, fortified by a second glass of wine, Liz noticed that Jason was no longer pale; his face was quite flushed. He coughed frequently. The lemon meringue pie — his favourite, specially prepared by Lilly every time he stayed with them — was almost untouched. He fidgeted with the candy by his plate.

'Are you feeling OK Jason?'

He shook his head. 'Headache, Liz. And my ear feels funny again.' He put his hand over it. Liz got up from the table.

'Come on, Jason. You've had a long day. Let's get your case unpacked — put your pyjamas on and we can watch television until it's bedtime.'

While he was cleaning his teeth, she conferred with Lilly in the kitchen.

'I'll come and feel his forehead. I always knows when a child has a fever . . . he certainly did seem excitable.'

After a quick touch, Lilly went straight to get the thermometer. Leaving Jason, thermometer in mouth, gazing at the television screen, making him promise not to move or take it out, Liz went to Dick's study. He was writing on a yellow note pad and looked up as she came in.

'Lilly and I think Jason has a fever,' she said coldly. 'He's also complaining of an earache. I'm taking his temperature now. Unless it's extremely high, I'll wait until the morning to call Pete.'

Dick got up.

'Poor kid. He did say he had a funny feeling in his ear on the plane . . . I'll come right away.'

Liz barred his way at the door.

'But before you do, I'd like to say that your failure to sit down to dinner with your son tonight was a disgrace. Have you completely forgotten how to treat other people? It was insensitive − and cruel.'

She turned quickly and went straight back to Jason.

'I'll get Dr McEwen in the morning, Lilly.' Liz frowned. She was crunching an aspirin in a small amount of orange juice. 'The fever isn't very high, but I hope that ear isn't going to flare up in the night.'

Lilly was collecting her things, putting on her hat, getting ready to go home. 'Would you like me to stay over, Mrs Conrad? I'd be glad to.'

Liz replaced the juice in the refrigerator.

'Thanks, Lilly, but we'll be fine. I'm afraid Jason won't be able to do justice to your turkey and pumpkin pie tomorrow.'

In their bedroom, Liz found Dick and Jason sitting on their bed, watching television. Jason was curled up next to his father, yawning.

'Here, Jason. Drink this. It's only aspirin.' Jason downed it with a grimace.

'The ear hurts, Liz. But I think I'll go to sleep now.'

Liz settled him in the spare bedroom, Jason's room when he stayed with them, where the snoopy covers were brought out whenever he visited.

'I'll leave the light on in the hall. Call me if you want me. Okay?' She gave him a quick kiss. 'Night, night. I'll send Dad in now.'

Dick had dinner in the kitchen while Liz made coffee.

'Linda didn't say anything about him being unwell when I picked him up. But he was coughing all the way down.'

'These things blow up quickly with kids.' She poured the coffee, but looked worried. It was the first time they had spoken normally since Sunday.

Liz was thinking, it can't be easy, raising a child and keeping a career going at the same time. It can't be. All the reasoning, all the peppy articles in magazines like *Gibsons'*, don't tell you how not to tear yourself apart when you're in a meeting and wondering what's happening to a seven-year-old back home who's in bed with an earache. Whoever was sitting on his bed, bringing him juice, however competent, it wasn't you – his mother.

That was the crunch; it must be.

Thousands and thousands of women coped with these feelings. In a sudden access of doubt, Liz wondered – could I?

Jason had a restless night. Liz heard him coughing in the early hours and went in to check. His forehead was burning. She gave him another aspirin and stayed with him for a few minutes as he tried to get comfortable. She knew, although he did not say so, that his ear was hurting badly. When he lay still, she tiptoed from the room.

Pete came at nine the next morning.

'I'm sorry, Pete . . . ruining your Thanksgiving,' Liz said, meeting him at the door of the apartment.

'Poor Jason, not me. Let's have a look at him.'

Pete diagnosed an acute ear infection and gave him a shot immediately.

'That should get things started.' He opened his bag. 'I'll leave some antibiotics and something for that cough. And a prescription. Keep on with the aspirin every four hours.' On his way out, he said to Liz, 'That's a sick kid you've got there. He needed treatment. Believe me. Keep him in bed. Liquids only or he'll start vomiting. I'll come and take another look at him tonight. Sixish.' He wrapped himself in a huge sheepskin coat.

'Thanks, Pete.'

'Look, it's an excuse to get away from the home front, a houseful of kids playing rock music. Did you see Mattson, by the way?' He glanced towards the closed door of Dick's study.

'Yes.'

'And is the old man co-operating?'

'He doesn't want a child, Pete. And he won't. Not another one. He told me so — in no uncertain terms. That's that.'

Pete put an arm round her shoulders. 'Mind very much?'

'Yes.'

'He's a goddamned fool.'

———————

Jason's illness was quite severe. After Pete left that night, Liz suggested that Dick 'phoned Linda in Boston. 'She's his mother. She should know. He won't be well enough to travel back on Sunday and he's not leaving until Pete agrees.'

———————

By Sunday evening, Jason was on the mend and out of bed. The fever which had zigzagged up and down for days had finally gone. He 'phoned his mother, asking in detail about his cat. Where was he? Was he asleep? He and Liz did intricate puzzles, played board games and watched television together. Once he had begun to recover, Liz rather enjoyed her housebound vacation from the office.

Dick worked as hard as ever. 'Phone calls from all over the world; messengers arriving to fetch or deliver bulky manila envelopes. A breakfast meeting at the Plaza at 8. But every evening the three of them had an early dinner together and Dick dispensed the nightly dose of medication before Jason's bedtime.

'How about a few days in the islands over New Year?' Dick asked them both on Wednesday while they were eating. The following day, with Pete's permission, they were driving Jason back to Boston.

'Sounds great,' Liz replied. 'Jason?'

'I don't know Liz . . .' He sounded doubtful.

'The weather should be good. You could swim in the pool or the sea. And the beaches are beautiful.'

'Not like the Cape,' Jason said quickly. 'And that's where I'd like to go best.'

'But not in the middle of winter, Jason.' Dick poured a glass of wine for Liz and himself.

'But why not? I've never seen the sea when it's really wild and stormy.' He jumped up from the table, eyes alight. 'Waves like this, Dad.' He stood on tiptoe, hands raised high above his head. 'As high as our house, maybe, and *crashing*!'

Liz laughed at him and told him to calm down and get on with his meal.

'It would be terribly cold there, Jason. And we could get snowed in . . . Still, the house is fully winterised.' She turned to Dick. 'Caroline and Alex spent a week there last February. Remember?'

'It's a crazy idea,' Dick said with finality.

A few days later, Dick was to leave for Paris. He would be away for about a week, he said, as Liz piled shirts into his case. He had to spend at least a day in London. He would try and see Jessica. Or give her a call. Did he have her number? He would be at the Ritz in Paris, Claridges in London.

'Lucky you,' Liz said coolly.

The night before he left, in bed, he reached towards her.

79

'I want to make love to you, Liz.' His voice was muffled against her bare shoulder.

'No,' she said briefly. And again, 'No.'

Dick sighed and turned on his back. Hands beneath his head, he stared up at the ceiling. Beams of light, the city's lights, flickered in the blackness.

'Is it that Sunday? What I said — in the Park?'

'Yes.'

'I apologised. Deeply. I could only do that.'

'For what you said?'

'For the *way* I said it.'

'But you meant it?'

'Yes.'

'You're a very hard man, Dick.' She was lying on her side; eyes wide open; crying. But not moving, not making a sound.

In a little while Dick said. 'Thank you for looking after Jason. I'm really grateful. You took such good care of him.'

'I liked it. I was sorry he was sick. It must have been a disappointing trip for him. But I liked looking after him.'

He would know now — that she was crying.

When you live with someone, intimately, you both know so much

He knew.

He began to touch her; soon, she moved. Swallowing bitter words, softened, throbbing, where he touched her . . .

That, too, he knew.

'Liz, I love you . . . I'm sorry, sorry . . .'

But she was lost in the ritual of their love-making.

Much later, Dick whispered, 'Liz, look . . . I *have* been thinking . . . maybe . . .' Given the time and place, his voice had an unexpected note of urgency. 'Liz . . . can we talk . . .?'

But he saw that she had already slipped silently into sleep.

CHAPTER 12

The next Saturday, when Dick was in Europe, Caroline brought the twins into the city for the day.

'Great. A shopping expedition and we'll have lunch. I haven't seen any of you for weeks,' Liz told Caroline on the 'phone.

Although it was only early December, New York was already in the grip of hysterical Christmas fever. The store windows along Fifth Avenue had turned into brilliant mechanised showcases. That Saturday morning, the sidewalks were jammed. The more sentimental carols gushed from loudspeakers and charitable Santa Clauses – absurdly bearded – jangled bells and stamped their boots in the freezing cold.

It's bizarre, Liz thought, as she pushed her way through the crowds. And weeks still to go before it's all over.

She met Caroline and the twins, early, outside Bloomingdales. By noon, they were exhausted. Holding on to both the girls, Liz shepherded them all across the street to a quiet restaurant.

'God, what a crush . . . Let's have something to eat before we face those herds again. Girls?'

Watching Laura and Lisa, identical in their pleated skirts and matching sweaters, long fair hair tied back neatly, Liz thought: they do Caroline credit. Natural, mannerly and well-behaved. They totally belie the European myth of the brattish American child. Would Kate be like them – when she was twelve? In answer to her inevitable seasonal question they said, in unison,

'What we'd really love, Aunt Liz, are sweaters. Shetlands

with Fair Isle yokes. They're *adorable* . . .'

'Girls . . .' from their mother.

'Then you shall have them. From Dick and me. What colour? Ah, here comes some coffee.'

Revived, they collected their shopping bags and set off towards Saks.

'Why don't we walk across town and get the bus down Fifth?' Caroline suggested. Chatting, their fair heads bent towards each other, the twins walked on ahead. 'And we can talk – for once,' she added.

'They are such sweet kids,' Liz said, watching them. 'So unaffected. They do you credit, Caro.'

'Now, maybe . . . but remember when they were little: *And* the boys?'

Glad to be on their own, without husbands or children, they laughed. They thought of the chaotic weekends Liz had spent at home with them, forever bathing or dressing or changing one child or the other; thankful to get back to New York on Sunday evenings.

Although only a year apart in age, Liz and Caroline were quite unalike, Caroline much the smaller and darker. Decidedly the less good looking of the two. But they both had wide, generous smiles; a willingness to see the funny side of things.

'You've always liked kids. Even those weekends didn't put you off. Seriously, haven't you and Dick ever thought?'

'I'd love one. I'd do anything to have a baby, Caro. Now – before it's too late. Dick won't hear of it. Simple as that.'

'But if *you* want one . . . I mean, why not? Somehow I always thought you would.'

'So did I. But apparently it's not to be.'

It was a subject too painful to discuss even with Caroline – and she said so.

In silence, they crossed Park Avenue. The twins were still in sight ahead.

'Any chance of Jason joining us all for Christmas? We'd love to have him. You and Dick know that.'

Liz shook her head.

'Thanks, Caro. But he'll be with his mother. He comes to us for the rest of the vacation though. We'll come out and see you for the day. It would be nice for Jason to be with the kids.'

'What about his mother — Linda?' Caroline asked, curious.

'I hardly know anything about her. Which rather surprises me sometimes. Dick doesn't talk about her. Jason doesn't much, either. Whenever I meet her, very briefly, she seems pleasant. Shy. A bit colourless. She teaches school. Really, that's all I know.'

'She certainly doesn't sound the ideal wife for Dick.'

They laughed. 'You can say that again,' Liz agreed. 'Or vice versa.'

'Does Jason look like her?'

'No. More like Dick. But she's rather pretty. Long, dark hair. Nice features.'

'She never makes Jason's visits a problem?'

'Never. And she's very precise about times and plans. His clothes are always neatly packed.'

'But she's somehow like a missing person?'

'Exactly.'

That evening, at about 7, the 'phone rang in the apartment. It was Dick, from London.

'I got in this morning from Paris. I'm meeting the British contingent for dinner here tonight, but I've just spoken to Jessica. I'm dropping by her house for a drink first.'

'Give her my love. Tell her I'll 'phone tomorrow. I was going to anyhow.'

'Will do, Liz. So what are you doing over there?'

'Drinking.' She had just opened a bottle of chilled white wine. 'I spent the day with Caroline and the twins. It was fun.'

'In Westchester?'

'No. Here. They came in for some shopping.'

There was a brief, expensive silence.

'How is the great merger coming?'

'OK. Cracking along very smoothly, in fact. Agreements drawn up on all sides, the legal boys jumping . . . so far, so

83

good. I'll be back next week definitely. Not just sure of the day yet.'

———————

The next day, Sunday, and another transatlantic 'phone call. From Liz, this time, to Jessica in her small house in Chelsea.

'Hullo, hullo . . . and you timed it just right. For once, Kate isn't yelling.'

'For once?'

'That's right . . . it's been a rough three months, I can tell you.'

'But Kate's fine. And you're surviving. She'll get easier.'

'Oh sure . . . look, Dick was here last night . . .'

'I know. He rang. Said he was going to see you.'

'I can't understand him at all. Honestly. That jargon . . .'

'What?'

'Words with strange endings . . . everything sounding very complicated. You know. *Jargon*.'

'Oh – jargon. Yes. That's Dick. He's got it all worked out. Life, everything.'

'Nothing he said – but I had the feeling that things weren't too rosy between you.'

'You could say that.'

'Mmm . . . and can I guess a particular bone of contention?'

'You can.'

'Pity . . . look, I'm taking Kate to Fontwell for ten blissful days over Christmas. Mother is sure to have another go at me over the christening .'

'*Not* to take place without me, please.'

'Certainly not – and Christopher says he needs your support . . . what about the spring?'

'Sounds fine to me – and I'll have all those minty-fresh spring issues of the mag, behind me . . . if I have the strength to pull them all together.'

'You will. Look, let's aim for late May, then. The weather might be good – and it's the loveliest time of year at Fontwell.'

———————

In the afternoon, Liz walked over to Martha and Jim's apartment for a cup of tea and a chat. When she came back, she found herself dialling Boston. Jason answered.

'Hi, Jason, it's me – Liz.'

'Hi, Liz.'

'I'm alone in the apartment – Dad's in Europe – so I thought I'd 'phone. What are you doing with yourself?'

'Nothing much. Hanging about.'

He sounded dejected.

'No more coughs or earaches?'

'All gone. I'm fine now.'

'And how's Mr Woo?' (Mr Woo was Jason's black cat.)

'He's okay.'

'And how is your mother?' Liz enquired politely.

'Mom's out. With Harper Higgins.'

'With *who*?'

'Harper Higgins. He's her new friend,' he explained patiently.

'I see . . . you're not alone there are you?'

She could hear the note of alarmed parenthood in her voice.

'Betsy's here. We're starting to play Monopoly.'

Betsy was the teenager next door. He liked her.

'Oh – good . . .'

'And Liz?'

'Yes, Jason.'

'I had a card from Dad – from France. When he gets back, will you ask him again about going to the Cape over New Year? *Promise*, Liz?'

So they did, after all, spend the New Year vacation at the Cape. And despite Dick's irritation – his assertion that the whole idea was absurd – it turned out a success.

Liz and Dick set out early to drive to Boston to pick up Jason.

'And to think that we could have been on the beach at St Lucia,' Dick said, breaking an hour-long silence, taking a hand off the wheel to indicate the stretches of frozen ground on either side of the parkway. 'Your decision . . .'

'And Jason's. And if you're going to Europe again next week, there really wasn't time to make it worthwhile,' Liz answered, reasonably, refusing to be pressured into a dreary argument.

And these arose so easily between them now. Disharmony and tension — new elements in their relationship — reflected in bitter words. On both sides.

The cold, pale sun — low in a clear winter sky — glittered on the surfaces of ponds and streams as they shot past.

Before stopping for lunch, they picked up Jason. He was waiting for them in the sitting-room. Through the window, Liz saw him disappear the moment the car came in sight. Seconds later, the front door opened and there was Jason, struggling into his blue anorak. His bag was ready on the porch, Liz knew that he was excited.

They both got out of the car, glad to stretch their legs after the drive. Linda materialised from the hall, handing Jason his scarf and woolly hat. She was wearing black drainpipe jeans and an outsize, shapeless sweater, clearly handmade. She had on dangling ear-rings which appeared to be made of corn husks.

Mildly surprised, Liz thought: she really does look strange for a schoolteacher in her early forties with a seven-year-old son. No wonder she didn't exactly relish her life with Dick in New York.

'Have a good time,' Linda said as they headed back to the car. And raising one arm. 'Peace.'

Peace?

Dick made no comment but Liz caught his look of extreme displeasure.

They drove straight to the nearest Macdonald's. Quite content to be wolfing down hamburger and apple pie with Jason, Liz, watching Dick, had a momentary sense of guilt.

It was, after all, his vacation as well as theirs. He had been working like a demon. Sipping a rum cocktail on a West Indian beach was what he had pictured on this, his first day away from the office in weeks; not gulping tepid coffee in a fast-food joint in a Boston suburb.

When, if ever, this merger came off, she would try to plan

86

a few days away for them both. It was what they badly needed.

Later that cold afternoon driving across the deserted roads of the Cape – Liz and Jason anticipating their first sight of the sea – Dick said sourly, 'If we come down with acute frostbite and are snowed in for weeks, don't blame me either of you.'

Liz turned round and gave Jason an exaggerated wink. Secretly, she was as pleased to be going to the cottage as he was.

'The sea,' Jason cried. 'Look, Liz, look . . .'

They stocked up with groceries at the supermarket. The man who ran the general store had kept an emergency house key for years, and he had already turned on the heating in the house. Jason's only disappointment that evening was the sea. In the fading light of the winter's day, it looked like glass, not the raging tempest he had imagined.

To Liz's relief, the house seemed dry and reasonably warm. The old chintz covers and the pine panelling gave it a homely look. There were logs and firewood left from last spring and soon Dick had the huge fireplace blazing. They would have what Jason called 'a feast': shrimp in hot sauce, steaks, and a rather battered Christmas log which Lilly had baked specially. Determined to make the best of the situation, Dick had brought up a case of wine.

They were lucky with the weather. It held. Although bitterly cold, it remained clear and sunny. The snow Dick had prophesied did not fall.

For two days, muffled up to their eyebrows, they walked on the empty dunes where cutting winds had flattened the coarse grasses. They collected pieces of driftwood, smoothed pebbles and amazingly curved shells.

'Remember, Liz, remember in the summer . . .' Jason shouted, pointing out where the lifeguard sat, where they bought ice cream.

Liz realised, pleased, that both she and the cottage were already a part of Jason's childhood.

Relaxed and good humoured, released from all his city tensions, Dick unearthed last summer's frisbee. He and Jason tossed it on the beach, watched it soaring and diving and soaring again; rotating gracefully, dipping perilously close to the water.

They came in for lunch, still laughing, both with a good colour.

'Bloody Mary's coming up,' Dick shouted towards the kitchen where Liz was heating soup. 'Sound good?'

'It does to me,' Liz shouted back.

In the evenings, in front of the fire, they tried out the new games which Jason had been given for Christmas. And on New Year's Eve, the champagne already opened, Dick suggested to Jason that he 'phone his mother.

'Wish her a happy new year. She'd like that,' Dick said.

'From all of us,' Liz added.

'No point,' Jason shrugged.

'Why not?' Dick asked.

'She'll be out anyway. With Harper Higgins.'

'With *who*?'

'Harper Higgins, Dad. He's her friend. Liz, it's your turn.'

'Who the hell is this Harper Higgins?' Dick asked over their last glass of champagne. It was already the new year. Jason had been in bed for hours.

'No idea. Jason has mentioned him before. Once.'

'*Harper Higgins*. Jesus. Not a name you'd forget in a hurry. And I thought Linda looked pretty strange, too. That get-up. And *Peace* . . . You don't suppose she's decided to become a middle-aged hippie, do you?'

Much later, warm, content, almost asleep, Liz thought: Why can't we be happy – like this – in New York . . .

CHAPTER 13

Because, it appeared, they could not.

An innate clash of wills, a particular disagreement in outlook, cemented by words which could not be erased.

They had dropped Jason in Boston. Linda, recognisable as the shadowy figure who opened the door, did not appear. Jason waved from the porch until they turned the corner, a small figure dwarfed by anorak and boots. Somehow forlorn, Liz thought sadly.

The drive down to New York was companionable enough, but as soon as they were back in the apartment, the grate of disharmony set in. That same evening, a minor domestic conflict ensued.

A British client, a merchant banker, 'phoned. He was over from London and had been trying to reach Dick for days. Was there any chance they could have dinner together? With his wife, of course, who he would — by the way — so enjoy meeting . . . His daughter was dead keen on journalism . . . He was returning to London the next day.

Overhearing the conversation, Liz sighed. She had anticipated a quiet evening; a pause between the peace of The Cape and the clamour of the office the following morning.

'One moment, just let me ask my wife . . .'

His hand over the mouthpiece Dick said, 'Liz, a guy I know from London . . . he entertained me over there . . . wants to know if we can have dinner.'

'I'd rather not.'

'Look — he's a good contact. In this business you never know when you'll need one. Or where. I think we should . . .'

'I really don't feel like going out for dinner. Not tonight,' Liz repeated – stubborn, cold.

The prospect of such an evening stretching ahead appalled her. She could picture it exactly. The stilted talk; the polite responses; surreptitious glances at watches. And what, really would be gained? She resented this stranger's impingement on their home life. Even more, she resented Dick's automatic response to any business, any client, any contact.

Priorities again. His or hers?

They had just got back from a holiday weekend; he would see him in London or next time he was over. Why couldn't he say that? It seemed simple enough.

'Ask him for a drink if you like,' Liz said, 'but I'm not going out to dinner. That's final.'

And I sound so graceless, she thought miserably. All the good feelings from their days at the Cape – the ease, the laughter, the salty wind stinging their faces – evaporated.

She left the room.

The Englishman came for a drink and stayed on, pontificating, through two hours and four scotches. Deliberately, Liz had not changed. She was wearing the same grey flannel trousers and beige sweater that she had put on that morning. But her looks – her style – still impressed. Ignoring Dick, the banker spoke at her exclusively. Occasionally, she made some monosyllabic reply. When she could stand it no longer, she said, 'Excuse me, but we had a long drive from Massachusetts . . . I'm really very tired . . .'

'I think you could have been a bit more attentive to Jamie Montagu,' Dick said over scrambled eggs in the kitchen. 'He's a big man in the City over there.'

'So he said.' Dick gave her a steely look across the table. 'I miss Jason. He really enjoyed those few days with us. He didn't seem keen on going back, not even to his cat. I hope he's happy . . .'

Dick left for Paris on Concorde in the middle of the next week. The day after, the East coast was hit by a ferocious storm, the first of many that winter. New York was paralysed. The airport closed, offices shut early. There was a ghostly hush over the city as the snow dropped softly, covering everything. The traffic slowed.

Jason 'phoned.

'Hi, are you snowed in up there?' Liz asked.

'Pretty much. School was closed. Tom and I made a *gi-normous* snowman.'

'New York's snowed in, too. I'm looking down onto the street now and practically nothing's moving.'

'Same here. Mom's mad. She couldn't get out to go to her meeting.'

'What meeting?'

'Oh − the one she and Harper go to all the time.'

After a brief pause, Liz said, 'So how's school going?'

'Good. I'm onto the next reading book. I'm in the top reading group in the class now.'

Just before leaving for the office one morning, Liz 'phoned Dr Mattson's secretary and cancelled her appointment. Pushing it to the back of her mind, she had deliberately left it until the last moment. Now, facing it, she realised how angry she felt towards Dick. And how helpless.

The irony of her situation struck her forcibly. Here she was, Liz Conrad, trapped between her sex − and her success. And what was she going to do about it?

The immediate answer appeared to be − work. Her head bent, sitting undisturbed in her office, she sifted through copy, developed ideas, planned articles. She killed several pieces she had commissioned. Painful − and costly − but they didn't work. Emerging from her office like a whirlwind, she wanted letters typed, a writer or an editor reached on the 'phone, back issues of the magazine photocopied.

At meetings, she was in full control. She suggested schemes for widening circulation, rejected layouts, criticised art work. Every page of every issue had to look right, to say or show exactly what she intended.

She knew instinctively that in order to project – to sell – a magazine, like a person, needed a strong, cohesive personality.

For the moment, anyway, she WAS *Gibsons'*.

Dick came back from Europe and was in New York for five days before flying to Tokyo.

'You're fast becoming the interesting stranger in my life,' Liz told him when they were having dinner by themselves in a restaurant one evening. It was Dick's fifty-second birthday. Liz was wearing a new black dress, which fell from the shoulders in apparently simple folds. Her mane of hair, lightly streaked, surrounded her face like a halo. She looked beautiful.

Earlier that day, she had appeared, coast to coast, on a prominent chat show. Liz Conrad, editor of *Gibsons'*, discussing women in the media. She had been pithy and informative. 'I'm going to get you back, Liz – and soon,' the host had said out of the glaring lights which never bothered her. 'You're a natural.'

Looking at her in the restaurant Dick said, 'Do you know, Liz, how proud of you I am? To see you fulfilling your talents, working so creatively.'

It was the closest he had come to personal talk since his outburst in the park.

'Since certain areas of my life are so spectacularly unfulfilled, then it's just as well, isn't it?' she replied brightly. She raised her glass towards him.

'Cheers. Happy birthday.'

For most of January and February New York was partially snowbound. Dry snow and ice hardened into mounds all over the city; greyish rims lined the sidewalks. The big freeze continued for week after week. There was no sign of a thaw. At night, the city practically closed down. Theatres and restaurants were empty, parties were cancelled. No one had any thought but of getting home – out of the biting cold – and staying there.

One Sunday, Jessica rang. Dick had just returned from his second trip to Japan in two weeks and was sleeping off the effects.

'*You* sound cheery,' Liz told her, catching the buoyancy in her voice.

'I am rather. And Kate's sleeping through the night at last. A triumph.'

'The Yukon now extends down the East coast of North America . . .'

'So I hear. Pretty bleak and rainy in the UK too. But listen, we've fixed the christening for May 30th. Sunday. How does that sound?'

'Great. A treat to look forward to. It will go down in my diary in the office first thing in the morning.'

'Really?'

'Really.'

Neither mentioned Dick, though Liz fancied that Jessica hesitated. But she said, 'How's that glossy mag of yours?'

'All right. In fact, the issues we're working on now seem to be coming along nicely. I'm considered quite a dragon round the office these days.'

'Send me some copies, Dragon Lady. The shop's ghastly. We're in the middle of a sale.'

'I can't wait to see it.'

'Soon. Is Dick still away?'

'No. He just got back from Japan. Again.'

'Well — give him my regards.'

She had lunch with Martha who arrived at the restaurant from her exercise class. She was positively effervescent.

'It's marvellous, Liz. *Everyone* goes . . .' She mentioned actresses, TV personalities, the widow of a president. 'And people like me. None of us get enough exercise. It's too cold to walk, we're busy . . . you're sitting at that desk all day.' She looked critically at Liz's hips.

'You may be right,' Liz admitted. During the winter, she knew she had put on a few pounds again. And she wasn't getting enough exercise. All too often, after working late, she collapsed into a cab, avoiding even her usual walk to the bus stop.

93

'OK I'll try. But nothing too strenuous. I simply can't afford time away from the office with a bad back or strained limbs.'

'Liz, you won't. He starts everyone off very gently. You'll see . . .'

She went with Martha, straight from the office. To her surprise, she enjoyed it. The next day, she felt stiff but relaxed. Gradually, her tolerance built up. Pleased with her improving performance, trimmer, she had a heightened sense of well-being. When she told Caroline, she said,

'It's only what you've been telling your readers to do, after all . . .'

Liz laughed.

'True.'

The beginning of spring — the long-awaited thaw, a mild day of sunshine — coincided with the finale of Dick's deal.

He had pulled it off. It had taken months — long flights, incredibly intricate paperwork, the spectre, always, of collapse. But he had had the patience, the perseverance, the grit. And he had been lucky.

He was exultant. It was as though some inner compulsion had at last been satisfied. The impact was such that editors moved it off the business pages. (The names involved, after all, were in every kitchen in the western world.) For two days, it made headlines. Editorials pontificated and radio and television commentators pondered the implications.

He was quoted in a newspaper profile as saying, 'I can look at balance sheets somebody brings me — look at some of the numbers — and I'll know at once if there's something wrong. I'll give it back, ask them to check it again, say it doesn't feel sound. Nine times out of ten, I'm right.'

And Liz, too, was both pleased and relieved.

'Can you take a vacation now — a long one?' she asked. 'You know Kate's christening is on May 30th. I'm planning to go for about ten days. Pam booked me into Claridges weeks ago. You know the Vanes would love us both . . .'

'I'm not sure of my schedule yet, Liz. Lots of details still to be tied up,' he said vaguely. 'You go off to England and have a good time — we'll get away together soon.'

'Okay.'

Easter passed with a visit from Jason. Unlike his Thanksgiving trip, he was in lively form. They watched the spectacle of the Easter Parade along Fifth Avenue. They went skating at Rockefeller Centre. On Easter Monday they drove out to Westchester to spend the day with Caroline and her family. Jason had a wonderful day, climbing in and out of the boys' treehouse in the garden, jumping off the ladder. The twins mystified him.

'They're exactly, exactly alike,' he kept repeating on the way back. 'Can we go there again, Liz?'

———————

A green and windy April merged into May.

Another birthday. *Thirty-eight*.

Liz remembered the anxiety, the panic, she had felt last year with astonishment.

Was it she, Liz, who had 'phoned Pete one stormy day last September – mouth dry, hands shaking?

To think that she had once felt so strongly – about anything.

———————

She and Dick were very cool to each other, very polite. Dick was still working late and away a lot. A night in Boston, two in Washington. A quick trip to the Coast. He was heavily involved in the aftermath of the deal; much of his other work had been neglected and needed his attention.

Alone after a press reception or a book launch or a first night, Liz was frequently invited to go on to dinner by friends. Often, she accepted. One evening, coming home after a late supper at the Plaza, she found Dick in the apartment, still dressed, watching television.

'Dick . . . I didn't expect you back until tomorrow.'

'No? My secretary called Pam to say I was taking the early plane up from Washington. She must have forgotten to tell you. Hi, anyway . . .'

Worlds apart now.

We're drifting – drifting, drifting, drifting, Liz thought bleakly.

———————

But when Pete McEwen and his wife, Marj, gave a large cocktail party on their twentieth wedding anniversary, they were both in town and went together. The rambling apartment, way up on Park Avenue, was jammed. It was a cheerful and noisy crowd. Dick was claimed by old friends from his Boston days. The McEwen's three teenage children circulated among the guests, pouring champagne and handing canapés. They all had their father's frizzy red hair and appeared to be dressed in garments bought in second-hand clothes shops. They looked confident and good-natured.

'We managed to get all three monsters cleaned up for the occasion.' Pete, glass in hand, was as shambling and untidy as ever. He looked very happy. He put an arm round Liz's shoulders and kissed her on the cheek.

'Hi gorgeous . . . how's the great man?'

'Fine. On top of the world. You read the papers, too.'

'Sure. He's a clever so-and-so. Always was. The bottom line in putting two companies together is greed and power . . . blah . . . blah . . . blah . . . End of quote. So why isn't his beautiful wife looking happier?'

'You know that. Past history. Not discussed. I presume Dick thought it was a sort of pre-menopausal hiccup that I'll get over.'

'Still mind?' Pete peered over the top of his glasses.

'Being rejected by my husband? Very much. And I mind what it's done to us. To our relationship. I mind that. I always − liked Dick so much. I miss the liking.'

'And a child, Liz?' Pete asked quietly. 'You still want to have one?'

'Yes. It takes two, though, unfortunately.'

Pete groaned. 'Okay. Look. With your permission, I'm going to have a talk to that husband of yours. I love you both, but if you don't stop chasing these goddamned careers of yours to the exclusion of human relationships, you're going to wind up in trouble. Both of you. I'll talk to him. Okay?'

'Sure. But you may be too late.' She held out her glass for more champagne. 'Hey, I'm off to London next week. To visit with my English friends. The Vanes. You'd like them.

And I'm going by myself, as it happens.'

'I'll tell you something, Liz.' Pete hiccuped. The noise and gaiety of the party surrounded them but Pete's face was serious. 'If you were my wife you wouldn't be going off to London — or any other place — alone. Dick's not so bright. Over you, *he's dumb*!'

CHAPTER 14

London

The plane banked; Liz's ears popped, losing sound. A patch of countryside was visible through the clouds. She peered down. So green — lush as a rainforest — and appearing so small-scaled. Toytown. Neat criss-crossed fields, cars moving slowly along winding country roads. Mist partially hid the landscape; there was no glimmer of sun.

Leaving the office after a hectic week had, after all, been astonishingly easy. The magazine was running superbly, all the hard work and planning of the long winter months blossoming into one excellent issue after the next. Striking covers; good copy; a first-rate serialisation. Circulation was rising steadily. Even the advertisers were pleased, for once.

'Go on, Liz, enjoy your vacation . . . you deserve it,' everyone said over a farewell drink in her office.

'I know you have friends in England, but it's too bad Dick can't go over with you,' Pam added wistfully.

Dick was off the following day to a conference in Japan. 'You won't change your mind?' he asked uneasily. 'Or meet me in California on the way back? The Vanes would understand.'

Liz declined. She had made these plans months ago, she said. She couldn't let Jessica down now.

All her preparations for the trip had been last-minute. She received a hastily written card from Jessica, reiterating the day of the christening, underlining it three times. The previous week, she had stayed on at the office until after seven each evening. Trying to pack last Saturday morning, everything in her closet had looked dull. Inspired by the warm spring weather, Liz had raced out to the shops. In a small boutique on Madison, her favourite, everything she tried on fitted and was becoming. Two suits, a silk dress and matching jacket, a heavy white cotton skirt and lacy blouse. A shirt picked up the blue in a skirt, belts and scarves materialised adding shape and colour.

Clutching the bulky packages, Liz walked out of the shop humming to herself. She had the money. God knew, she earned it. So why not? Now for shoes and possibly a handbag. She headed for Gucci.

The night before she left, she telephoned Jason to say goodbye.

'Okay Liz. Have a good time. It's not for so long, I guess.' He sounded resigned, patient, like a little old man, Liz thought, smiling. She could picture his expression, curiously adult for a small boy, rather like the strikingly mature faces of children in medieval paintings.

'It will soon be time for the Cape again, Jason,' she told him, wanting to cheer him up.

'I've thought about that,' he responded, brightening. 'And I've bought a new kit to mend the lilo.'

Not for the first time after speaking to him, Liz wondered whether she should worry. She was undecided. He *seemed* happy enough: a pleasant house with a garden, his cat, his friend Tom, his improving schoolwork.

And yet . . . She sensed that he was often forlorn, needing affection. He rarely mentioned his mother. Linda remained a shadowy personality. And who on earth was this Harper Higgins person?

The plane was banking steeply now. Through aching eardrums Liz could just make out the captain mouthing encouraging words about the imminent improvement of London's weather as they flew on through the greyness. The passengers sat bone-weary, stiff, bored. Any excitement they may have felt on take-off — seven hours back across the Atlantic in the New York night — had long since vanished.

By the time Liz had negotiated the long line at passport

control and extricated her luggage, a thin drizzle was falling. Waiting in the queue for a taxi, she pulled her cashmere coat tightly round her. And to think that in New York she had debated whether or not to bring it!

In the taxi, she yawned and stared sleepily out of the window. Huddled under umbrellas, people were going to work; the traffic was building. Splashes of dampened blossom — pink, mauve and yellow — brightened the dreariness of the urban sprawl. The gears of the taxi grated painfully; the windscreen wipers started.

Cold, tired, longing for the comfort of bath and bed, it occurred to Liz to wonder, more than once, what she was doing here. On holiday. Alone. She could after all, have been on her way to Japan; or met Dick in California or persuaded him to fly off to Spain, to the Marbella Club (he liked it there) or even the South of France. And here she was, jolting into the crowded thoroughfares of London's West End on a dull, drizzly May morning.

Because of Jessica.

Reaching the hotel, her spirits rose. She was about to be very pampered — and she was going to enjoy it. Porters wafted her up through the spacious halls into her room which reminded her of nothing so much as a superbly comfortable country house. In the middle of Mayfair. And it was warm. And coffee and croissants would be brought immediately and in the bathroom, immaculate towels were arrayed on a hot towel rail.

The 'phone rang. It was Jessica.

'I'm glad you called. I was seriously considering returning on the first plane to my native land . . .'

'Not possible. Sun is predicted and a heatwave for the weekend. Fontwell looks magical.' She sounded happy and confident. 'Look — have a rest and then come over to the shop. You know where we are. Come between 12.00 and 1.00 and we'll go round to the pub.'

'Sounds good. I'll do that.'

'And is — is Dick with you? Or coming over?'

'No. No, he's off to Japan — to a conference.'

'I see. And Liz . . .'

'What?'

'It's marvellous to have you here.'

———————

After a gloriously hot bath, Liz drew the curtains and got into bed. The sounds of London, even on a busy weekday morning, seemed muted, almost countrified, after New York's shrill cacophony. Soon she looked at her watch. Eleven thirty. She must have dozed, or even slept, a little.

And Jessica's prediction was correct after all. Pulling aside the curtains, she saw that the grey, cloud-swept early morning had become a warm and sunny day. Umbrellas had vanished. Women in light dresses and sandals crowded the pavements. Across the street a barrow was loaded with spring flowers.

Suddenly unaccountably happy, Liz fished a clean cotton shirt out of her case. Ten minutes later, she was ready; dressed in a beige summer suit, striped shirt and new Gucci shoes. She brushed out her hair remembering that it was several shades lighter than when Jessica saw her in New York last year. Any uncalled-for remarks and she would say that Kate deserved a smart, blondish godmother.

As the taxi crawled down Park Lane, Liz looked about her with pleasure. Through the dappled greenery of the park, she could discern a troop of Household Cavalry, the reds and blues of their uniforms, sunshine striking helmets, and white plumes cresting. There was an air of excitement, of expectancy, in London that morning. Up and down Park Lane, people walked animatedly, macs and overcoats discarded, the whole city seemed to be breathing a communal sigh of relief at the blue sky and the warming sun.

Released from the snarled traffic, the taxi bowled round Hyde Park Corner and sped across the formal elegance of Belgravia; back-doubling through terraced streets and leafy squares, past window boxes of red geraniums and brightly painted front doors.

Oblivious of her sleepless night and her jet-lag, Liz watched it all with pleasure. She had once known the area intimately; had lived just a few streets away, passed through this particular square on her way to work each morning. It still seemed familiar after ten years; cleaner, more attractive, more liveable than New York, although she knew she was seeing it at its best that shining spring morning.

Soon, she would be with Jessica; thank God she had not been tempted, at that last moment, to fly off to Japan with Dick, waiting, waiting for meetings and conferences to end, no chance of a genuine vacation together.

The taxi stopped briefly to allow a uniformed Nanny, two immaculate small children in tow, to cross the road.

There'll always be an England . . . Liz hummed, smiling to herself, leaning back and swinging one foot. (She appreciated the spaciousness of a London taxi after the back-breaking New York cabs.) The Nanny walked on smartly. Some things never changed, Liz reflected indulgently, despite an empire lost, war, inflation, rising unemployment.

Her life in New York, the office, the forthcoming issue of *Gibsons'*, even Dick, seemed a world away. And only hours before she had been in its midst. She remembered Jason. She must keep an eye out for some bits and pieces which would amuse him. A T-shirt for the Cape and a model of a London bus. Hamleys was the best place. And was he really all right, with his closed, too adult face and those wary, watching eyes? And if not, why not?

Gears ground. They were cruising slowly down a narrow street crammed with shops. Pulling up to the crowded kerb with difficulty, the driver opened the sliding window.

''Ere y'are, Luv.'

Liz emerged onto the pavement, thrusting some notes into his hand. Excited, she turned away, leaving an enormous tip.

'Ta very much, Luv.' He touched his cap respectfully.

As the taxi moved off, Liz found herself looking into a smart shop window. Several exotically striped and coloured hand-knitted sweaters were displayed among posters and pots of spring plants. Liz looked up. Here she was, no doubt about that. *Bubbles* was painted above in vermilion letters.

She went inside.

'*Liz* . . .' Jessica, waiting, saw her at once and bounded to the door. They hugged briefly.

'And here I am at last. Honestly, I never thought . . . let me have a look at you.'

Jessica's appearance was as attractively individual as ever. Her skin was flawless; she looked radiant. She was wearing a lacy sweater over a voluminous cotton skirt, pulled in by a wide belt, and flat red pumps. Her fair hair was in a knot on top of her head.

'Well?' Jessica smiled at her expectantly. 'Changed out of recognition by the traumas of unmarried motherhood?'

Liz shook her head.

'You look terrific,' she said. 'Same old Jessica.' But there were changes; she saw at once. There were creases round her eyes which had not been there before. Her figure, still slim, had lost its youthful angularity.

'You do too. I like the – er – tawny hair . . .'

So she had noticed. Liz laughed. 'I didn't think you would. Now – show me round.'

Jessica's inimitable touch was apparent throughout the shop. The place was much larger than Liz would have guessed from the street. Sunshine poured in through the bay window at the back. Colour was everywhere. A rainbow of pumps, of the kind Jessica was wearing, was arrayed along one wall. Shiny belts festooned an old coatrack. Sweaters and T-shirts were stashed in red shelves running from floor to ceiling. Cotton skirts, tops and trousers were pegged on what appeared to be a clothesline.

In one corner there was a display of embroidery canvases and silks; in another, a tiny coffee bar and two or three comfortable chairs. Attended by a pretty young girl dressed in the same style as Jessica, two customers, apparently mother and daughter were choosing summer cottons. Settling them in chairs with cups of coffee, the assistant began to put the outfits together on hangers – adding a belt or a waistcoat or a slouchy felt hat. The two women watched intently, approving, offering suggestions.

'I'm impressed. Truly,' Liz whispered to Jessica, inspecting a sweater. And she was, too – much more than she had imagined.

'*It works*,' Jessica mouthed back. 'Carol – who's selling – is a marvel. They'll end up buying masses, those two. They've been in before. US sales have been a tremendous help. The catalogue, too. I must show you the new one for summer.'

Jessica's pride and satisfaction were evident. She looked at her watch. 'Let's push off to the pub now. Carol can hold the fort until I get back. My other girl, Jill, is on holiday.'

'But I've only just got here. I want to look, even *buy* . . .' Liz protested.

'Tomorrow. Come back.' Jessica made a face at Carol, who nodded, grabbed an old leather shoulder bag from behind the till and whisked them out into the street. All her actions were as quick and decisive as ever. Letting out a sigh, Jessica grinned at her sideways.

'That's better. Now we can talk. You approved?'

'Amazing. It's so attractive. And you're doing well?'

'Not bad. Can't complain. We had a slow start this spring . . . but this weather is a bonus. It really brings out the buyers. This way.'

She steered Liz, her reactions slowed by the time change, through the lunchtime crowds, round the corner and across the road to the pub. It was almost 1.00 and the place was jammed. Seeing one of the outside tables empty, Jessica said:

'Here. Let's grab this. You sit − I'll get us something to eat and drink.'

Thankful to be sitting. Liz fumbled in her bag for dark glasses. Walking from the shop she had felt, momentarily, disorientated. The crowd of young people spilled out of the pub and onto the sunny pavement. Funny to hear all these upper class English voices again en masse, Liz thought. Once, when she had lived here, they hadn't seemed foreign in the least.

Minutes later, Jessica was back with double gins ('Lots of ice. I remembered.') − bottles of tonic and sausage rolls.

'Feeling a bit rocky?' she asked.

'A bit.'

'It's normal. Practically no sleep and the time difference. Drink up. You'll feel better.'

'Or worse,' Liz replied, drinking anyhow.

'And eat. These rolls are home-made and delicious. Mustard?' She spoke through a full mouth. 'No trouble about your coming over? With Dick, I mean?'

Liz shook her head.

'None. He's off to Japan in any case.'

'And how are things — between you?'

Liz shrugged, toying with a sausage roll.

'I don't know. I just — don't — know.' Over Dick she felt — and sounded — helpless. 'He won't consider a child. He's too old, I'm too old, it would change our life-style, there's Jason. Same old stuff. *My* feelings don't count. *He* doesn't want a child — and that's final. Pretty brutal about it he was, too. We're both working flat out, Dick travelling a lot . . . we live together but we don't talk very much,' she finished briskly.

'You say brutal. Really?'

'Well — verbally at least.'

'A word beginning with S?'

'You guessed.'

'*I know.*'

'How?'

'Hugo. After Kate was born. I haven't seen him since, by the way. And I shan't again.'

They were silent for a few moments then Jessica said, 'I'm sorry. About Dick. I think he's right for you. I told you that in New York. I sense he's got what my Pa would call — bottom.'

'He has. And I'm sorry, too. Very.' Liz sighed.

'Look — can't you try not to think about it all while you're here? It sounds cowardly advice I know. But there are times when turning off can help. Unexpectedly.'

'Don't worry.' Liz was feeling brighter after the drink took hold. She smiled warmly at Jessica. 'I'm going to enjoy it all. You, Kate, that fabulous hotel, Fontwell . . .'

Jessica laughed.

'As I told you, Kate will be unveiled for you tomorrow night. She's *lovely* . . .'

Her face softened, almost visibly. With love, Liz thought, stricken.

She said, 'I've tried not to imagine her. I know she's very fair.'

'White-blonde. Like mother was. And Chris. Oh — by the way, he's coming for supper tomorrow night, too. We can make arrangements for the weekend. And he's intrigued to see you again.'

'Christopher?'

'That's right. He's working in the City now for our very pompous uncle. After Vanessa died . . .'

'Of course. I remember now. It's just that I always associate him with Fontwell.'

'You'll see quite a change in him. He's so good looking that sometimes even I get a shock. Decidedly dishy . . . the young-man-about-town all right. But terribly remote. Aloof. He has been since Vanessa . . . Mother says time will do it. Sometimes, I wonder. To change the subject, I've got a new gentleman friend,' she teased.

'Yes?' So there was someone. Perhaps that explained her glowing good looks, not motherhood alone.

'Yes indeed. You'll meet him tomorrow night, too.'

Mysterious Jessica.

'A party. Can I do − or bring anything? Now that I'm suddenly so leisured?'

'You can not. My nice French girl Louise is a marvellous cook. And it will be such fun to be together with all my favourite people.'

Jessica always had the knack of catching people's attention, of attracting the best. Now, she summoned a youthful pub employee who was gathering up glasses and ordered coffee.

'I always knew you'd manage, Jessica. With everything. Even the baby. I told Dick so last year.'

'Well, it's been pretty hard going, I can tell you. No point in pretending otherwise. Kate yelling her head off in that tiny house. Rushing back from the shop at lunchtime to feed her. I was *always* exhausted. For months. The tiredness was the worst.'

'But your mother helped?'

'Only at the beginning. She can't leave Father − he's far from well as you'll see − and in any case I wouldn't want her to. The girls at the shop were super. Before I got Louise, they babysat quite as much as they worked in the shop. And that's another thing . . .'

'The shop?'

'Yes. You only saw the surface this morning, all running smoothly, looking pretty, stock for next autumn ordered,

106

etc, etc. But last winter with the sale, cajoling lady knitters down with flu to get the orders filled . . . looking at new lines. And Kate . . .'

'But you'd do it all again.' It was a statement.

'Yes.'

'You've more guts than I have.'

'Different. I just wanted it — a child — more. More than anything,' she said quite fiercely.

Jessica looked at her watch.

'Help. I must go and relieve Carol. We're often busy at this time of day.' They started to walk back towards the shop.

'If you can manage it, do give Mother a ring. They're both looking forward to the weekend, the christening, having us all there.' They strolled along the busy pavements, glancing into the windows of boutiques, pointing out what interested them, remembering the time when they first met, when Liz was constantly in tears at Jake's absences. A different lifetime, it seemed.

'By the way,' Jessica asked. 'How's the little boy?'

'Jason? Okay — I think.'

'But you're not sure?'

'No. I'm not. He's become rather withdrawn for a seven-year-old. He has always been a "thinker", but he was such a bouncy kid until recently. Maybe it's just a stage.'

'You're fond of him, Liz.'

'Very. Really close. Funny, isn't it?'

'Rum old life,' said Jessica.

They parted company in front of the shop. Through the open door, Liz could see about a dozen customers inside.

'I'm going to walk for a bit and then go back to the hotel and collapse in a heap,' Liz said.

'Good idea. Keep going for as long as you can. You'll sleep better tonight. I'll be home after 6.00. Give me a ring.'

'I will. And tomorrow I really want to come and have a good look round Bubbles and buy something.'

'No problem,' Jessica smiled.

'And then I'll drag you out for a good lunch. On me.'

'Super. Have a good wander.'

With a quick wave, Jessica disappeared inside.

Liz walked on into Knightsbridge and turned right towards Harrods. The stiff drink and the time with Jessica had dispelled her exhaustion. Having nothing in particular to do – no urgent 'phone calls to return and no copy to pull into shape – felt strange. And relaxing. Dawdling along, she felt curiously peaceful. She could even smile at her more than ten years younger self, stuck in that Chelsea flat, an ocean away from family and friends; glimpsing Jake, briefly, between assignments, throwing out his line of empty whisky bottles.

She had not seen him once since the divorce. Looking back, she realised that the break-up must have been a relief to him. He was ambitious in his work; he couldn't afford ties. Since, he had acquired the reputation for being the best newspaper reporter in the business, flying round the world covering wars and famines, earthquakes, space shots and royal weddings. He had not remarried. Liz had often seen him on television and thought, with wonderment, of that brief time when they were joined together in matrimony – if not much else.

In a daze, she made her way through the food halls of Harrods, through what seemed like miles of expensive perfume and men's clothing. Outside again, she bought a card to send to Jason, blinking in the sunlight, hesitating before the traffic which streamed along Knightsbridge.

Her thinking was becoming confused. She wondered about the time. Had she remembered to change her watch on the plane? Crossing the sea of traffic cautiously, she found herself in Hyde Park. She was beginning to feel very tired indeed. But the warm air, the beds of spring flowers, pleased her. She walked on . . . across Park Lane, through the streets of Mayfair, until the massive red pile of the hotel came into view.

All day, Mr Conrad had been trying to reach her from New York, she was told solicitously as she passed through the lobby. Liz nodded and smiled feeling decidedly lightheaded. The moment she entered her room, the 'phone rang. Picking up the receiver, she collapsed onto the bed.

Clearly, it was Dick. A hollow, confused sound, much crackling, then,

'Liz?'

'It's me.'

'Where on earth have you been? I've been trying to get you for hours.'

'Out. With Jessica.'

'All this time? You must be exhausted.'

'I am rather. I walked back from Knightsbridge. Glorious weather.'

She kicked off her shoes. The noise on the line was deafening.

'Where *are* you?' she shouted through the din.

'At Kennedy,' he shouted back. 'My plane's boarding.'

'For Japan?' Liz asked, uncertain.

'Sure. But Liz, there's something I want to say. Something important.' Miraculously, the line cleared. She could hear him perfectly. And it was good to hear his voice. She had always responded to its resonance, its steadiness. It pleased and comforted her now.

'What's that?' she asked.

'This. Look, it's been a lousy year, a sort of lost year, between us. I want to tell you that I know this.'

Taken completely by surprise, Liz hesitated. She was wary.

'But in many ways, Dick, it was a good year. The deal that came off after all that work and worry . . .'

'Liz, I'm not talking about careers. Yours or mine. And you know it.' That makes a change, she thought. She said:

'No?'

'No. I'm talking about us. About the misunderstanding between us. I was wrong in my thinking, wrong — inexcusable — in what I said.' Liz thought, we have been living together week in, week out. Quite polite and civilised but drifting apart. And now — between Kennedy Airport and a hotel room in London, across three thousand miles of ocean — we are, or seem to be, communicating. Life could indeed be very strange.

'You really mean that, Dick?'

'Yes. I do.'

'But why? I mean — what's happened?'

'Lots of reasons. Pete principally. I had dinner with him and Marj last night. Marj went off to bed and we stayed up and had a few drinks and talked. He's a good friend.'

'He certainly is. To both of us.' She was still mystified.

'We need some changes of direction. I see that now. Will you remember, Liz — what I've just said?'

'I'll remember.' Her head was spinning.

'And Liz?'

'Yes.'

'Another thing. Jason 'phoned me last night. I think he had been crying. Very upset and overwrought. I calmed him down as much as I could and asked to speak to Linda. She was out. You guessed it. With Harper Higgins. God knows what's going on up there . . . but I think we may have to intervene.'

'I do, too.'

A loudspeaker droned in the background.

'Hey, last call for my plane. I must go. But Liz — don't forget what I said. I love you very much.'

'Likewise. And I'll remember.'

'See you soon. My best to Jessica. And take care.'

'You too.'

After he had hung up, for some minutes Liz sat there, looking at the receiver crackling in her hand and smiling.

It was time for some change in both their lives. Dick was right about that. And perhaps, after all, it wasn't too late.

CHAPTER 15

After supper in her room, Liz slept at once. When she
awoke, she groped for her watch beside the bed. Nine
o'clock. She had slept straight through the night. Sunlight
streamed in between the curtains; the traffic rumbled.
Newspapers which she ordered with her coffee were full of
stories of 'Londoners Beat The Heat' – pretty girls in the
parks wearing bikinis and the marvel that 'soaring
temperatures' were here to stay for the moment. After
summers in sweltering, air-conditioned New York, Liz
laughed. Fontwell and the Cotswolds would be at their
glorious best this weekend.

The unaccustomed luxury of an empty day stretched
ahead. No appointments, no deadlines, no administration.
The whole day; and hers to do what she wished with it.

She 'phoned Jessica who was in a tearing hurry, rushing
off to the shop. (Liz could hear Kate protesting loudly in the
background.) She would see her later in the morning. 'And
don't be too late,' Jessica ordered sternly.

Still in bed, she spoke to Jessica's mother, Katherine
Vane, in the country.

'We are *so* looking forward to the weekend, Liz. So lovely
to have you with us, the christening – a very special
weekend. And we're even laying on good weather for a
change, I believe.'

Later, Liz walked down Bond Street, past St James'
Palace and over to the National Gallery. With the buildings
newly cleaned, Trafalgar Square looked noble. The
fountains played, splashing and sparkling in the sun. Certain
paintings are like old friends, Liz thought, after an hour in

the gallery and waiting for a bus, looking around, re-acquainting herself with the sights and sounds of London . . .
The bus came at last and she climbed upstairs. Unused to the height and the swaying motion, she watched dense flights of pigeons swooping about Nelson's Column. She was enjoying being a tourist in London again. She tried to remember where The Scotch House was – the twins and their sweaters . . .

For the first time, she thought back to yesterday's telephone conversation with Dick. Had she, muddled by lack of sleep, misunderstood him?

He had faced up to their growing emotional estrangement, put it into words. Shown more courage in that than she had. He minded.

He had spoken of change. What change?

A child? Had he come round to understanding *her* feelings? To appreciating the enormity of his denial?

For the first time for months, they had spoken of things that mattered between them.

Hope rekindled.

Don't think, she cautioned herself as the bus sped on towards Knightsbridge. Jessica was right. I'm away from it all. *Don't think* . . .

When Liz arrived, the shop was crowded. With a wink to Jessica who was selling hard, Liz concentrated on the clothes like the other determined shoppers. She picked out a blue and white cotton skirt and a matching T-shirt, blue pumps like Jessica's and a stunning hand-knit sweater which had caught her eye yesterday. She took them into a curtained cubicle to try on.

Coming out, she found Jessica waiting for her, bag slung over her shoulder.

'Well?' she enquired – brisk, professional.

'They're fine. I'll take them . . .'

'Good. Let's leave them over here for the time being and push off. I've got extra help today, but I don't want to leave Carol for too long.'

Over pasta and a glass of wine in a nearby Italian restaurant, they had a relaxed and amusing lunch. They recalled other meetings, old boyfriends, Jake's eccentricities. A weekend in Paris, where Jessica had joined Liz and the Senator. 'And we spent most of the time avoiding the Press and drinking champagne,' Jessica recalled. 'Nothing remotely cultural . . .'

On the way back to the shop, Jessica recommended a hairdresser and a shop near her hotel where she could buy some jokey gifts for Jason. As for Kate's christening present:

'Something pretty. And please, Liz, not extravagant.'

'We'll see. Oh − I spoke to your mother. We had a long chat. She sounded very crisp and lively.'

'But you'll see them both very aged, I fear,' Jessica said, suddenly serious. 'Vanessa's death, Pa's health . . . and *I've* put them under a lot of pressure. I do know that. Their support of me and Kate has cost them dearly.'

'Do they know Hugo?' Liz asked.

'No,' Jessica replied, quickly and definitely. 'Nothing. Not even his name.'

I can't remember, not for years, getting dressed to go out − on a week night − so unhurriedly, Liz thought as she ran her bath. She had the sensation, it had been with her all day, of moving through a dream; pleasantly removed from reality. Light years away from her ordinary life. From Dick.

And Dick would be in Tokyo now.

Jessica wanted her to come to the house early, before Kate went to bed. She was excited at the thought of meeting her god-daughter, and curious to see Jessica with her baby. This was an aspect of Jessica she could not picture.

Her new beige silk dress and jacket, boldly patterned in blue and pink was perfect, she thought, pleased, looking at her image in the mirror. She brushed her hair. Burnished and shining, it sprang back from her forehead. She groped in the wardrobe for sling-back shoes, chain bag; she was ready.

The vast lobby downstairs was quiet. It was too early for the discreetly wealthy visitors to begin making their way to restaurants and theatres. Liz got into a waiting taxi. The sky touched with pink. Groups of people gathered outside pubs, glasses in hand, making the most of the balmy weather, the long light evening.

Jessica's house was in a narrow street near the King's Road. ('An eighteenth century artisan's dwelling,' Jessica described it, adding, 'Everything's wonky, nothing fits. But it's solid as a rock.') Liz's knock on the yellow door was answered immediately by a young woman in jeans. Louise.

'Please come in. Jessica is in the kitchen with the baby.' She had a pleasant, smiling face. Her accent was very slight.

As Liz remembered, the kitchen was on the right of the narrow hall passage, in the front of the house. Jessica was talking on the 'phone – it was clearly a business call from her tone – a chubby baby, Kate, held firmly and casually on her hip.

Mother and child; the most natural sight in the world, Liz thought. And that's how Jessica looks with Kate – natural.

Still talking, Jessica made a face at her above Kate's head.

'Shan't be a moment,' she mouthed.

Smiling, Liz approached Kate who was eyeing her with some interest.

She is, as Jessica said, lovely, Liz thought. Wisps of hair that was almost white, enormous blue eyes, pink toes curling.

'Hi,' she said, extending a finger. 'Hi there, Kate.'

She suddenly felt a little shy. Except for Caroline's mob, she was unused to babies. Kate took her finger and put it straight to her mouth, gurgling and dribbling. Liz laughed.

'Okay then, we'll speak tomorrow.' Jessica slammed down the 'phone. 'Bloody man.' Then, 'That's a funny way to greet your godmother, Kate.' Jessica removed Liz's finger and gazed down at her daughter affectionately.

'Jessica, she's adorable.'

'Nice, isn't she? Here, take her.'

'She won't mind?' Liz held out her arms.

'Not she. Anything for a bit of attention. She's a friendly sort. Here. Have this.' She draped a towel over Liz's shoulder. 'Don't let her dribble on that beautiful dress.'

Kate felt solid and comforting to hold. And surprisingly heavy. Still gurgling, she stared up at Liz with wide blue eyes.

'She's chubby, Jessica.' Liz saw, with delight, that her elbows were dimpled. She felt her plumpness beneath the thin white cotton nightie.

'Fat, you mean. That's right, isn't it Kate?' Arms folded, Jessica watched them contentedly.

'Kate's going to show me round . . .' Still holding her, Liz walked into the adjoining dining-room.

The old longing, the hopeless, helpless frustration which she had believed dormant, came rushing back. Breathless, she swallowed rapidly. Her chin rested on the soft top of Kate's hair. Infuriatingly, her eyes misted. Lucky – gutsy – Jessica.

The moment passed.

Blinking, she saw that the table was laid for four – cream napkins, candles and a bowl of fresh roses.

'The house looks pretty, Jessica,' Liz called over her shoulder, her poise recovered. Jessica was still in the kitchen, assembling glasses.

'Thank God I bought it when I did, before prices went through the roof. And thank God for that small legacy from my great-aunt . . . I could never have managed it otherwise.'

'You've had it redecorated.'

'Last year. Just before Kate was born.'

It was painted white throughout. Inexpensive, practical furnishings were mixed with a few good pieces from Fontwell – the dining-room table, a chiffonier and several fine watercolours. Kelim rugs covered the floor. The effect was stylish; Jessica's style.

'Pa complains you can't swing a cat here . . .'

'Can I take Kate outside?'

'Do.'

Open french doors led onto the small patio garden. Ivy cascaded down the walls. There were pots of geraniums and several rose bushes in tubs. The last time I was here, Liz remembered, I met Hugo. She could see him now, a large man, his head thrown back, holding forth . . . Kate's father. Tactfully, she kept her memory to herself.

'It's so warm, I thought we could have drinks outside,' Jessica said, putting a tray and glasses on the wrought iron table. 'Let me have her. She's heavy.' She disengaged Kate from Liz's arms. 'Come upstairs with me. We can chat while I change.'

Carrying Kate over her shoulder, Jessica led the way. They passed the sitting-room on the first floor. Louise emerged from the bathroom on the half landing above.

'Enjoy yourself,' Jessica said. And to Liz, 'Louise has classes two evenings a week. Not that there's much wrong with her English that I can hear.'

Liz agreed. Louise smiled deprecatingly and said: 'I have made the vinaigrette. Only the potatoes need to be done and they will not take a long time, I think.'

'Thanks, Louise.'

'*Dors bien*, Kate.' Louise wished them a happy evening and ran down the stairs, her ponytail swishing.

'Super girl,' Jessica said. 'And she's good in the shop, too.'

'You're lucky.'

'Long may it last. I really need her.'

The nest of tiny bedrooms was on the third floor. Jessica spread a blanket on the floor of her room and put Kate down on it. She produced a rattle and soft toys. Liz sat down with her, trying to engage her attention with the toys. But she pushed them away and began to grizzle.

'She's tired,' Jessica said. 'And it's been hot all day.' Sitting at her dressing-table, she was putting up her long hair in an eccentric Greek style which was supported by combs. 'I must keep her up until Chris gets here. He adores her. Then we'll pop her into bed.'

Downstairs, the bell rang.

'Speak of . . .' Jessica began.

'I'll get it. You finish dressing in peace. Come on Kate.' Liz scooped her up. 'Let's go and see your uncle.'

She opened the front door with some difficulty. Kate was squirming in her arms and needed holding.

'Christopher?'

'Liz?'

The reason she gasped, Liz told herself later, was that the blonde young man standing on the doorstep resembled nothing so much as the current Golden Boy of the American cinema. And the last time she had seen him, he was almost a schoolboy. Jessica did warn her. I should have listened, she thought.

As Christopher was carrying two bottles, and as Kate was still wriggling vigorously, there seemed no possibility of shaking hands. So they touched cheeks, briefly, Christopher saying:

'Good Heavens, Liz, it's been years . . .' and Liz replying, just a shade too quickly;

'Yes, years, at Fontwell . . .' And they were standing in the narrow hall, Christopher bending down − 'Hullo there, Katie, Kate' − his fair hair falling over his forehead.

And of course he's exactly like his mother, Liz was thinking. The same cheekbones, rather long mouth, pale, pale eyes. And tall, too, she realised, as he straightened.

'Jessica is changing. She'll be down in a minute.'

'Let me dispense with these.'

He put the bottles of wine on the dining-room table, pushing his hair back with one hand. Smiling, he held out his arms to Kate.

'Come on then,' he said, taking her, holding her high in the air as she giggled wildly. 'Let's have a look at you, young lady.'

Liz noticed his narrow, elegant hands and wrists, the immaculately cuffed shirt. And she remembered, vividly, the gangling student. Playing tennis at Fontwell. With Vanessa.

Jessica clattered down the stairs and joined them.

'Hullo, Chris. I see you two have met − or re-met.' She was wearing a vivid pink cotton dress and strappy sandals. She inspected the wine Chris had brought.

'Good, good. But the wrong colour. We're having a fishy meal tonight. I'll keep them. Thanks, Chris.'

Seeing her mother move away to the kitchen, Kate burst into tears, rubbing her eyes.

'Definitely bedtime,' Jessica said firmly, taking her from Christopher. 'Off we go, Kate. We'll all come up for goodnights.'

In a procession, they trooped up to Kate's tiny nursery and Jessica deposited her in her cot. Her eyes were almost closed already. She found her thumb and a misshapen velvet rabbit. Strands of fine hair clung damply to her forehead.

'It's hot up here,' Jessica whispered, only partially closing the ruffled curtains. 'I'll come up later and cover her.'

'We could all do with a drink,' she said on the way down. 'Last Christmas, Pa thought I looked so "poorly" that he got his wine merchant to deliver half a dozen bottles of champagne. Not that he can afford such extravagant gestures, the old love. Anyhow, I've saved it. Do the honours, would you Chris?'

The three of them sat on the patio. Above, the sky was darkening; sweet, fresh scent wafted from the roses. They heard laughter from people sitting outside the pub on the corner. They talked about times together they all remembered — the picnics, tennis parties. Watching the hunt move off — Christopher and his father riding — on a brilliant, frosty New Year's day. Vanessa's name was not mentioned.

Jessica stood up and refilled their glasses.

'Plenty more inside. I've got to go in and do something. Tony should be here any minute.'

Tony. So that was the name of the mysterious new friend.

Sitting there alone with Liz, Christopher said suddenly, 'Liz — do you remember Vanessa at all?'

'Yes — yes, I do.' She saw Christopher was looking at her intently.

'Can I ask — how?'

It was a question she had not expected. She flushed uneasily, groping for the right words.

'It was a quite a few years ago, of course . . . but very dark, very vivacious. Rather lovely and wild. I remember — I remember you always together,' she finished.

'Thank you. I hope I didn't put you on the spot. It's just that — the family won't talk about her. Ever. They think it helps, I know. But it doesn't. It makes it worse.'

The front door bell rang.

'It's understandable, though,' Liz said. 'It must be so painful for them and they think they are sparing you pain.'

'Yes, anyhow — thanks.'

He threw her a dazzling smile.

For a twice married woman, nearly ten years older, I shouldn't feel quite so affected by his admittedly handsome presence, Liz thought lightheadedly. But, as it happens, I do.

Jessica stepped out onto the patio, followed by a rather stout middle-aged man. Tony. Liz braced for the second shock of the evening. He was close to sixty, Liz guessed, with a magnificent head of silver grey hair. He was wearing a formal dark suit, an expensive 'name' tie.

Well, she thought, *well* . . .

She held out her hand, smiling, welcoming him into the private world in which she and Christopher had been sitting.

After the introductions, Jessica told Tony that he was late and to 'drink up because the spuds are almost done'. She spoke rather sharply; familiarly.

Downing his champagne, Tony chatted affably. He had only returned from a trip to the States last week, he said. He loved the place; couldn't get there often enough. Liz couldn't place his accent although Christopher told her later that he was from the Midlands; his family had a silver-plate business in Birmingham, which he had built up into a thriving company.

As he was speaking, over his shoulder, Liz could see Jessica lighting the candles on the table. Moments later, she called them.

'Not a murmur from Kate?' Liz asked, sitting where Jessica indicated.

'Fast asleep. I just checked.'

It was getting dark; in the candlelight, the silver gleamed against the mahogany surface of the table. Expertly, quite without fuss, Jessica served a perfect summer's evening dinner. Cold asparagus with Louise's vinaigrette; fresh salmon with cucumber and tiny new potatoes.

The foursome was convivial. Liz's holiday and the warm weather lent an air of gaiety. Tony emerged as a good conversationalist, with the knack of telling a quick, entertaining story. He got the tempo just right; their laughter echoed round the narrow room which was lit by the flickering candles. Although Christopher seemed reserved at the start, Tony paid him particular attention, drawing him out, leading him on to tell them about yet another insurance scandal in the City.

After her initial dismay, unfair, she knew, Liz found herself warming to his persuasive personality. She understood his business success. And she could tell from the way she questioned him that Jessica had a healthy respect for his opinions. His quick mind appealed to her.

They spoke of Dick's work — Tony showing himself knowledgeable about the recent merger — and then Jessica mentioned *Gibsons'*. Turning to Tony she said in a teasing, rather proud, manner, 'She's built it right up, our Liz has. Put it back on the top of the heap again. Clever girl.'

Christopher was refilling their glasses; moths fluttered about the candles.

After a pause, Liz heard herself say, 'I have. That's true. But I've done it now. I'm thinking of giving it up, resigning. Doing something different.'

The words came out so confidently, that Liz almost looked over her shoulder. Were they spoken by her — or somebody else?

'Not *seriously*?' Jessica stared at her across the table. She was serving the dessert, a bowl of magnificent strawberries on a bed of creamy meringue.

'Seriously,' Liz smiled back at her.

And I do believe I am serious, she realised, picking up her glass. Funny that I didn't know before, that it suddenly surfaced here, round this table of Jessica's in Chelsea. Miles and miles removed from *Gibsons'* lush offices on the fortieth floor in New York City. Change, Dick had said, a change of direction. Perhaps.

She was aware that Christopher was looking at her quizzically. She turned to him and their eyes met. It was a moment of extraordinary intimacy. Shaken, Liz looked away.

'I think I can understand that,' Tony, on her right, was saying in his reasonable manner. 'You probably feel you have already achieved — created — what you set out to do.'

'Exactly.'

'Good God.' said Jessica getting up to fetch the coffee.

The conversation changed and became general again. Louise came in, rushing breathlessly upstairs. Tony looked at his watch. Jessica polished off the last of her wine and started to yawn.

'Time gentlemen. Work tomorrow.'

'Will I be able to get a taxi?' Liz asked, pulling her jacket round her shoulders.

'No need,' Christopher replied swiftly. 'I'm dropping you back.' Liz felt his hand touch her arm, lightly.

'Fix up with Chris about going down to Fontwell tomorrow. They're expecting you both for dinner. I'll come on Saturday as early as I can,' Jessica told her. They moved towards the door. Christopher and Tony were behind them, still talking.

'Chris was in good form tonight,' Jessica murmured, 'Unusually good. He is rather dishy, don't you think?'

Dishy?

'Lovely, lovely evening, Jessica,' Liz called, standing outside with Christopher. Jessica saw them off, standing in the doorway. The light glowed behind her. Her precarious hair-style had collapsed onto her shoulders. Liz thought she looked very pretty; soft, uncharacteristically vulnerable. Tony put an arm round her and she leant against him. Unquestionably, he was staying the night.

'My car's round the corner.' Christopher guided her towards a sports car parked in the next street.

'But you live in Kensington. I'm taking you right out of your way.'

'My pleasure.'

He smiled at her quickly, shyly, engaging the gears, nosing the car through a maze of one-way streets.

'It was a great evening,' Liz said. 'Such fun.'

'I enjoyed it. Jessica does these dinners well.'

'Always did. And Kate's a honey.'

'Indeed. A great joy.'

After rounding Sloane Square, Christopher drove fast through the emptied streets.

'And Jessica seems to be managing, the shop, the baby . . .'

'Absolutely. Despite her zany ways, she's really very capable. Very down-to-earth. All the same, her suddenly producing Kate wasn't exactly easy for my parents to come

121

to terms with. I'm sure you understand that. They're very conventional people.'

'But she says they've been marvellous — very supportive.'

'So they have. But there's no point in pretending they wouldn't like to see her comfortably married. Frankly, I would too.'

'Jessica would say, fiercely, *that's not the point*.'

They laughed together, hands accidentally touching as Christopher changed gear, intimate in the small enclosed space.

'I understand that,' Christopher said, serious again. 'Nevertheless, what *is* she going to tell Kate — and when? I gather she doesn't see Hugo at all now. So Kate will grow up knowing nothing about him. But it will have to be faced. And it's a lot trickier than divorce or adoption.'

'Yes. Yes, it is.' Liz was quiet. 'But I'm sure Jessica has thought it through.'

'I wonder.'

'I thought Tony was nice. I was surprised at first. He wasn't at all what I was expecting . . . whatever that was . . .'

'He's a very decent chap. And he's done extraordinary things with the family business. Did Jessica tell you everything about him?'

'Nothing.'

'He's separated from his wife. Two grown-up children. Years older than Jessica, of course. I don't see her with him permanently, do you?'

'Frankly, no.'

But with Jessica — with anyone — who knew?

'It's not terribly late,' Christopher said suddenly. 'Let's go and have a drink.'

It occurred to Liz that they had already had plenty to drink that evening, but she found herself pleased (or was it excited?) that he had asked her. He parked the car.

'A square I can't remember. I've lost my bearings,' Liz said, looking up at the dark outlines of plane trees, hardly moving in the warm night.

'Berkeley. But without nightingales.'

Liz laughed. 'Pity. It sounds so romantic.' She took his

arm as they crossed over to a canopied entry. Steps led down to the basement.

'Good evening, Sir.'

To Liz, it was like entering a spacious private home. Prints and pictures on the walls, chintzy chairs and subdued lighting gave the feeling of a large house in the country. There seemed to be a preponderence of older men with very young, dazzlingly dressed, women. Liz thought the men all looked like prototypes of Dick's British business contacts; like Jamie Montagu. Settled in a corner with drinks (two glasses of champagne appeared almost immediately) Christopher said, 'It's a bit of a haven here.'

'A very luxurious haven.'

'Very. Vanessa and I always came on special occasions. Birthdays and so forth . . .' The tension showed on his face.

'Do you miss her all the time — still?' Liz asked quietly. She felt very close to him; they had been intensely aware of each other all evening. Now, the atmosphere of the club invited intimacy.

'Yes. Some days — some hours — are better than others. Like tonight.' He suddenly looked so young, so stricken. Touched, Liz thought: is there to be no comfort for him? And with such looks. The height, the fairness, those marvellous cheek bones. She had noticed people watching him, discreetly, as they walked in. 'Dishy,' Jessica had called him; now she knew its meaning.

'Tonight was better?' Her voice was hardly audible. Dangerous, she thought, dangerous. All this champagne . . .

Christopher didn't answer. He said, 'Let's dance.'

The floor was crowded and very, very dark. A Gershwin tune. Liz moved against him, close, her elbow somewhere behind his neck. The insistent beat; fragments of familiar lyrics.

'Liz . . .' His arms tightened. Turning, her lips brushed his cheek.

'Liz . . . Liz . . .' murmured against her hair, his thigh touching the smooth silk. Chris . . . Chris . . .

That tune again; eyes closed; hardly moving.

CHAPTER 16

Liz awoke frequently during the night, disturbed by vivid dreams and churning emotions. Kaleidoscopic, it all came back. The satisfying feeling of Kate cuddled against her shoulder, the strangeness of being in London again. The expression on Jessica's face when she spoke of resigning her job; moths fluttering round the candles. *Christopher*. His voice; his touch; the length of his leg against hers as they danced.

And one hell of a lot too much to drink she said to herself, fully awake, switching on the light and reaching for a glass of water. She saw that it was four o'clock. Outside, it was perfectly still. There was no possibility of sleep for the moment, she knew. She was totally alert. And she hadn't got back so very late after all. They had only stayed at the club for a short time. Christopher returned her to the hotel, seeing her into the lobby and leaving at once, quite formally, without so much as a brush on her cheek. He would telephone in the morning, he said stiffly. He would know, then, when he could get away.

Liz smiled to herself. The excitement was there still. Steady, she said aloud, steady.

She considered, and rejected, calling Dick in Tokyo.

Why was Jason crying when he 'phoned Dick? Why did she sense that he needed them?

She opened a book.

Soon, she fell into a dreamless sleep until morning.

When Jessica answered the 'phone, Liz could tell at once

that she was out-of-sorts.

'I've got to go and see that bloody man, the accountant,' she fumed. 'And Carol's threatening a migraine and Tony's gone off to some ridiculous trade fair – just when I need some advice . . .'

'How's Kate this morning?' Liz enquired, tactfully. She knew Jessica was worried about something in particular to do with the shop; she also knew she was powerless to help.

'*She's* all right. Sitting in her high-chair chucking her breakfast overboard.' At the mention of Kate, her voice lifted. 'Look, we'll be down on Saturday – tomorrow – as early as I can manage. Sorry about the moans . . .'

Christopher 'phoned just as Liz was about to go out. She wanted to find a present for Kate that was just right. Sweaters for the twins, something for Jason – cards to write to Caroline, friends, people in the office.

'Hi,' Liz answered, casual, friendly. 'Thank you for such a fun evening.' That seemed neutral enough, she thought, remembering.

'Look, I'll pick you up. At the hotel. About 3.30. Will that be convenient?' Very cool and clipped, he sounded. Liz could hear the clacking of a telex in the background. He must be at his office in the City.

'Fine. I'll be waiting downstairs.'

One of the many uniformed minions in the hotel lobby told her, that afternoon, that the heatwave was expected to last through the weekend. So Madam would be seeing the countryside at its best. Liz smiled and agreed, watching for Christopher's car. Across the lobby, a well-dressed American, a man in his fifties, stared boldly, admiringly. Liz looked away. Unaccountably, she felt slightly nervous, her hands clammy. It had turned sultry and even her thin cotton skirt and blouse clung to her skin. She would be glad to be out of London's airlessness.

She spotted Christopher as he was crossing the street. He was dressed for the country – open-necked shirt, sleeves rolled up to his elbows, grey slacks. He looked very boyish, very jaunty.

'Hope I'm not late. Diabolical traffic already, I'm afraid. Everyone's trying to get out of London. Is this all you've got?'

He swung her case as they walked to the car. Liz saw that the top was down.

'I'll close it if you like,' Christopher offered.

'Leave it. It's fine,' she lied, thinking: there's an example of our almost ten-year age difference for you . . . She tied on a silk scarf and put on dark glasses. There was a coppery glare to the sun.

They inched their way through central London and turned onto the motorway for Oxford. Unfettered, the powerful sports car shot forward. Liz watched Christopher's hands on the steering-wheel, saw the speedometer jump.

When they spoke, they had to shout against the noise of the engine and the torrent of rushing air.

'Did you mean what you said last night – about giving up your job?' Christopher yelled.

'I'm not sure. I might,' Liz shouted back.

'Jessica looked horrified.' He glanced at her briefly. He was smiling.

'I know. I saw.' She laughed. The speed and the deafening noise intoxicated her. Liz had a sudden urge to lean over and kiss Christopher's cheek. Soon, she would be in the Cotswolds, on the ridge, looking down to where Fontwell nestled in its green valley.

She felt deliriously happy.

The car slowed. They could speak normally again; Liz's exhilaration passed.

'The end of the motorway? That was quick.'

'I really put my foot down,' Christopher said, negotiating a roundabout. 'The rest of the going is rather slow. You remember it, I expect?'

'Yes. It's very familiar.'

And such a long way from New York . . .

They had left the heavy skies in London. The sun broke through, stippling the fresh leaves. Past Oxford, Christopher turned off onto narrow country roads. Hedgerows were dusted in hawthorne. Cow parsley studded with wild poppies lined the roadsides. Flinty stone walls flashed by, a field of yellow mustard. To their right lay a valley, a river meandering through; cottages, a church spire, an imposing country mansion.

'Don't you miss all this, in London?' Liz asked.

'I'll come back. One day.' Even on those twisting roads, he drove with assurance. He must know every inch of the country round here, Liz thought. 'Managing the land is beyond Dad now. The place is going to pieces, I'm afraid. Worrying . . .' He frowned.

They were driving along an escarpment which dropped steeply to their left. A line of blue hills was visible in the distance. Up an incline, through a village, then: 'Here we are.' Christopher swung the car through imposing gates and Fontwell lay in the hollow beneath them.

'Breathtaking' was how the guides described it from that spot as the charabancs rolled down on days the house and garden were open to the public.

'The same,' Liz said, 'just the same,' seduced yet again by its beauty, its air of hushed tranquillity. Its timelessness.

'Yes.' She sensed his shared pleasure, his pride. He drove slowly down towards the old house. Savouring the moment, Liz noted sunlight on the weathered grey walls, the pond, the dovecote. Lawns, herbaceous borders filled with colour. The walled garden to the side, the tennis court, yew hedges, a cluster of cottages and the church beyond. A steep green hill, rimmed by a coppice, rose behind.

As they descended, Liz had the sensation of floating into a well remembered dream.

Katherine Vane came out of the front door, which was thrown wide open, the moment the car stopped. Her arms were held out.

'Liz.'

They embraced warmly.

'I can hardly believe I'm here,' Liz said. She pulled off her scarf. Her hair was windblown from the journey. 'Magical as ever. Nothing has changed.'

'*We* have,' Katherine Vane said, smiling. 'You wait and see.'

'Really not,' Liz told her honestly. Not with that bone structure and English skin, she thought. Short hair more white than blonde now. Like Kate's. 'And it's been four years . . .'

There was a commotion behind them by the car as the dogs spotted Christopher, jumping and tumbling all over him, yelping delightedly. Freeing himself, Christopher put his arm round his mother and bent to kiss her cheek. To Liz, their likeness was startling. And their eyes were pale, like aquamarines, not really blue at all.

'Christopher darling, I've put Liz in Jessica's old room. Miles away from the rest of us, including Kate. Put her things up there, would you?'

In the hall, they met Tom Vane. He seemed, to Liz, bent and rather shrunken, a shadow of the bluff squire she remembered. Illness and personal tragedy had visibly taken their toll. They chatted briefly – 'splendid to hear a good Yank accent again, Liz' – and walked up the wide, shallow stairs, across the gallery and down a corridor. At the end, a door was open. Jessica's old room which Liz knew so well. The same pink and white striped walls of years ago. Faded, but still pretty.

'Lovely,' Liz said. 'Like old times.'

'I hope you'll be comfortable. Anything you need – shout. We count you as family, Liz, not a guest.'

'I'm glad, Katherine.' There was a bowl of roses, the palest, creamy pink, on the dressing-table. Kneeling on the windowseat, Liz saw the sweep of lawn stretching below; to the left, the yew hedges and the church. The early evening sun cast long shadows. 'Such peace, Katherine. That's how I always think of Fontwell.'

'Not always so peaceful. Liz. Such a lot has happened since you were here. And we get all your news from Jessica, of course: *Gibsons'*, your new husband. Such a pity he couldn't come . . . But tell me, what do you think of my Kate? She's rather a pet, isn't she?'

'She's absolutely adorable.'

'*We* think so.'

Smiling, Liz watched Katherine Vane affectionately. Speaking of her granddaughter, her face glowed with pleasure. She was slim as a young girl in her pale linen dress. Poised; assured. 'And Jessica? I *think* she's all right, don't you, Liz?'

'She's fine, Katherine. She was always her own person. Very strong.'

'And a rebel. Although I've never understood why. I don't find her — easy these days. Standoffish. Almost bitter towards us, at least.' She sighed. 'But I can't go on worrying. Now, Christopher . . .'

Looking down at that moment Liz saw him walking across the lawn with his father. They were deep in conversation. The sight of him, so unexpected, disturbed Liz. The two men stopped and looked up at the house. Tom Vane was pointing something out — the roof? a chimney? — with his stick.

'But he's still such a young man,' Liz said, turning to face Katherine Vane, keeping her voice impersonal. 'He has everything ahead of him.'

'True. But he and Vanessa, as you know, literally grew up together. They were always a part of each other's lives. I think this has made her death especially hard for him. And he has been very brave. Her illness, Vanessa's, when we first heard, we simply couldn't believe it.'

'It was unbelievable,' Liz said quietly.

'And I sometimes think hearts do break. None of us can get close to Christopher. He says he's quite enjoying the City — although he's badly needed here. As you say, he is young. He will mend. Time . . .' Her voice trailed off. It was very quiet in the bedroom. Outside, in the warm air, the doves cooed softly. The eyes of the two women met and held in a long look.

'In time,' Katherine Vane finished briskly, 'and if he gets the help he so badly needs. Now, Liz darling, I shall leave you. Drinks about seven in the drawing-room. Did I give you enough decent hangers?'

'One of my specials, Liz?' Tom Vane asked as Liz walked into the drawing-room before dinner. She felt cool in her blue silk dress; refreshed by a bath and the peace of Fontwell.

'Sounds good to me,' she answered politely. It was, she knew from experience, a gallant attempt at an American martini. To refuse would have been churlish. Now, changed

129

for dinner, immaculately groomed, Tom Vane was recognisable as the former Guards' officer in the silver framed photograph on a sidetable.

Christopher was standing in front of the fireplace, one arm resting along the mantelpiece. He looked at ease; less grave than his London self. He, too, had put on a tie, Liz noticed. Behind his father's back, he winked at Liz, raising his glass and grimacing.

'These cocktails of yours don't improve with practice, Dad.'

'Nonsense, my boy.' He measured carefully. 'Here you go, Liz.' Putting his arm round her, he led her over to one of the huge sofas which flanked the fireplace. Clouds of white lilac were arranged behind. 'Now come and tell me what's been going on in your life in New York. I've heard great things from Jessica, in fact, she sent us an article about you – their *Times* wasn't it? – and we thought how jolly clever you were . . . you're looking very handsome, by the way, my dear . . .'

Soon, Katherine Vane came in. Firmly refusing a cocktail, she asked Christopher to pour her a sherry. Unusual for her, she looked a little flustered.

'Drink up everyone. I'm afraid we're going to dine rather early. It seems there's a fair in Cirencester and such help as we have is intending to go.'

The panelled dining-room at Fontwell was always considered the finest room in the house. But its original grandeur had taken on a cosy shabbiness – family portraits dulled with age and fading brocade curtains; the crest on the silver worn thin. Looking round the table during dinner, it was easy to see, Liz thought, where Jessica got her knack for entertaining. Here, at Fontwell, from her mother. The meal was simple – roast lamb and crisp, fresh vegetables – served by a young girl, obviously trained by Katherine Vane.

'Quite a decent claret this,' Tom Vane said, pouring the wine fussily. Across the flowers and the ivory candles, Liz saw Christopher watching her. Their eyes met and she caught her breath.

'I do hope Jessica gets away early,' she said smoothly, turning to Katherine Vane. 'London was terribly hot and stuffy today.'

'Damn place isn't fit for humans to live in,' Tom Vane remarked from his end of the table.

'Tommy dear . . . not good for Kate, this weather. Babies never like the heat.'

'Whether or not my dear sister turns up early tomorrow, I'm taking Liz off on a Cotswold picnic,' Christopher said. 'That's definite.'

'You must,' Katherine Vane said quickly, looking from Liz to Christopher and back. 'Can't waste this heavenly weather and the short time Liz is with us.'

Thick cream from the farm was served with the strawberries. Christopher was saying, 'But Dad, if we did sell a piece of land to raise liquid assets, there would be a good many tax advantages.'

In the drawing-room, sitting in a straight-backed chair beneath a strong light, Katherine Vane took out her embroidery.

'Hand me my specs, would you, Liz dear? More coffee?' Christopher and his father had disappeared into the study. 'I'm delighted Chris seems to be taking an interest in the place again,' she continued, holding up silks to the light. 'Tommy is finding it harder and harder to cope. Our manager is rather a bungler, frankly. He's aged, do you think? Tommy?'

'A bit. But he seemed very cheery tonight.'

'Having other people does him good. Gets him out of his rut. But what about you, Liz? Tell me about *Gibsons'*.'

'Well — I guess you could say I've done a rescue operation. It was going downhill rapidly when I took over. Now, it's back on top again. I've been lucky. I've had a good team. It's worked. Advertising and circulation way up . . . I hope a lot of people find it a good read. It seems — they do!'

'It sounds awesome. Such an accomplishment. Tell me, isn't it the most terribly hard work?'

'God, yes. In fact, it has taken over my life to such an

131

extent that I'm considering giving it up. It suddenly came to me at Jessica's last night. *I've done it*. Why go on? Does that surprise you, Katherine?'

'I don't believe so. Should it?' She measured and cut several lengths of silk. 'I mean, you've got a nice new husband, other things in your life . . . Jessica liked your Dick.'

'I know. I like him, too,' she agreed, laughing and throwing back her hair. 'We're really very good friends. We understand what each other's life is about. We match, somehow.'

Scent from the lavender beds wafted in through the open windows; insects flew about the light.

'Forgive me asking, Liz, but I always pictured you with children. Much more maternal than Jessica, I thought. No?'

Liz put her chin on her hand. She spoke very quietly. 'Of course I want a child, Katherine. More than anything. I knew that, yet again, when I saw Kate. I *ached* . . . But what do you do when you have a husband − quite a lot older, already with one child from a former marriage − who won't?'

'Dick? But why not?'

Liz sighed. 'So many reasons and they all sound plausible. They don't help the aching, however . . . let's see − a child would change our lives, restrict freedom to come and go . . . mean problems with nannies, schools and camps to be found . . . Oh, and he thinks I'm too old to start.'

'Surely not. Sad for you, I think, Liz.'

'It feels sad, often. Empty. Although life, work, goes on of course. There have been awful times, awful moments when I've thought I was going mad . . . I was so frightened, Katherine . . . the sight of a pram . . . I remember once, on 72nd Street, a pram with a baby sitting up and I simply *yearned* . . . friends' babies, children playing in the Park . . . A year or so ago I came across an article in a French magazine interviewing women of around forty who had just had babies. I read it so often, it fell to pieces in my hands. *There*. Now I've told you.' She tried to smile; her throat felt tight.

'My poor Liz.' Katherine Vane put down her sewing and

looked at her. 'As bad as that?'

'Worse. Impossible to describe. Unless you've felt it. The panic — sweating, literally — as the months go by . . . but I haven't felt so intense about it all recently. Resigned, almost.'

'But how does this make you feel towards Dick?'

'Resentful. Cold inside. *Rejected*. That more than anything. Although I do think, perhaps, that he is beginning to see what it is doing to us — to our relationship. It has been very destructive. He has been under the most tremendous business pressure, really embattled. A huge merger which he masterminded. But this is over now, so perhaps . . .'

'I see.' Katherine Vane picked up her sewing, her hands moving deftly above the canvas. 'You know, do you, that Jessica has never told Tommy or me the name of Kate's father?' She sewed calmly, haloed in light.

'I know that.'

'In fact, it wasn't until she was five months pregnant that she told us about the baby at all. She simply stayed away, made excuses. She said after that she was terribly sick to begin with and determined to go through with it. And that was why.'

'But Katherine,' Liz got up and helped herself to more coffee, 'in New York last year she told me you had both been angels. Completely supportive.'

'We've tried to, certainly.' She snipped a thread, smoothing the canvas on her knee. 'And it hasn't been easy. You can appreciate that. Living as we do here, part of rather a conventional country existence. I realise that Jessica, in her impatient way, believes that only her generation knows a thing about life and loves and affairs of the heart. Naturally, that is absurd — particularly to those of us who spent the war separated from our husbands.' She looked directly at Liz. And Liz thought: what a stunning beauty she must have been in those days, nearly forty years ago now. Living in London, working at the Admiralty, Tommy overseas. 'However, I am *not* accustomed to the flouting of surface conventions. You, Liz, so much younger, brought up in a different moral climate, may think this hypocritical.'

'I don't. I understand. On the whole I think I feel the

133

same. But I admire Jessica – her guts, her courage. She wanted a child, Katherine, wanted one so badly. I couldn't believe my eyes when I saw her last summer in New York. And yet everything she said made sense to me – really, it was exactly the way I felt – feel – myself.'

'Was it, Liz?'

'Oh, *yes*. And seeing her with Kate seems so natural. It's as though she has had her always. I envy her that, Katherine.'

Katherine Vane sighed. 'In any event, we have tried to be understanding and helpful towards Jessica. And we adore Kate. Yet she persists in this coldness towards us which hurts us both terribly. You'll see.'

'Will I?'

'I'm afraid so. I can't talk to Jessica like this, Liz. I can't get close to her. Ever.' Impulsively, she leant forward and touched Liz's hand. 'About a child. And Dick. It's not like you, Liz, not to fight for what you want. Not if you want it badly enough. Now is it?'

Liz shook her head. She was smiling

'I suppose not . . .'

'Well, then . . .'

Katherine Vane adjusted her glasses and held the canvas up to the light. 'That wonderful blue looks charming on you, Liz. Like a hyacinth. And I've never seen you looking better.'

'Or fatter,' Liz laughed.

'Nonsense, darling, you're a tall girl. All in proportion. Tommy says all the men find these skinny young things too boring.'

They heard voices outside the drawing-room door. Tom Vane said something inaudible and Christopher laughed.

'I've enjoyed our talk,' Katherine Vane said. 'And you've done Chris the world of good. He seemed much more like his old self tonight.'

CHAPTER 17

It's going to be a scorcher, Liz thought, wandering out into the garden after breakfast with a mug of coffee. She sat on the bench by the sundial, closing her eyes, putting her face up to the sun. It was very still; she could feel tiny beads of sweat on her upper lip.

'That's a pretty outfit, Liz.' Katherine Vane joined her. She carried gloves and cutting scissors and she was wearing an enormous, rather faded, straw hat. 'Did you get it from Bubbles?'

'Mmm. Cute, isn't it? The shoes too. Just right for this weather.'

'She's got such a good eye, Jessica. It's marvellous to see the shop really established. I believe she's selling quite a lot of things in America now.'

'She is.' Liz sipped her coffee. The twin herbaceous borders, bursting with colour, stretched ahead of them towards a shady arbor in which a Grecian statue languished. 'Only the British can garden,' Liz murmured. She felt languid; dreamy; not quite in touch.

'You must come with Dick next time, Liz. And bring the little boy, Jason. It's a paradise here for children in good weather — fishing, swimming in the lake, tennis, the horses.'

Jason would love it; she must show him Fontwell one day. He and she always enjoyed the same places. It was a bond between them.

Tom Vane was walking across the lawn towards them. He, too, was wearing a battered straw hat. (So much for the secret of an English skin, Liz thought, amused.)

'Christopher is on the 'phone to Jessica,' he called out.

135

'She was in a bit of a panic. That accountant chap got the wind up her. Chris is sorting it all out.'

'Oh no, Tommy. When will she be here?' Katherine Vane asked, dismayed.

'Late afternoon, she thinks now.'

'Not until then? In that case, I must go and reorganise some things in the kitchen. You and Chris take anything you want for a picnic, Liz,' she said over her shoulder.

'We will.' Turning to Tom Vane, Liz said, 'Your garden looks blissful this morning. I'm sitting here admiring — lazily.'

He sat down heavily beside her, took out a handkerchief and mopped his forehead.

'It's hard going these days, now that we're so short-handed. Katherine has developed into an obsessive weeder. I must say, when you get a show like this, it's worth it.'

'I'll say.'

'Good chap Chris, you know, Liz. Got his head screwed on all right. He's giving Jessica some very sound advice in there.'

'He's been through a lot, Tom. Vanessa . . .' She still had the sense of unreality; the dreaminess.

'He'll come round, he'll come round.'

———————

Late in the morning, Christopher and Liz set off. Foraging in the kitchen they had collected some bread, cheese and pâté and unearthed an old wicker picnic basket which still retained plastic plates and knives.

'We won't bother about anything to drink,' Christopher told her. 'We'll go to the pub. I know a good, short walk through some woods.' He looked doubtfully at her shoes. 'Nothing too arduous.'

As they drove slowly above Fontwell's hollow, Christopher pointed out his cottage at the end of a wooded lane.

'Vanessa adored it,' he said. It was the first time he had mentioned her name since they got to Fontwell, Liz realised. 'She planned the whole conversion. I'll show you round on our way back. I always stay there when I'm down.' So that

136

was where he had slept last night.

High up on Cotswold ridges, they drove past grey stone walls, yellow fields of mustard, patches of dense woodland. Long roadside grasses brushed the car. The warm air rushed past their faces. Christopher slowed and turned the car in by a gate. Liz saw that they were on top of a hill. Below lay a valley, a sprawling village, misty in the heat haze.

'I thought we would walk down towards the pub from here, picnic somewhere in the woods.'

'Fine. Let's go.'

Christopher took the rug and the picnic basket and swung easily over the gate. Helping Liz, he took her hand, leading her across a field and into a dappled beechwood. The floor was carpeted with blue; fragrant; deliciously cool.

'Bluebells. Past their best by a couple of weeks, but very pretty all the same,' Christopher said.

'Magical,' Liz agreed, breathing in the woody scents. Above them, the trees were trellises of most delicate green, through which the sunlight glinted. Beyond a stone wall, far off, the other side of the valley rose mistily. They walked on until they came to a stream.

'I thought we could pitch camp here and walk on to the pub to get a drink. It's not far and the views are spectacular,' Christopher said. He put down the rug and the basket and held out his hand again. 'Come on.' He was smiling rather shyly; characteristically, his hair had fallen onto his forehead. Liz moved to follow him, meaning to take his hand, but instead, their arms ended up round each other.

Liz felt lightheaded; without a care in the world. It seemed very good to her to be walking through these woods on a fine spring morning with Christopher. Neither of them spoke.

Reaching the pub, Liz asked for cider. She sat on one of the seats outside while Christopher went inside. The sun was hot on her arms, her face, her bare legs. She listened to the strong country accents around her as people walked out carrying their pints. Squinting, she watched the larks calling and falling in the perfect blue arc of the sky.

Somewhere, in another world, she had a different life.

They walked back by another, longer path, pointing out to each other the landmarks and sudden dramatic views. When

137

they got to the spot where they had left the picnic, they spread out the rug and opened the basket.

'Hell,' Christopher said, brandishing an opener. 'We forgot glasses. And there aren't any cups.'

'Who cares?' Liz took a swig of cider from the bottle he had opened. She was thirsty. 'It tastes just fine.'

Over lunch, which they both ate ravenously, they talked about Jessica.

'She's not good at figures. I don't think she realises how successful the shop is.' Christopher tore another hunk of bread. 'But she needs working capital and she needs to borrow more from the bank. It's no problem. Any business does it.'

'Is that what she's been so worried about?'

Christopher nodded. 'That's been the main difficulty. But she's got a good accountant to advise her. Tony. And me. The trouble is, getting her to listen.'

'She badly needs a vacation to get away . . .'

'Badly. She's very ragged – nervy – which isn't surprising after all she's been through this year. Unfortunately, she's been taking it out on the parents.'

'Your mother mentioned this to me last night. Not knowing about Kate's father hurts them dreadfully. Why should Jessica want to hurt them?'

'God knows.' Christopher looked gloomy. 'I'm devoted to my sister, but she can be bloody awkward.'

When they had finished eating and scattered crumbs for the birds, Liz kicked off her shoes and splashed her feet in the stream. Affected by the heat, they lay back on the mossy ground, looking up through the layers of shimmering greenery. They heard only birdsong and the occasional car in the distance.

They were inches apart; drowsy; conscious of each other's nearness. They did not speak.

After some time, they packed up and walked back to the car. Hot silence blanketed the afternoon. The sound of the engine starting shattered the stillness. Christopher drove back down the lane near Fontwell and straight to his cottage. Without speaking, he handed her out of the car. He fished the key from under a stone and they went inside.

Liz had the impression of quite a long, low room. There were softly coloured chintz chairs and curtains; books lying about in piles, photographs everywhere.

'Liz . . .' It was the first word spoken between them since they had left the picnic. Languid with the heat and the strong country cider, Liz looked at him. His face was burnished from the sun; she thought he was extraordinarily handsome. He took her hand. 'Liz . . .' he said again. Her eyes were fixed on the blond hairs on his arm. Leading the way, he guided her up the stairs to a small bedroom at the back of the cottage. It was quiet there, very still, almost dark after the brilliant sunlight.

As though mesmerised, she said nothing.

Christopher pulled her towards him and kissed her. Sense, conscience − reality − deserted her. Her body softened, leaning; her eyes closed; her mouth opened.

Abruptly, he turned away from her. She stared − disbelieving. Then, she understood. There was no decision; only instinct.

'Chris . . .'

He was standing apart. She moved to him, her face pressed against his back, her arms on his. 'Christopher . . . darling . . . Christopher . . .' Her pressure on his arms propelled him. Slowly, he turned back to her. His expression was taut and strained. She sensed his helplessness, his vulnerability.

She knew. Quickly, she pulled her T-shirt over her head. She smelled the scents and perspiration of their bodies. All the time, she was conscious of the warmth, the shadowy room, flowered wallpaper, a bed in the corner.

'Liz, please, help me . . .'

He was afraid.

'I know, I know, I'll make it right,' she breathed.

Everything appeared to Liz like a film in slow motion. Her hair fell to her shoulders; her breasts, she knew, were full and beautiful. Her eyes never leaving his face, she touched them and her nipples hardened.

'Christopher . . .'

As a sleepwalker, he bent towards her.

'Here, here . . .'

139

Childlike, she put him to her breast, cradling him, touching his neck, his hair, his cheek. Carefully, caressingly, she removed his shirt. Her skirt fell to the ground. His hands moved down from her waist. He stirred against her thigh. She knelt on the cold floor, heard him call her name over and over.

Lying together on the bed, she helped him still.

All around the green, shadowy room heaved softly, like cool waters. Somewhere, not far away, Liz heard a car.

'Darling Liz . . .' His voice had changed, grown more urgent. And his hands, his mouth, the tension of his body. His shoulders were above her, his mouth on hers. Pressing, moving. Moving her.

'*Christopher.*'

She gasped and she came to him and he took her triumphantly.

The peaceful room, green and still again, enclosed them.

Minutes passed. Christopher's head was buried against her. Raised on one elbow, Liz ran her fingers along his back, admiring the length and slenderness of his body, the muscular arms and shoulders. He had cried unrestrainedly. She knew that she was the first woman he had made love to since Vanessa.

He slept. Very carefully, very quietly, she got up. Retrieving scattered clothes, she dressed quickly. She glanced at the bed. Christopher had not moved. He was sleeping deeply. She tiptoed from the room and down the stairs. She saw that the cottage was quite small, one large room below and two bedrooms above.

Opening the front door, she came face to face with a photograph — an enlarged snapshot — of Christopher and Vanessa, arms around each other, laughing. Liz turned away.

On the doorstep, another shock. She stopped. Her body froze. A bottle of milk and a basket of flowers stood by the door.

She had heard a car nearby. *Katherine Vane.* Who else? She would have seen Christopher's car, known they were together in the cottage.

Liz began to walk quickly up the lane. She glanced at her watch. Four o'clock. It was still hot, even on that shady path. She glimpsed Fontwell through the trees.

Gradually, the full impact of what had happened between her and Christopher struck her. How could she have allowed it — *wanted it* — to happen: Older, so much more experienced. Her cheeks were burning. Oh God; Oh God. The heat, the cider. The look — the touch — of Christopher. All her senses roused.

And the rest of the weekend before her. Facing them all. How?

And Dick, said a small voice inside her. And Dick.

At the end of the lane, she turned left, following the path down the hollow towards the house. It was a ten minute walk. Reaching the house, she was relieved to find nobody about in the hall as she went to her room.

She washed and brushed her hair. Straightened her clothes; splashed her face with water. Dabbed on cologne. She felt calmer, more composed. She smiled secretly. But for Katherine to have visited the cottage!

Through the window, she could see Tom Vane sitting by the table beneath the cedar tree, reading a newspaper. It must be time for tea. It would be thought strange if she did not appear. Bracing herself, Liz went downstairs.

'Liz . . . hullo there . . .' Katherine Vane called out in her light, musical voice. 'I'm in the kitchen. Making tea. Come in.' Liz made her way through a series of pantries to the cavernous kitchen.

'The heat,' Katherine Vane said, looking up from arranging cups on a tray, smiling brightly. 'You managed a bit of a rest, I hope. And was the picnic fun?'

'Marvellous. I never remember how beautiful the Cotswolds are until I see them again.'

'They really are, aren't they? Too wonderful. Earl Grey with lemon, I think, in this weather.' She poured steaming water into a silver teapot.

'I saw Christopher was showing you the cottage when I dropped a couple of things over for him. It's charming, isn't it?'

'Delightful. Very pretty, very cosy.'

'Actually, it's two tiny cottages knocked into one. Vanessa was clever at that kind of thing. She and Christopher did a lot of the work themselves. Did he tell you? Take the tin out, would you, Liz? Tommy can't do without his Chocolate Olivers.'

So there was to be no awkwardness, no difficulty; not from Katherine, at least. Liz had the strangest feeling that she was behaving towards her with even more than her usual warmth. She sensed a subtle change of attitude. Fanciful, perhaps.

In procession, they took the tea things out onto the lawn. It was shady and sweet smelling beneath the cedar. Tom Vane was still wearing his old straw hat. The dogs lay panting at his feet.

Neither Tom Vane nor Katherine, Liz noted thankfully, asked for Christopher. They must assume he was still at the cottage. He had, after all, his own and quite separate life.

'Thank you.' She took a cup from Katherine Vane; she felt cool and happy and relaxed. Jessica and Kate would be there soon, any moment now.

Nearby, a green and shadowy room with flowered wallpaper, a bed pushed into the corner . . .

As they sipped their tea, Tom Vane huffed on about a certain Labour politician he disapproved of. Katherine Vane, although agreeing, made soothing sounds and offered biscuits. The dogs opened weary eyes, twitched, and slept again.

Behind them, the house was bathed in golden rays. Shadows crept across the lawn. Clouds of gnats hovered around their heads.

CHAPTER 18

They were still sitting under the cedar, glancing through the papers, when Jessica's car came sputtering down the drive.

'Here she is. At last.' Girlishly, Katherine Vane jumped up and started to run across the lawn. Tom Vane and Liz followed. The small, battered Renault, frequently used for transporting merchandise, drew up with a screech of tyres which sent the gravel flying. Jessica got out. She looked hot and dishevelled. And cross, Liz saw. She was wearing what appeared to be a man's shirt over her jeans, sunglasses pushed up on top of her head.

'Quite the bloodiest journey ever. Cheers, folks.' Kate, who had apparently been asleep in her carrycot in the back, woke up as the car stopped and began to wail.

'Poor lamb.' Opening the door, Katherine Vane extricated her. The baby's hair was wet, plastered to her forehead, and there was a heat rash down one side of her face. But once in her grandmother's arms, surrounded by a circle of admiring grown-ups, her cries ceased. Liz tickled a pink foot. Tears still running down her cheeks, she began smiling angelically, clutching at Katherine Vane's hat with chubby fingers.

'When did you leave London, Jess?' Tom Vane asked.

'Soon after lunch. When I'd got rid of the dreaded accountant. And on a Saturday. Hi, Dad.' She gave her father a peck on the cheek. Liz and Katherine were totally absorbed in Kate. 'Traffic everywhere. Queues of cars, roadworks, breakdowns. The lot.' She grinned at Liz. 'Now you see what I mean by not-so-good days. I hope you're enjoying your leisure. Sorry I couldn't make it earlier.'

'You missed a marvellous day. A picnic up in the Cotswolds. It was really hot.'

'So I see. You've caught the sun. Where's old Christopher?'

'Up at the cottage,' Liz said quickly, joining her.

Jessica glanced over at her daughter, now gurgling seductively at her grandmother. 'I must say, she was very good. A trooper. Look, I badly need a bath, a drink and a natter. Let me see to Kate first.'

She dragged a plastic holdall from the car. Tom Vane was carrying an assortment of her luggage into the house.

'Mother, I think Kate's probably feeling hungry and thirsty. Certainly thirsty.'

'We'll see to that, won't we Katie-Kate,' Katherine cooed. Then, to Jessica, 'Oh darling, you've got those awful clogs on. How do you drive in them? You know they infuriate your father, clomp, clomp, clomp on the stairs . . .'

'Oh Mother, the moment I get here, you start nagging about something. I'll take them off, for God's sake.' She kicked them onto the drive, stuffed them in the holdall and stood barefoot. Liz saw that her face was flushed with anger. 'I hope that makes everyone happier.'

There was a difficult silence. Katherine Vane, holding Kate, stood still as a statue.

'By the way,' Jessica went on after a few moments, quite normally, 'Tony Langdon is staying at a relative's establishment near here and wanted an escape hatch. I asked him for dinner tonight. Is that all right? I can easily put him off.'

'Tonight?' her mother asked coolly. 'Why, yes, of course. Only he must be here by 7.30. We're dining at 8.00, no later. Now what do you think Kate wants to eat?'

As Jessica followed her mother into the house, Liz heard the dogs rousing. She turned and caught sight of Christopher, sprinting easily down the path from the cottage which paralleled the drive.

All of a sudden, she knew the meaning of the expression weak at the knees. Her instinct was to flee — anywhere.

Christopher had changed into a white tennis shirt. Glad of the exercise after a lazy afternoon, the dogs yelped and raced towards him. Panting slightly, he caught up with Liz outside Fontwell's massive front door. He put his hands on her shoulders, forcing her to look straight at him. She quailed.

Her hair was full of light from the early evening sun — golds, greys, browns. She wore no make-up at all. Freckles dusted her face.

'There are two things,' he said gravely, 'that I forgot to tell you. The first is that from the moment I saw you at Jessica's I've been thinking about how beautiful you are — and little else.'

Liz gasped. 'Secondly, I love the way your nose wrinkles when you smile. Which is often.'

She smiled then.

The tension broke and they laughed. In huge relief, Liz thought: so everything is going to be all right after all.

When they went inside, they found the great old house stirring into life. After the day's bright sunshine, the hall was dark and cool. As she stood there with Christopher, Liz heard voices from the kitchen — the cook and the maid from the village. Jessica. Kate was protesting loudly and impatiently; laughter followed. Katherine Vane appeared, her arms full of flowers, colourful and sweet-smelling.

'There you are, Chris. Darling, would you go and help your father with the drinks and the glasses? He's dithering about in the cellar . . . and I haven't done the table yet, or cheered up the flowers. Jessica's going to ask you if you would mind bathing Kate, Liz. Sponging her off a bit. Jessica longs for a bath herself after that ghastly journey.'

Following the somnolent heat of the afternoon, there was an air of purposefulness about the place; pleasurable anticipation of the evening ahead. Cooking smells began to emanate from the kitchen, although Liz knew that Katherine Vane had already made the soup and dessert, planned every detail of the dinner menu; picked the fruit and vegetables from the garden that morning.

From the dining-room, Christopher called out to his father with slight impatience, 'But I've brought them up already, Dad. I'll open them a couple of hours before we eat.

145

Okay. Now. And which port, do you think? Tony knows his stuff over drinks.'

Later, sitting in the bathroom with Kate on her lap, drying between her toes while she wriggled, Liz heard Jessica phoning Tony in one of the corridors upstairs, giving him directions, telling him quite sharply what time he was expected. '*Of course* I'm behaving myself,' she ended impatiently. '*Ciao* . . .'

There was a knock on her bedroom door. 'Come in,' Liz called. Jessica came in, wrapped in an enormous towelling robe of her father's, whisky glass in hand.

'You were an angel bathing Kate for me, Liz.'

'We both enjoyed it. She's a great splasher. By the way, I left her door open in case she cries.'

'I saw.' Jessica settled herself on the bed, watching Liz put rollers in her hair at the dressing-table mirror. 'It's marvellous to have you here. Like old times.' She took a sip of her drink. 'You can't imagine how desperately I needed a bit of peace and a bath.'

'I could see that when you got here. Clogs and all.' Liz turned to face her, smiling.

'Mother and Dad do drive me mad. I know how good they are, how hard they try. Quite honestly, the christening business is purely for them. And a marvellous excuse to get you over, of course. I suppose I was rather vile to Mother, over the clogs. We've never got on terribly well. God knows why. All my life everyone – *everyone* – has told me how wonderful she is. Only *I* find her so irritating. The fact is, I'm simply not the daughter they envisaged having.'

'Why do you say that?' Liz enquired through a mouthful of pins.

'Because it's true. Not orthodox enough for them.'

'They're very admiring of you even if they feel they don't quite understand you.'

'Perhaps,' Jessica said, indifferent.

'They find you a bit cold. Standoffish.'

'Mother been at you?'

'She mentioned it. And the mystery of Kate's father . . .'

Somewhere in the house, a 'phone rang. 'I hope that's not Dick,' Liz said. They listened. Jessica handed her glass to Liz. The shout which they had half expected did not come.

'Why on earth not, Liz? You're not screwing that one up, I hope?' Liz shook her head.

'Certainly not. But — I want distance for a bit. Apartness. I want to figure out where I'm going from here. Choices.'

'Fair enough. And what's all this about *Gibsons'* — giving it up?'

'I don't know, Jess. Choices again. I'm in limbo. And that's where I feel like being for the moment.'

'Have you been thinking about this for some time?'

'No. Not consciously, at least.'

'What prompted it, then?'

'I don't know,' Liz answered truthfully. It was hard to explain, even to Jessica. It suddenly seemed, away from it all, an absurd way to live. She said, 'The tension the worrying, the long hours, the tiredness, the endless administration. Always the possibility of the magazine going sour again. It wouldn't take much, believe me. A downturn in the economy, some scared advertisers. It was something Dick said, when he 'phoned the other day. I thought: what's it all for?'

'You do realise that everyone, but everyone, in New York would think you had lost your senses. Especially Dick. Liz Conrad of *Gibsons'* — Superwoman of the 1980's. After printing that article the *New York Times* might sue you.'

Liz threw back her head and laughed. 'That's funny, Jess. Really. To hell with *The Times*. How's that for sacrilege? Listen, I talked to your mother about it last night. She understood.'

'You and she always got on. She's a great fan. But she *is* cocooned in Gloucestershire. Not exactly in the swim of the New York success league.'

'No decision yet. Just thinking. Aloud.' She took another sip of Scotch handing it back to Jessica. 'This goes down well. Now tell me about Tony. I liked him.'

'Did you? Honestly?'

'Yes. I wasn't sure at first. But he grew on me.'

'Everyone says that. Including me.'

147

'I think you respect him.'

'As a matter of fact, I do.' Jessica stared into her glass. 'Do you realise he's exactly five years younger than my father?'

'I suppose so. Does that matter?'

Jessica shrugged. 'His divorce comes through this summer and he's making marrying noises. Kate and the conventions and so on.'

'Well?'

'Like you, I just don't know. Marriage strikes terror, rather. I don't see my having Kate has anything to do with it. More to the point, he wants us to go off to Greece on holiday this summer. That does sound blissful.'

'You should, Jess. You need a rest. Badly.'

'Kate, the shop . . .' Jessica closed her eyes briefly. Liz saw the fine lines, the strain.

'It could all be managed.'

'I daresay. Look.' She stared hard at Liz. 'I've seen you with Kate. Strong maternal instinct and all that. You should have a baby, you know.'

'Maybe.'

Remembering the time, tearing off to change, Jessica stuck her head back through the door.

'By the way,' she said blithely, 'you've certainly cheered up old Christopher. Good work.'

'No thanks, Dad, I'll stick to scotch,' Jessica said briskly, refusing Tom Vane's offer of a 'special'.

'Not the first of the evening, Jess,' Christopher said pointedly.

'Shut up, Chris, and mind your own business.' Jessica poured herself a stiff drink.

'Children, children,' Katherine Vane murmured vaguely, snipping off a drooping head of white lilac. She glided through the drawing-room in a long skirt of rustling taffeta, which everyone in the family knew was at least twenty years old. Her exquisite diamond-drop earings glimmered.

'Hullo, Liz darling,' she said as Liz walked in, 'why, you're looking quite brown.' She was wearing a white cotton

148

skirt and lace blouse. The wide collar suited her handsome neck and arms; her skin was warmed by the sun. She glanced at Christopher. He had changed into a blazer and grey flannels. Absurdly, she thought how attractively his hair grew above his blue shirt collar. He gave her a brilliant smile. Radiant, pulses racing, she smiled back.

'Scotch, Liz?' Jessica asked. 'Just ice?'

'Please.' Tonight, a 'special' was to be avoided. Noticing Tom Vane's slightly crestfallen expression, Liz went over to him. 'What about a game of billiards later, Tommy?' she coaxed. 'You always beat the rest of us, I remember.'

'So I did.' He brightened. 'I don't see why not? What about it, Chris? Does your friend Mr Langdon play at all, Jess?'

Through the open windows, beyond the formal garden, Liz saw last shafts of sunlight striking the still surface of the pond. The colour of the sky reminded her of Kate's feet after her bath. She said so to Jessica who smiled quite tenderly and agreed.

'I hope Mr Langdon won't be late, Jessica,' her mother said, looking anxious. 'There's a fair on at Cirencester, you know.'

'He won't be. On time to the minute.' Jessica spoke confidently. They heard a car. 'That's him now. I'll go and bring him in.'

At first, Liz thought Tony looked even more out of place at Fontwell than he had at Jessica's house in London. She couldn't pinpoint the nuances precisely. Perhaps it was only the faint, but unmistakable, regional accent. (She had forgotten the town Christopher mentioned.) But his exceptionally full head of silver grey hair had a theatrical look. Liking him, these unfortunate first impressions dismayed Liz.

Katherine Vane's reaction to her daughter's lover, a man close to her own age, was manifested only in slight over-effusiveness.

'*Please*, Mr Langdon, don't let my husband foist one of his eccentric cocktails on you. The family has learnt . . .'

'As a matter of fact, Mrs Vane, I rather enjoy cocktails myself,' Tony replied easily. And to Tom Vane, 'Thank you, I'd like one very much.'

'Glad to see someone appreciates a decent drink,' Tom Vane muttered.

'Good old Tony,' said Jessica.

It turned out to be an evening visited by gaiety, everyone looking, and feeling, at their best. Effortless talk was punctuated by laughter all round the table. The candles glowed more brightly as daylight faded. Heavy cut glass sparkled. The beautiful old room — the silver, the intricate panelling — gave an other-worldly atmosphere. The air was cool and fragrant after the fierce heat of the day.

Cold soup, handed with freshly made croutons, was delicious. 'And such an irresistibly pretty colour, I always think, this delicate green, don't you agree?' Katherine Vane said to Tony Langdon on her right in her vague, rather dotty way. Those pale eyes missed nothing, Liz thought, watching, wondering what she made of him.

She was seated on Tom Vane's right, next to Christopher. Jessica sat opposite. Liz marvelled at the change even a few hours at Fontwell had made in her. Challenging a statement of Tony's, teasing, she was quite unrecognisable as the tired, unkempt woman who had emerged from the Renault that afternoon. Her hair fell, smooth and fair, to her shoulders. She was wearing a gold dress, one of her own designs, she told them. And did they approve? And would it sell if the price was right?

As at Jessica's house, Tony's conversational skill astonished Liz. One by one, he drew them out, engaging interest, stimulating discussion. When he spoke, he charmed them all. Even Jessica's brusqueness melted. Relaxed at last, she bent towards him to catch what he was saying, a hand on his arm, dark eyes softened.

Christopher took charge of the wine. Under cover of the general conversation, throughout dinner, he and Liz exchanged looks and smiles. Beneath the table, their hands touched frequently.

Tom Vane carved.

'Marvellously thin. Well done, Dad,' Jessica said, turning round to the sideboard, holding up her glass for Christopher.

'I hope it's all right for everyone, not too pink,' Katherine Vane added.

After dinner, Katherine Vane, Jessica and Liz looked in on Kate. She was sleeping like a cherub, had hardly moved since Liz put her down. Leaning over the cot, Katherine Vane covered her legs with a light blanket. Liz was struck forcibly by the thought: *her granddaughter, and she does not know the name of her father*. She drew a sharp breath. The reality of the situation appalled her. How could Jessica have repaid their love and their loyalty in this way? Shown them so little trust?

'Such a pet,' Katherine Vane murmured as the baby stirred. Outside the room, she said: 'Shall we take the coffee straight up to the billiards room do you think?'

'Yes, let's,' Jessica said. 'Dad wants a game. It would be fun.'

'In that case, perhaps you would go down in due course and tell the men . . . I like Mr Langdon, Jessica.'

'*Tony*.'

'Tony. He's most charming. But isn't he a little old for you, darling?'

'Honestly, Mother, for God's sake . . . *Another* lecture?' Angered, Jessica went clattering off downstairs.

A moment or so later Liz said, 'I remember your lovely earrings, Katherine.'

Katherine Vane touched one absent-mindedly, 'Beautiful, aren't they? They belonged to Tommy's grandmother. Liz?'

'Yes?'

Katherine Vane was looking at her intently. 'Tell me, did I do something – at some time – very wrong with Jessica? Or is she just – Jessica?'

'I don't know, Katherine, I don't know.'

In the billiards room, removing their coats, Tommy Vane and Christopher started to play. Christopher had entered the room carrying a decanter of port. For some reason, his father's battered straw hat was stuck on the back of his head. He was nicely tight, Liz concluded, as she brought in the coffee. Katherine Vane poured. The game was going badly. Both Christopher and his father laughed a lot, sighting their cues with arms long out of practise. The table was dusty and the surface roughened. The port passed back and forth between them.

Some time later, Jessica and Tony reappeared. Taking a coffee cup from her mother, Jessica announced, 'Tony wants us over at his cousin's for drinks tomorrow evening. Sixish. You and Chris, too, Liz. Can we leave Katie-Kate with you and Dad, Mother dear?'

Near midnight, Liz heard the centuries old floorboards outside her room creaking. There was a loud whisper, 'Liz . . .'

She opened the door. Christopher stood there, grinning. He had taken off his tie and was carrying his shoes. He was still wearing the straw hat. Laughter welled up in Liz; and excitement.

'Christopher – *quiet* – not here . . .'

He closed the door behind him, dropped his shoes with a thud and took her straight into his arms.

'Yes. Here, American lady.'

She could feel his warmth beneath her thin cotton nightdress. Pushing down the straps, he nibbled her shoulder.

'Lovely Liz.'

'Lovely Christopher.' Teasing, a bit breathless; but she meant it. He was.

'Lights out. *At once.*'

She sat on the bed as he undressed, moonlight silvering her hair, the outline of her throat, her arms, her shoulders. Pillows were a dark mass behind her. Bending, he kissed her breast. They both noticed the hat and started to laugh. It tilted forward. Reaching up, Liz sent it spinning to the floor and their lips touched and their laughter ceased.

During the night, he woke her. There was a full moon shining through the curtains, but the air felt damp and chill.

152

Liz reached for a blanket.

'Wait . . .'

Christopher was kissing her inner thigh. He looked up. 'I love you, Liz,' he said.

'I love you, Christopher.'

CHAPTER 19

The church smelled dank. The stones beneath their feet were grooved with age. Katherine Vane had decorated the font with sheaves of yellow and white flowers. Standing next to Christopher, holding Kate, Liz called out her names – Katherine Elizabeth – in response to the vicar's formal question. Kate resisted the drops of water on her forehead with a loud yell. She was hot and rather cross that morning and the proceedings were beginning to make her restless. As the grizzling started, Christopher distracted her attention, dangling his car keys within her reach. She quietened. Liz looked at him gratefully.

Jessica stood to one side, appearing openly bored and sceptical. Despite her mother's entreaties, she had insisted on wearing clogs with her fairly crumpled cotton skirt. Apart from Katherine and Tom Vane, the only others present were two elderly aunts, from Katherine Vane's side of the family. Both wore hats and gloves although the morning was exceptionally sultry. The old ladies were flushed and obviously uncomfortable. Katherine Vane gave them anxious, sideways looks.

After the ceremony, they straggled back to the house in procession. The sky was heavy and overcast. Liz and Christopher walked ahead, Liz still holding Kate. Some way behind, Jessica and her father strolled along, chatting. Inching their way came Katherine Vane and the aunts. She held each firmly by the elbow.

'I honestly think Mother thought the old girls were going to keel over, then and there,' Christopher said. 'God knows what *they* make of the situation – Katie-Kate's absent father, unmarried niece. They're very much of the old school, procreation of children, till death do us part and so forth. Here, let me take her. She's quite a weight.'

He took Kate easily from Liz, hoisting her against his shoulder.

'Watch out. She's decidedly damp,' Liz warned.

'Nothing on that pretty dress, I hope?'

Liz was wearing a new deep pink dress of thinnest cotton. A bit overdressed for such a family occasion but wonderfully cool. She felt ridiculously pleased that Christopher had noticed.

'It's fine. You like babies, Christopher. You're good with them.'

'I suppose I do. They feel natural to have around. Like dogs.' They both laughed. Joining in, Kate babbled and pulled Christopher's hair.

'And you, Liz?'

'Let's not talk about it.'

'No?'

'Painful subject.' Liz looked away, over towards the pond and the summerhouse. After a few moments, Christopher said quietly:

'Liz, do you know what I feel about a child – now?'

'Yes. Don't say it.' She stumbled slightly, the path was rutted. Christopher put his arm around her and kept it there.

And it was Jessica, Liz thought, of all people, who had written after Kate's birth that 'nothing in this life seems to work out quite as it should, does it?'

As they approached the house, Christopher told her, 'The other night at Jessica's, I was incredibly nervous, turning up. Terrified that you had turned into one of those overpoweringly successful American females one dreads. Sorry! And the door opened and there you were with Kate. Amazing . . .'

'I thought Kate stood up to all the mumbo jumbo very well,' Jessica said loudly in the hall at Fontwell, taking her from Christopher. The aunts, red faced and breathless, gave her looks of extreme disapproval. Liz saw they were carrying ivory backed prayer books.

'She *is* a poppet,' said Aunt Dot, approaching Kate

155

nervously. 'Would she come to me for a moment, do you think, Jessica dear?'

'You wouldn't want her, Aunt Dot. Honestly. She's dripping wet. I'll go and change her and bring her in after she's had some lunch.' Thumping up the stairs, Jessica took Kate off to their bedroom.

'How informal the young are these days, Katherine,' said Aunt Dot witheringly, her eyes on Jessica's creased cotton and bare legs. 'I thought you said she had a most satisfactory young nanny.'

'She does. In London, but it's her weekend off. She has to because of the shop you see. Now, Dot and Mary, dears, let's settle ourselves in the drawing-room. Tommy has gone to get us lovely glasses of champagne. What about your hats, do you think?'

'If I do the lettuce and the spuds would you do the dressing and the rest of the salad, Liz? Here.' Christopher threw her a plastic apron.

'Sure. We laid the table after breakfast. So it's just the potatoes — they won't take more than a few minutes — and the cold meat from the larder. We make a good team, Christopher.'

'Sure do.'

He exaggerated her accent and gave her a quick kiss on the neck. Immediately after, Tom Vane walked in.

'Got the glasses, Chris, have you? Your mother's holding the fort with the aunts and they're all dying for a spot of something.' He opened the refrigerator and took out a bottle of champagne. He was pouring, when Jessica came back with Kate. She plopped her into the highchair which Katherine Vane had borrowed.

'Take these into the drawing-room, would you, Jess? And do pay a bit of attention to Dot and Mary . . . good of them to make the effort to come over and all that.'

'Oh Christ, Dad, must I? Kate needs lunch . . .'

'I'll see to her,' Liz called from the sink. 'Just tell me what.'

Jessica sighed and removed various jars from the refrigerator.

'Okay. If I must. Liz, give her some of this – and milk. Plus bits of whatever it is you're chopping.' She put a can of lager on the tray with the champagne and banged out through the swing door muttering, 'Bloody old disapproving cows.'

'She needs a good holiday, poor Jess,' Tom Vane said, searching for another bottle. He looked worried. 'We do our best, you know, but she's very chilly with us. It grieves your mother, Christopher.'

'What she needs,' Christopher said deliberately, 'what she needs, Dad, is a bloody good hiding – and some manners.'

'Yes. Well. Difficult life for her, you know, Chris. Lots of problems ahead, responsibilities and so forth. Well – I'll take this into the others shall I?' He followed Jessica out.

'Good girl, Kate. She's starving, poor child,' Liz said, fixing her bib.

'I meant it. Every word.' Christopher dumped the dried lettuce into a salad bowl.

'I know you did.' Liz spooned puréed carrots into Kate's open mouth. 'Maybe Tony could help.'

'He's too nice, too docile. Do you think I'm wrong?'

'What you said to your father? I guess not. But I think you may be about Tony. She wasn't like this – defensive – in London.'

'So why here? And I assure you, she always is. Rude. Unco-operative. Looks a sight. Like now. And she *never* does in London. Zany, possibly. But stylish.'

'Perhaps, seeing all this – Fontwell, your parents, their settled, very conventional life, she gets frightened. For Kate. For herself.'

'She should damn well have thought of that before,' Christopher said irritably.

Through the kitchen window, Liz could see heavy grey skies. It was unbearably humid. There was thunder about. She realised that she had a faint, persistent headache. Too much to drink? The weather?

She wiped Kate's mouth and sticky fingers.

The gaiety – the happiness – of last evening has quite disappeared, she thought sadly.

In the drawing-room, Jessica was sitting on a sofa beside Aunt Dot, looking disgruntled, swinging a clog from a scarlet toenail. A glass and a can of beer were on the table in front of her. Liz, removing the apron and giving her hair a quick comb in the kitchen mirror, carried Kate in. She put her down on the floor and took a glass of champagne from the tray.

'Isn't she adorable? Look, Dot, I was telling you, the same woman in the village who made dresses for Jessica did that smocking. She's a marvel. She does quite a bit — knitting and embroidery — for the shop, doesn't she darling?'

'That's right. She's good. But damned unreliable.'

'And you always dressed Jessica so beautifully, Katherine.' Aunt Dot glanced at Jessica. 'As a child, of course, I mean.'

Jessica drank some beer and pushed a toy towards Kate who was crawling rapidly along the floor, making for the nearest light switch.

'Here, Kate,' Jessica intervened, heading her towards the sofa.

'Liz, darling, you've been such a help. Thank you so much. Where's Christopher?' Katherine Vane turned to Mary, the less vocal of the two aunts. 'Christopher and Liz have dealt with the lunch.'

'And fed Kate,' Jessica added.

'That too. Such a comfort. If only we had you with us more often, Liz.'

She means it, too, Liz thought. As Jessica rightly said, they always understood each other. And she's slept badly, Katherine, Liz could see that. She looked pale and exhausted, dark circles under her eyes. Glass in hand, she smiled at Liz quite lovingly. 'We're all so grateful to you, Liz,' she said softly, 'so grateful.' Liz flushed. *She knows. About Christopher. And she's pleased*. Her mind whirled.

Moments later, Christopher came into the room, poured himself some champagne and refilled glasses.

'To Kate,' he said. Smiling, they all repeated the toast, lifting their glasses, watching Kate as she disappeared behind the sofa.

'To Katherine Elizabeth, to be precise,' Tom Vane added, bluff and proud.

'The spuds are on, Mother. Do you want to start carving, Dad?'

Taking Liz's arm as they walked into the dining-room, Aunt Dot said, 'Now that's a pretty frock, dear. It reminds me of one of my mother's. She used to wear it with long beads – in the twenties. Funny how all these fashions come back. Katherine tells me you have the most wonderful job in New York. So clever and enterprising of you.' She gave Jessica, on the floor playing with Kate, a final look of disdain. 'And *isn't* Christopher a splendid young man, don't you think?'

After lunch, Liz and Jessica vetoed Christopher's half-hearted suggestion of tennis. Too energetic, they agreed. It was hot, grey and still. Occasionally, thunder rumbled.

'What time is Tony expecting us, Jess?' They were washing up. Tom Vane had taken the aunts home. Katherine Vane had gone to see someone in the village.

'Sixish. As long as we leave just before six. I'll get Kate bathed and fed. This weather gives me the willies. If only it would storm and get it over with, for God's sake.'

One by one, they drifted upstairs to rest or read the papers. The oppressive weather had even felled the dogs who lay about the hall, panting, not moving when Christopher took the stairs in his tennis shoes, quietly, two at a time.

He knocked on Liz's door and went in. Turning the key in the lock, he undressed and lay beside her. She had drawn the curtains and the room was dim. For a while, they slept.

Footsteps in the corridor outside woke them. Liz tensed. She waited for a knock or the handle to be turned. Neither happened. The footsteps retreated.

Jessica.

Had she sensed, somehow, that they were together? A faint breeze pushed at the curtains; rays of wan sunlight played through the room. Somewhere in the house, a 'phone rang. Again, Liz tensed. She was certain Dick would 'phone today. Was that him?

Apparently not. No shout came from below. Still half asleep beside her, Christopher read her thoughts.

'Jessica tells me Dick is very high-powered. Dynamic. Wizard of the financial world. I know the firm, of course. True?' His voice was muffled against her.

'True the way all clichés are. Yes and no.'

He had undone her cotton wrapper and was kissing her stomach deliciously. Her eyes closed, not moving, she said, 'You're tickling me.'

He lay on top of her, kissing her eyelids, the side of her nose, moving slowly down her cheek.

'*Stay*,' he whispered.

Joy – or was it pain? – rushed through her.

'I can't,' she whispered back. 'You know.'

He kissed her mouth. She lifted her arms and ran her fingers lightly down the length of his back.

'Let's take your car, Chris. I haven't been in it for ages. I might even drive it.'

'If you like.' He shrugged. 'It means walking up to the cottage.'

'Okay, Liz?' Jessica asked.

'That's fine with me.'

Jessica put her head round the drawing-room door. Tom Vane was asleep, his mouth open, snoring, newspapers strewn about him. Katherine Vane got up and joined them in the hall.

'Mother, I think Kate's down for the night. But if she starts yelling, you might see what she wants. Her door's open.'

'Of course, darling. I'll look in on her soon anyhow. We'll expect you when we see you. And there's masses of food in the kitchen. Two cold chickens, salad things. Enjoy yourselves. And remember me to – er – Tony.'

Walking up the path to the cottage, Christopher said, 'I don't think it would hurt you to thank Mother, just occasionally, Jess, for all the support she gives you over Kate. *Or* treat her in a rather more civil manner.'

'Look, Christopher. I don't want any lectures from you.'

Jessica's voice was so hard and bitter that Liz was shocked. 'And I don't think you − or you, Liz for that matter − are in any position to preach to me about how to behave in other people's houses.'

Jessica was walking slightly ahead. In one stride, Christopher reached her and pulled her arm. They all stopped.

'You're asking for trouble, Jessica.' He sounded furious.

'Let me go. Take your hands off me, Christopher.' Her face was very red.

'Trouble, Jessica. And I mean it.'

She pulled away without answering and walked on up the path, very fast, heels flashing, bunched hair bobbing on her shoulders.

Liz and Christopher exchanged looks and followed.

By the car, outside the cottage, Christopher took the keys from his pocket. 'Who sits where?' he asked.

'I told you. I want to drive,' Jessica said imperiously. 'Liz sits in front with me. You hop in the back. Got it?'

'Very well, Jessica,' Christopher said, resigned. He tried, and failed, to catch Liz's eye. 'And where exactly are we going?'

'Beyond Northleach. I know the house. I've been there before. Let's have the top down.'

'Do you mind, Liz?' Christopher asked. She shook her head and looked at Jessica, genuinely concerned. What, really, was the matter?

Seeing Liz struggle with her seat-belt, Christopher turned towards Jessica. 'Belt up, Jess.'

'*When I'm ready*. I want to feel her out first.'

Christopher stared down at Jessica's feet. 'And those clogs don't seem ideal gear for driving sports cars, if you don't mind my saying,' he remarked with polite irony, vaulting into the back seat.

Jessica ignored him, got into the car, slammed the door and put the key in the ignition. She started to rev the engine. Liz turned round to Christopher.

'What happens if it rains?' They were all wearing light summer clothes. Christopher looked up at the dark grey skies. The wind was getting up. It was going to rain, all right, and hard.

'Don't worry. We'll stop and put the top up.' He put his hand on her shoulder as Jessica drove the car down the lane and up onto the main road. The car picked up speed. Air rushed past their faces and blew their hair wildly. Christopher's hand tightened on Liz's shoulder.

They drove through the narrow, twisting streets of the village, taking a left turn between grey stone buildings towards the hill which led out of the valley. At first, shifting the gears to which she was not accustomed, Jessica drove slowly, almost experimentally. The low-slung car purred round bends, over a bridge and crept up the hill edged with beech trees. They reached the crest; beyond lay a network of roads, almost lanes, which latticed that part of the Cotswolds.

This was countryside which Jessica had known since childhood. Unhesitatingly, she rounded sharp bends, forked left and right, shot down into a deep gully. An escarpment fell away on their right. White heads of cow parsley foamed beside them, so close they could touch their milky froth. There was little traffic about.

First, fat drops of rain fell.

The car emerged onto a ridge; a straight length of road stretched ahead. Lightning forked above them. Jessica put her foot on the accelerator. The car leapt ahead.

'Take it easy, Jess,' Christopher shouted, leaning forward. 'For God's sake . . . you're driving too fast. These roads are dangerous.' The wind caught his words, spiralling them up and away, lost in the churning air and the roar of the engine.

Jessica did not reply. She drove faster.

But Liz heard. She looked at Jessica sideways. Her face was rigid; intent. Her chin lifted. Wind had torn her hair from the ribbons at her neck. Her hands gripped the steering-wheel so tightly that her veins stood out.

Liz felt afraid. She turned towards Christopher. He was shouting in Jessica's ear, frantic now.

'Stop this . . . for Christ's sake. *Listen to me, Jessica.*'

It flashed through Liz's mind: she would listen to Tony.

Facing Christopher, by now as desperate as he was, Liz did not even see the other car before the impact. Briefly, she was conscious of Jessica braking and veering. Too late. The noise was horrendous, deafening; at first, it shut out all other sensations. Then screams, screaming tyres, metal crunched like paper, smashing glass. A crashing jolt — and another — and another.

Somewhere — where? — more screeching tyres, another crash.

It was dreadfully still. For seconds, all consciousness was lost. Liz opened her eyes. She was wrenched on her side. The branch of a tree was only inches away. This puzzled her. She hurt. Christopher's face, terribly white, was beside hers.

'Liz, Liz, are you all right? Can you help? . . . Jessica . . .'

With a tremendous effort, she turned. Jessica had been thrown partially out of the car. Her legs were twisted. Her head and arms hung down over the side. She did not move.

Liz felt sick with horror. She groaned. Very cautiously, Christopher was undoing her seat-belt. He lifted her into the back. Her left arm and shoulder hurt excrutiatingly. Her face felt wet and sticky.

'Jessica?'

'Can you manage, Liz — can you help me? We must get her out. Gently. In case of fire. *At once.*'

Responding to his urgency, she nodded. Christopher half handed, half carried her onto the road. Standing upright took all her willpower. The car, the road, the hedgerow, swam around her.

Jessica. She must help.

Christopher was speaking. 'We must move her. Very carefully. Over there.' He nodded towards the grassy verge opposite. He was very calm, deathly pale. He appeared unhurt.

'Ambulance . . .' Liz slurred the word.

'Yes. But we must move her first.'

He put his hands beneath Jessica's shoulders, lifting her, freeing her from the crumpled steering-wheel. They saw her face. She was terribly cut. Strands of long blonde hair were matted in blood.

Liz retched.

'Her legs,' Christopher said sharply. 'Take them.' Liz began to cry. Blindly, she helped Christopher carry her to the

163

roadside. They laid her carefully on the soft grass. Once or twice, she moaned. Liz noticed some obstruction — a car? — at an awkward angle further down the road.

'Ambulance,' she said again to Christopher. And at that moment, a car appeared from the direction in which they had been travelling. It stopped almost beside them. Two men, both quite young, jumped out. Liz saw the horror on their faces. She and Christopher were kneeling beside Jessica.

'We need help,' Christopher said. Tense; deadly serious. He spoke directly to one of the men. 'Drive to the farm about a quarter of a mile down the road. You'll see the gate on your right. 'Phone for an ambulance. It's an emergency. Just one of you go.' The car shot off. To the other man, Christopher said, 'The second car — there — give me a hand, would you?'

The other car. Liz had forgotten. She saw it lying half into the hedgerow. Christopher was speaking to her rapidly, 'We must see what we can do. You stay with Jessica. I'll be right back. The ambulance will be on the way.'

Liz nodded. She was trembling uncontrollably. Desperately, she tried to think of some way to help Jessica. With her good arm, she took her sweater which was tied round her neck and put it beneath Jessica's head. Jessica moaned and opened her mouth as if to speak. No sound came. Wild flowers, brilliantly coloured, grew among the grasses where she lay.

Liz put her hand up to her face. It was sticky with blood. She started to cry again.

Thunder rumbled; miraculously, the rain held off.

'Jessica,' she sobbed, 'Jessica, Jessica . . . it's going to be all right . . . we're getting help . . .'

After a little while, Liz looked towards the other car. Christopher and the man were carrying a body from it. Liz thought it was a man and she believed he was dead.

She crouched over Jessica, crying, calling her name over and over, stroking her flaccid hands.

Desperately, she wanted Jessica to speak to her, to say she was all right; that the nightmare was over.

She wanted Dick.

CHAPTER 20

By the time the ambulance arrived — she had lost all track of time — Liz was hysterical. She was shaking and crying; calling for Dick in despair. Looking grim, Christopher had his arms round her. He leapt up as the ambulance came in sight. He turned to the two men who had helped them and shook their hands. 'My name is Vane,' Liz heard him say, 'Christopher Vane.'

Jessica moaned as the attendants transferred her to a stretcher. Watching intently, Liz and Christopher saw that she opened her eyes briefly. They flickered and closed again. In the ambulance, they sat very close. A heavy blanket was placed round Liz' shoulders, but she still trembled violently. Over and over again, she asked the attendant,

'Will she be all right? Will she be all right?'

'We'll have to wait and see, Miss. We'll soon have her in emergency at the hospital.' Patient, professional, feeling Jessica's pulse, covering her with another blanket. 'Her breathing's all right, so far.' Carefully, he held her jaw.

Liz glanced at Christopher. She saw the agony on his white face. Blood from her head wound had stained his shirt. Incredibly, he seemed to have escaped all injury. But he looked ghastly. Painfully, Liz became aware of what lay before him — the hospital, doctors, breaking the news to his parents. An accident . . . a car crash . . . Jessica seriously injured . . . She thought of Kate, asleep in her cot at Fontwell.

And he has been so good, Christopher, she realised in wonder. Taken charge. Reacted so stoically.

Making the effort, Liz found strength to control herself.

165

Calm at last, she put out her hand from under the blanket and grasped Christopher's. He took it, gratefully.

It came to Liz, then, in her acutely emotional state, that Jessica would live. She knew this with absolute certainty. She also knew that from this day, somehow, the direction of all of their lives would change.

As suddenly as it had visited her, the vision and the certainty vanished, leaving her cold and shaking.

The ambulance, siren wailing, was moving through traffic. They sat like statues, their eyes on Jessica, until they got to the hospital.

There, the nightmare started again. Hands reached out and Jessica was rushed away from them.

'We'll let you know as soon as she has been examined. Wait in here, please.'

The smells and sounds of hospital; the creeping fear.

Christopher started to give details of the accident — names, times, the road on which they were travelling, their destination. Liz saw him moisten his lips with his tongue, push his hair back off his forehead. The words they spoke made no sense to her.

She was taken off into a small room containing an examination table, a trolley of dressings and instruments. Overhead, there was a fierce light.

She blinked; the trembling started again.

Where was Jessica? What were they doing to her?

The doctor and nurse came in briskly. 'What have we here? Let's have a look at you.'

The smell of disinfectant made Liz feel ill.

'Not going to pass out on us, are you?' the doctor asked, examining her forehead.

Liz shook her head.

Doctor and nurse worked away diligently — scissors, swabs, sutures passing between them.

'It's a very nasty wound. Jagged. I'm doing the best I can, but there'll be a scar, I'm afraid.'

The pain seared.

'Wearing a seat-belt, were you, *I trust*?'

'Yes. Yes, I was.'

But not Jessica. She had not thought of that before.

166

'Good girl. You'd be in trouble otherwise, I can tell you,' the doctor said cheerfully. 'Where did it happen, by the way?'

'I don't really know. Up on the Cotswolds somewhere I guess . . . I'm staying with friends.'

'American, are you?' He looked at her, interested. 'Where from?'

'New York.'

'Fancy. My wife and I were over last year. Disneyland. The kids loved it. Not hurting too much, am I?'

'I think I'm going to throw up,' Liz said.

The nurse produced a kidney bowl. Blinded by pain, Liz leant over. The moment passed. 'I'm okay now,' she said, swallowing.

'We've almost finished. Then I'll take a look at your arm and shoulder.'

He gave her tablets for the pain which she slipped into her skirt pocket. He strapped up the shoulder. Painful, he thought, but not serious; very bad bruising. 'Better have it X-rayed all the same. Just to be on the safe side. And don't expect to feel very grand for the next few days. You won't. Sorry all this has messed up your holiday.'

He held out his hand. 'Cheerio. Full marks for being a good patient. And give my best to the Statue of Liberty.'

Liz thanked him and smiled wanly. The nurse, taking her firmly by the arm, walked her through a maze of corridors into a small, darkened room. Blindly, Liz followed the technician's directions. When it had been established that nothing was broken, the nurse strapped up her shoulder, briskly and painfully, and took her back to the waiting-room. Seeing her, Christopher jumped up.

'All right?' His face was livid in the harsh light.

She nodded. 'Stitches. Quite a lot. Nasty. But I'm okay.' He looked at her arm. 'Painful, but not bad. Jessica?'

'Nothing yet.'

They sat together on the hard black leather seats. Christopher was holding a paper cup of coffee. He offered it to her. She shook her head.

'I managed to get hold of our own doctor,' Christopher said. 'Luckily, he was at home. He's going to see Jessica a bit

167

later. He's an old friend.'

'Your parents?'

'Not until I know — something definite.'

'Of course.'

'I spoke to Tony. Didn't want him 'phoning Fontwell. Luckily, he hadn't. He assumed we'd started late and lost the way.'

And had Dick 'phoned? If so, he would have spoken to Katherine Vane; been told that she had gone out for drinks with Jessica and Christopher. And here she was, her head throbbing, sitting in the hospital in Cheltenham.

She was missing him — Dick — badly.

Agonisingly, the minutes passed.

'The police took a statement from me, by the way,' Christopher said. 'They'll want one from you, too, Liz.'

'The man in the other car?' The sight of a body being carried to the roadside came back to her. 'Dead?'

'Yes. Poor sod. Long list of dangerous driving convictions. He was driving like a madman. And on those roads.'

A few moments later, Christopher said very quietly, 'It was my fault.'

'*No.*'

'It was. Jessica was terribly overwrought. In no condition to drive my car. I knew that. I just didn't want a scene. More than we had already had. Because of that — pure cowardice — I put us all at risk.'

'I knew her state of mind just as well as you did, Christopher. She was in a foul mood the moment she got down from London. I was there. I saw. We *all* knew. Even Jessica. The responsibility lies with us all.'

And she minded, minded badly, about us, Liz thought. Considered our being together a breach of friendship, hers and mine. Jealousy? And was Christopher aware of this?

The effort of speaking had brought her back to her senses. She put her good arm round Christopher and held him.

'And those fucking clogs,' he muttered. 'No seat-belt. Imagine!' Soon after, the door opened. A young doctor in a white coat put his head round it. 'Mr Vane?'

Liz and Christopher were already on their feet.

'Yes?'

The doctor came in, looking from one to the other, obviously not quite placing Liz. He looked tense and harried.

'About your sister . . .' He looked round the room. 'Let's go over here.' They sat in the corner, the doctor pulling up a chair. Christopher faced him.

'My sister. How is she, Doctor?'

'I've examined her myself and she has been seen by a neurologist, Mr Vane. Her condition at present is stable.'

Relief stunned Liz. She clutched Christopher's arm.

'She is badly concussed,' the doctor went on. 'She appears to have a serious skull fracture. The neurologist, Dr Ball, will be able to brief you on that better than I. And he's still with her. Otherwise,' he frowned, 'the other obvious complication from such injuries is internal bleeding. So far, we've found no indication of this. But she is being carefully monitored. It can't yet be ruled out altogether.'

'Is she conscious?' Liz asked.

'No. She did regain consciousness and was quite lucid. But she has lapsed. This is to be expected. Her face is very badly cut. I expect you saw that.'

'Yes,' Liz said, wincing.

'No seat-belt?'

'She wasn't wearing one. No.'

'That law is meant to be kept. If the public saw what I've been seeing here these past months, they wouldn't go round the corner without one,' the doctor said bitterly. He looked at his watch and stood up. Outside, an ambulance whined.

'That's really all I can tell you for the present. I'm sorry. It could have been a lot worse.'

'You don't feel that my sister's life is in danger, Doctor, is that right?' Christopher asked, watching him closely.

'No. No, I don't. But as I said, her injuries are severe. We can't yet dismiss the possibility of internal bleeding. The next twenty-four hours are crucial. As it is, she will be an ill woman for some time. She will certainly need plastic surgery for her face.'

Liz shuddered involuntarily. 'Can we see her?' she asked.

'Better not,' the doctor said. 'Come back tomorrow. She's

sedated and heavily bandaged. You can 'phone the ward later on tonight, if you like. I'll write the ward number and extension down for you.'

He scribbled on a piece of paper and handed it to Christopher, who said, 'Our family doctor, Dr Clark, is on his way over to see her.'

'That's all right. But there's nothing else to be done for the present, I assure you, except to hope that no trauma occurs and that she begins to recover.'

'Thank you, Doctor.'

Gravely, they shook hands and the doctor bolted from the room. Christopher took Liz's arm and they walked out into the reception hall. They were both feeling giddy with relief.

'Look, I've been thinking what to do for the best over the parents, Christopher said. 'Now that we know Jessica's not in danger, I think I should 'phone. Break it to Mother . . . that way, she will be prepared when we get to Fontwell.' He glanced at Liz's forehead. 'It might be less of a shock. What do you think?' He looked desperately concerned and youthful.

Liz caught sight of them, standing there, in a large mirror. She was shocked. There was blood all over her silk blouse which had been immaculate just hours before. There was a large dressing above her left eye, bruising was beginning to discolour one side of her face. Her hair was dishevelled. Christopher looked white and gaunt; blood stains showed on his collar.

The Vanes. What was best? She tried to concentrate. They could not possibly walk into the house like this, without Jessica.

'Yes. I think you should 'phone, Christopher. That seems right. But you must speak to your mother — break it to her first — your father . . . his heart condition . . .'

'Quite. That's agreed then. Look, you haven't got any change, have you? I used mine up on the other calls.'

Liz looked down at her hands. For the first time, she missed her bag. She had left it in the car. Christopher said quickly, 'Don't worry, Liz. You'll get it back. The police are towing the car away.'

'It doesn't matter. There's nothing important in it.' She

suddenly felt intensely weary. 'Now where can we get you some change?'

The smallest problem, it seemed insuperable; if only she could sit down.

'*Christopher*.'

They turned. Tony Langdon was pushing his way through the emergency doors.

'I came straight over. How is she?' He looked terribly shaken. His normally ruddy face was as white as Christopher's.

'Tony. Hullo. Stable, thank God,' Christopher said, clearly glad to see him. 'But it was a near thing. She's badly injured, fractured skull, cuts.' Tony interrupted. 'Who's seeing her?' Intensely practical, even then, Liz thought.

'The duty doctor in emergency is the only one we've spoken to, so far. The neurologist is still with her. Our own doctor is on his way to the hospital. He may be here now.'

'What about your parents?'

'We decided to wait until we knew Jessica's condition. As a matter of fact, I was just going to 'phone Mother now — break it to her — only we've no change. Liz is minus her bag.'

'Here.' Tony fished a handful of coins out of his pocket.

'I won't be long.' Christopher turned in the direction of the telephones. He looked very young; terribly serious. Liz touched his arm.

'Good luck, Christopher. She's very strong, your mother. She'll — cope.' He squeezed her hand and went off.

'Come and sit down, Liz.' Tony put his arm round her and guided her over to a row of chairs. 'Feeling rocky?' He looked at her dressing, the strapped arm and shoulder. 'You look as though you've been in the wars, all right.'

'I feel it, too. God, it was awful, Tony.' She began to shake. How to explain, ever, that endless wait for the ambulance, the threatening storm, the silence; Jessica hurt and broken on the roadside; she, helpless, sobbing above her?

'I'll bet it was.' He spoke grimly. 'I looked at the car and had a word with the police on my way over. They

171

were measuring up, skid marks and so forth. Frankly, it's a miracle you weren't all killed.'

'Yes.'

'One question, Liz. And answer it, please. Before Christopher comes back. Was Jessica driving much too fast?'

'Yes. Not crazily like – that man. But much, much too fast. No chance to – avoid. Too fast for that. Not responsibly.'

'Thank you. Liz, you're cold. Here.' He took off his jacket and put it round her shoulders. Liz was grateful for the warmth. She remembered putting her sweater beneath Jessica's head. Hours and hours ago, it seemed. Tony was speaking,

'. . . and my brother is a surgeon in London. Whatever she needs, whoever is the best, we'll get it for her.'

And he would. Liz had sensed his competence from the first. Thank God!

They saw Christopher coming back.

'Mother was splendid,' he said quietly, 'absolutely splendid. Just as concerned about you, too, Liz. John Clark promised me he would go to the house after he's seen the doctors here. That will help her – and Dad.'

Now that the news was broken – knowing that although Jessica was lying somewhere in this hospital, at least her life was not in danger – Christopher looked visibly better. They walked outside. Liz saw that it was almost dark. She looked at her watch. It was half past nine. She had lost all sense of time. It was cool and windy and looked as though it had been raining. She remembered the beginnings of a storm as they started to drive.

'Look, I'm going to run you back to Fontwell,' Tony said. 'But you both look pretty shattered. There's a pub near here. I think a drink is in order.'

'Agreed,' said Christopher.

'I've got my car parked over there. But the pub's just round the corner. Can you manage the walk, Liz?'

'Sure.' After the glare of the hospital, the cool air on her face was pleasing. 'We look such freaks,' she murmured, remembering their blood-stained clothing, turning up

172

the collar of Tony's blazer.

'It feels good to be out of that hospital,' Christopher said, echoing her thoughts. Poor Christopher. The memories he must have of hours spent in hospitals with Vanessa — waiting, hoping. Now, Jessica.

The lighted pub was ahead of them.

I hope Dick 'phones tonight, Liz said to herself. *Please God let Dick 'phone*.

Tony drove them to Fontwell through sheeting rain. Liz's head was starting to throb badly. None of them spoke much. The whisky burned in Liz's throat.

Katherine Vane was waiting at the door of Fontwell, silhouetted against the light from the hall. Discarding Tony's blazer, Liz made a dash up the steps, splashing through puddles. Katherine Vane put her arms round her and held her. Neither woman spoke.

Behind her, in the drive, Liz heard Tony and Christopher talking briefly. Tony's car moved off. Although he had said nothing about it, Liz was positive he was returning to the hospital. For reassurance; to be near Jessica. To be sure that everything possible was being done for her.

Christopher came bounding up the steps behind them. Disengaging herself, Liz murmured indistinctly, 'I'm going to clean myself up a bit . . .' She didn't want Katherine Vane to see her bloodied shirt. She wanted Christopher and his mother to have some time alone together.

She walked to her room rather unsteadily. When she got there, she sat on the bed, snapped on the light and stared round. It seemed an age, another lifetime, since she had changed for the evening here; decided what skirt, what shoes to wear; brushed her hair, sprayed on scent.

Using her uninjured arm, her right one, Liz tore off the soiled shirt, washed her hands and face, and combed her hair. She managed to pull on a clean blouse, wincing as her left shoulder moved. The ache from her stitches was intense. Remembering the tablets in her skirt pocket, she took a couple. She felt quite alert, her exhaustion had passed. She would go down to Katherine, now. She and Christopher would have had time to talk. And they might 'phone the ward about Jessica.

CHAPTER 21

Downstairs, Liz found Katherine Vane in the study. The untidy room with its worn, dark leather furniture looked welcoming. Pools of lamplight glowed. Katherine Vane had a tray of tea beside her. She was composed and very pale. Again, Liz was struck by her and Christopher's startling likeness.

'Come in, Liz darling. Sit down and put your feet up. I've sent Tommy off to bed with one of his strongest pills. It seemed best. There's nothing more any of us can do tonight. Tea or a drink?'

Christopher came into the room carrying a plate of bread and cheese.

'A drink, please. I think.'

'Something to eat?' Christopher asked. Liz shook her head.

'I couldn't, thanks.'

He handed her a weak scotch and water. She sipped it. The pills she had just taken seemed to have stuck in her throat. They tasted sour and unpleasant.

'Let me look at those stitches.' Katherine Vane bent over, inspecting the dressing closely. 'Are they hurting?'

'Rather badly.'

'Poor darling. Your shoulder, too. I'm afraid you won't be too good tomorrow.'

'I've been warned.'

Katherine Vane poured herself more tea and sat opposite Liz. 'Christopher has told me everything,' she said. 'Everything,' she repeated quietly. 'We have to be grateful there was no tragedy. And, all of us, pick up the pieces and

175

carry on.' Her voice shook a little. Liz saw that Christopher, like herself, was nursing a glass of whisky. His plate of food was untouched. Gradually, the tablets started to work and the throbbing in her head dulled. Again, Liz had a feeling of unreality. Of *déjà-vu*. As though sitting here was part of a dream, seen and remembered from a long time ago.

'Did Kate wake up at all this evening?' Liz asked. And she thought: that is the first normal sentence we have heard for hours, Christopher and I.

'No. Not once. I've got a girl from the village coming to help with her in the morning, so that I'm free to go to the hospital. And I shall 'phone Louise and get her down. What about the shop, Chris?'

'I'll 'phone Carol in the morning. I've thought about that, actually. She's pretty efficient. She'll hold the fort for the time being. She'll have to.'

'That will be a relief to Jessica,' Katherine Vane said. 'We'll tell her tomorrow.'

In the depths of the comfortable armchair, Liz was beginning to feel drowsy. The 'phone rang. They all tensed. Christopher took it. Liz heard him say,

'One moment, please. For you. Liz. A personal call from New York.' As she took the receiver from Christopher, something whirred inside her head but did not click.

'Dick?'

'Hi . . . I waited until now to call because I figured you would be busy all day. How was the christening?'

She could have wept with relief at the sound of his voice; resonant; confident. Her words came with difficulty.

'Fine. The christening. We're okay.' After a brief pause, 'Liz? Liz, are you all right?' Because he had known at once, of course, that she was not. Katherine Vane and Christopher had drifted tactfully from the room. Feeling her knees sag, Liz propped herself on Tom Vane's massive, paper-strewn desk. Taking a deep breath, she marshalled her remaining energies and gave Dick a précis of the accident and Jessica's condition, in so far as they knew it, in the hospital. She omitted her stitches but not her increasingly painful shoulder.

'*My God*! When did you say this happened?'

'Tonight. About six. I'm not sure exactly.'

'Look, would it help at all if I came over?' Capable; used to taking charge. But he sounded horrified.

'No need. If there were, I'd say. I'll stay on for a few days . . . see how things go . . . Jessica . . . And then I'll fly straight back. I want to.'

At that moment, the whirring clicked inside her head.

'*New York*,' she shouted into the 'phone. '*New York? But you're in Tokyo*.'

'Liz, Liz take it easy. I *am* in New York.'

'*Why*?'

'Something came up. Nothing to be concerned about. I'll discuss it with you tomorrow. Not now, not after what you've been through today.'

'*Jason*?'

'Jason's fine. Calm down. Please, Liz. There is nothing to be alarmed about.'

'Then tell me. I want to know, Dick.' She sounded in control again. He hesitated.

'Very well. It's this. Linda has left Boston. For good. She's living on a commune in Southern California. I know it's a bit of a shock, especially now – for you – but it's true.'

Liz was stupefied. 'In California? Linda? But why?' And Jason, her mind drummed. Jason, Jason, Jason . . .

'Quoting from a letter I received via her lawyer – to find peace and freedom and new rhythms, etc, etc, etc. You can imagine the rest.'

'Dick – are you being serious?'

'Never more so. Meanwhile, in leaving, she has donated us the house in Boston, her alimony and child support, most of her material possessions. And Jason.' Despite her physical and emotional exhaustion, she reacted instantly.

'*Jason*,' she shouted. 'Where is he?'

'At this moment, he's making a Lego power station in his room – next to the study – where I'm speaking from.'

'You mean – *he's going to stay with us always*?'

'I mean just that. If you can – take it on, Liz.'

'You don't have to say that. You know. And legally?'

'Legally, too. I've made the first moves in that direction.

177

And listen to this. Linda went off with — you guessed it — Harper Higgins. But what you don't know is that Harper Higgins is a twenty-one-year-old drop-out with a long string of narcotic convictions!'

'You're kidding. You must be.'

'No way. It seems Linda stopped teaching months ago. The two of them have been rolling round that house stoned out of their minds. The lawyer caught up with me in Tokyo and I flew straight back and on to Boston. Jason was with the neighbours, poor kid.'

'So we were right all along. About him needing us. He *was* unhappy, but he couldn't say . . .'

'He's okay now. He seems perfectly calm and happy. Lilly has moved in for the present. We'll sort it all out . . . but what a hell of a thing to happen. Linda on a commune. Can you believe it?'

'Barely. Particularly now . . .' The study, the pools of lamplight; her mind churning with thoughts of schools and camps. Jason abandoned by his own mother . . .

'Changes. What I said from the airport — though I didn't exactly have this in mind. Remember?'

'I remember.'

'Liz, listen. While we've been talking, I've been sitting here wondering whether Jason and I shouldn't hop on a plane to London and get you. Together.'

'Don't do that. I'll be fine. Really. Jason has had enough drama. I want to stay on for a couple of days. I'm something of a basket case, pretty-shaken . . . and Jessica. She's bad, Dick.'

'I understand. We'll 'phone tomorrow. And get some rest yourself. I'm sorry to have dropped the domestic bombshell — on top of everything else.'

'I'd rather know. I'm glad you've told me. We'll manage. Jason will be fine.' Then, 'His cat. What happened to Mr Woo?'

'As a matter of fact — we were saving this one for you — he's here too.'

Liz started to laugh. Tears came to her eyes. She ached and ached all over. 'I'm so glad,' she said. 'I guess he wouldn't have liked it much on a commune in Southern California.'

178

'Liz,' Dick said quietly, 'Come home soon. Please. We need you.'

'I know. I will.' Liz replaced the receiver carefully. She could hear voices – Christopher and his mother – somewhere outside the door. Feeling dizzy, she sat down and put her head on her knees. There was a great buzzing in her ears. All the happenings of the extraordinary day appeared in brilliant, broken fragments. She imagined she saw a large black cat, stalking proudly.

Christopher found her.

'Come on, Liz. Up to bed. Good girl . . . Give me a hand, would you, Ma?' Supported by Christopher and Katherine Vane, Liz staggered back to her bedroom. She wanted to say to them: I'm sorry to be such a bore when you – *we* – are so worried about Jessica. She wanted to tell them that Jason and his cat were now hers. But the whisky and the pills had done their job and she couldn't quite get her tongue round the words.

'We'll leave her as she is. She needs to sleep,' she heard Katherine Vane say above her as she pulled up a blanket and closed the curtains. And she was falling, falling through the darkness into oblivion.

———————

But towards morning, the analgesia started to wear off. Liz was tormented by vivid and frightening dreams – of Jason and Jessica; a dark church; warm, rushing air; wild spring flowers by the roadside. Inexplicable fear. Groaning as she turned onto her injured shoulder, Liz woke. She felt bruised all over her body. Putting her hand to her face, she knew it was swollen. She looked at her watch. Six o'clock. The room was dim with grey light. Her mind was blurred.

With an effort, moving very slowly, she got off the bed. Astonished, she saw that she was fully clothed.

Then she remembered. *Jessica*. Had she come safely through the night?

All the horror of yesterday – Jessica's anger, the crash, the hours in the hospital – came back to her. She started to shake. She longed for a warm bath. All her limbs ached. But would she wake the household? She thought not; her room was quite far from the main bedrooms.

Lying back in the blissful warmth, slowly, her mind began to focus. Dick's 'phone call. Jason and his cat. In those few minutes, hunched on Tommy Vane's desk downstairs, the whole direction of her life had changed. And Dick's — which was what he said he wanted. And did he?

But Linda . . .

(Liz turned the tap to a trickle with her toe; every movement made her wince.)

What on earth had induced this apparently rather shy, middle-aged woman — a teacher in the local primary school — to leave her child and her home and start living on a commune, with Harper Higgins aged twenty-one; drop-out; drug addict?

Was it unhappiness? Some kind of drug induced personality change? Resentment which had built up over the years? Anger? 'Peace', she had said to them in Boston last winter, her hair flowing down her back. 'Peace'.

Liz guessed they would never know the answers.

What Jason had seen these past months hardly bore thinking about. Linda stumbling round the house in strange clothes; giving up her job; Harper Higgins. She remembered Jason's quietness, his sad little voice on the 'phone, the 'meetings' he said his mother and her 'new friend' were attending. His hysterical state when he 'phoned Dick last week.

But he was a loyal little boy. Confused and unhappy as he must have been, he had said nothing. Somehow, they would find a way of coping with this trauma — the loss — in his life. With them, he was safe. Soon, they would be back on the Cape for another summer. There would be different lifeguards on the beach, but equally bronzed, equally beautiful. College kids, barefoot in cut-off jeans, wandering into the general store. Coarse grasses sprouting from the white dunes. Barbecues on the terrace; sand everywhere. Sun burning mist off the blue-grey Atlantic. Jason loved it — and so did she.

School and friends for Jason in New York. They would manage that. Caroline would be full of practical suggestions. She had had enough practise, with her lot.

And *Gibsons'*? Liz thought she already had the answer to that. Daily, it became clearer to her. The details, whatever followed, she would decide all that when she got back. When she felt stronger.

And she suddenly wanted very badly to be home, to be in New York.

Dressing was difficult. Moving – even touching – her bad shoulder was agonising. She managed to pull on jeans and a sweater which buttoned up the front. Combing her hair, she saw that the left side of her face was badly swollen; there were dark patches beneath her eyes. She peered out of the window. The hollow surrounding Fontwell was swathed in soft, drizzly mist. Taking her tablets and her dark glasses, she made her way gingerly downstairs.

She heard voices in the study, Christopher and his mother. Standing in the doorway, she said, 'Jessica?' Katherine Vane, who had her back to her, turned, Christopher was slumped on the sofa opposite.

'Liz. So early? We've just spoken to the ward sister. Jessica had only a fair night, but no complications. No signs of internal injury which is the danger, John Clark thinks. He was here late last night. So far, so good.'

'Thank God.'

'Come here and let me breathe whisky fumes all over you,' Christopher said thickly. Liz saw that the decanter by his elbow was almost empty. He looked utterly exhausted. Glancing at Katherine Vane's ashen face, Liz wondered whether either of them had slept at all.

'Does everything hurt, Liz?' Katherine Vane asked sympathetically.

'More or less.'

'I'm making coffee. We all need it. I'll go and bring it in.' Slipping on her dark glasses, Liz lowered herself onto the sofa next to Christopher. Their bodies touched – easily, comfortingly. With a tennis sweater slung round his neck, his feet up on the table, he looked the image of Jessica's kid brother who she remembered from years ago.

'Christopher and I did sleep. A bit,' Katherine Vane said, coming in with a tray of coffee. 'But we heard each other bumping about – I came down – and we gave up.'

'But not on the talk,' Christopher said, leaning back with his eyes closed.

'No indeed,' his mother agreed. 'Milk, Liz?'

'Please.'

'We talked and talked. And decisions were made,' Katherine Vane said in a strong voice.

'*Choices*, Mother, *choices* were made,' Christopher amended, opening his eyes and reaching for a mug. 'I'm leaving the City, Liz. At once. I never had the slightest interest in insurance, anyway. I was running away and I thought I might get away with it. But I can't.'

'Still – it must have been right for you to get away – run away if you like – for a time,' Liz said tentatively.

'Well. That time is over. There's a job to do here and one I've been trained to do. Frankly, unless something drastic is done about the home farm, the place will go under. With taxes and labour what they are, we simply won't be able to continue. We'll have to sell up. That's that.'

'You won't let that happen, Christopher.' Liz made it a statement.

'I don't think so. I hope it's not too late. And I'm moving back into the cottage. Vanessa would approve of that.'

The three of them sat silently, in the dullish light, holding their warm mugs of coffee.

'She was very brave, Vanessa,' Christopher continued, as though talking to himself. 'Very brave. A fighter. She knew everything about her illness from the beginning. She pretended not to – she fooled us – but she did. I found her diaries – afterwards. But she fought that hellish bloody cancer to the end,' he finished violently. He got up and blundered from the room, slamming the door behind him.

'We talked a lot about Vanessa during the night. It was the first time, really, since she died,' Katherine Vane said quietly. 'I didn't know about the diaries. Chris found them in her desk. Before she went into hospital that last time they were planning a trip through France – poring over books and maps, deciding where to stay. She knew they would never go.'

'I'm glad that he was able to talk.'

'Yes. It helped, I think. And he must come back to Fontwell. So much needs to be done. It will give purpose to his life. Something to hold onto. Liz?'

'What, Katherine?'

'I rather dread seeing her — Jessica.' Her face was averted. 'I irritate her you know. We have such very different outlooks.'

'Katherine, Jessica has never needed you more than she does now. She is going to recover. That's what matters. All that matters.'

'Her face. Is it very bad, Liz? I prefer to know.'

'Quite bad. The doctor told us she was heavily bandaged. She will need plastic surgery. That's certain.'

Through the tall windows, Liz saw Christopher striding across the lawn in the drizzle, head down, hands jammed into his pockets.

'She and Kate must spend the summer here. Chris and I were discussing this. There's no question of her going back to London until she's quite well.'

'I think Tony Langdon will be a tremendous help. To Jessica. To all of you.'

'Yes. I liked him. I think he's wise — and tolerant.'

A clock chimed. Footsteps — Tom Vanes'? — sounded in the hall.

'Look,' Liz said, 'shouldn't we go up and see if Kate's awake?'

In the kitchen, an hour later, normality appeared to have returned to the household. John Clark had 'phoned to say that he had already looked in on Jessica. She was uncomfortable and rather confused, but there were no signs of internal injury. This, he felt, was progress. They all relaxed visibly.

The radio intoned the eight o'clock news. Kate, dressed and fed, sat in her playpen chewing happily on a rusk. Christopher was on the 'phone to the police about his car — a write-off, Liz learned later. Liz, Katherine and Tom Vane were having breakfast at the scrubbed pine table amidst a litter of morning papers, toast and pots of marmalade.

That was when Liz told them about Dick's 'phone call, glossing lightly over the drug aspect; explaining that she had to go back to New York as soon as possible.

'No wonder you almost passed out,' Katherine Vane said. 'All that on top of what you had just been through. And the stitches.'

'Good God!' Tom Vane exclaimed, peering over the top of *The Times*. '*A commune*? How old did you say the little boy was? Seven? You'll have your hands full, Liz dear.' He returned to his paper.

'What kind of a woman pushes off with some juvenile layabout and dumps her kid like that?' Christopher demanded, looking aghast and pouring himself a cup of coffee. 'It's − negligent.'

'We thought things weren't right for him at home,' Liz sighed. 'Not that we imagined anything like this. But he never told us anything, not even that his mother wasn't teaching any longer. He must have known. I suppose he didn't want to let her down.'

'This being the case, I think Jason is a very lucky little boy − having you and Dick,' Katherine Vane said serenely.

And what Liz also didn't tell them was that sometime during the past twelve hours − during the journey in the ambulance, she thought afterwards − she had made the final decision to leave *Gibsons'*.

CHAPTER 22

For three days, Liz stayed on at Fontwell. She felt very tired and emotionally drained. She found that she slept a good deal even during the daytime, although her sleep was disturbed. Her arm and shoulder were extremely painful. Christopher, Tom and Katherine Vane visited Jessica in the hospital for a short time daily. They reported her physically stable, but sedated and uncertain as to what, really, had happened to her.

Dick 'phoned frequently and Liz spoke to Jason several times. He had been told of the car crash and reassured by Dick that she was safe.

'How black is the black under your eyes, Liz?' he wanted to know.

'You'll see,' Liz told him. 'But it may be yellow by the time I get home.'

She helped Louise to look after Kate, taking her for walks, watching her crawl over the rug on the lawn. The heatwave had broken. Warm, sunny spells were followed by sudden showers. The amount of hard, physical work Katherine Vane did, indoors and out, astonished Liz. She also cooked dinner for them each night. During the meals, Christopher and his father discussed the farm. Liz, as Katherine Vane noted, had little appetite.

Louise helped her pack on Wednesday evening and the following morning she kissed Katherine and Tom Vane goodbye on the drive in front of the house. She was still wearing dark glasses but the swelling on her face had gone down. The accident had left them all subdued.

'Please come back soon,' Katherine Vane said quietly, her

hand on Liz's shoulder. 'And bring Dick and Jason. We would love to have them here. You know that.'

Kissing Tom Vane hastily on both cheeks, Liz climbed into the estate's new Range Rover. Christopher was driving her to Cheltenham station. On the way, she would visit Jessica in the hospital to say goodbye.

As they drove up out of the hollow, Liz turned. Her last glimpse of the mellowed stone of Fontwell was obscured by shimmering beech leaves. Christopher drove out through the gates and towards the village.

During the first part of the drive, they were both silent. It was the first time they had been alone together for days.

'This vehicle is one of Dad's ridiculous extravagances,' Christopher said at last, smiling, his hair blown in the wind. 'For what this cost, we could have repaired the worst parts of the roof at Fontwell.'

Liz sensed his commitment. Whatever happened to Fontwell and the estate was in his hands now.

'Will you sell your flat in London?'

Christopher nodded. 'I won't be needing it again,' he said.

They reached the outskirts of Cheltenham, gliding down a steep hill. Liz began to notice the Regency parades, the terraced houses and wide tree-lined streets. She had forgotten what a delightful town it was. Years ago, spending weekends at Fontwell, she and Jessica had shopped there on Saturday mornings.

Christopher dropped her outside the hospital, pointing out the way to Jessica's ward.

'I'll go and park and meet you here. You can't be long, in any case. She's still pretty weak,' he warned. 'And not always clear headed.' It was the first time Liz had seen her since the accident.

When Liz walked into the ward, she found Jessica propped up in bed. She was wearing a neck brace and, as Liz had expected, her face was heavily bandaged. But she was recognisably Jessica, all the same.

'Feeling a bit brighter today, aren't we?' said the nurse who accompanied Liz. 'Not quite so down-in-the-mouth.'

Jessica ignored her.

'Liz — it is you, isn't it?' She clutched Liz's arm. 'Are

186

you all right?' She spoke fuzzily.

'Sure.' Liz sat on the chair by the bed. The strangeness of seeing Jessica so helpless — the hospital surroundings — overwhelmed her. 'A bit sore all over,' she said, swallowing hard. 'Plus this . . .' She took off her dark glasses, exposing her bruises and her smudged eyes.

'Liz!'

'They're starting to disappear . . . I always wondered what a heavy-handed lover would be like.'

Jessica tried to smile. 'How's Kate?'

'She's splendid. Honestly. Surrounded by admirers. And Louise, I've loved the time I've spent with her. I'm going to miss her. Look, I got this for her christening and forgot to give it to you. It's a very modest little coral necklace. Victorian. I saw it in London and I thought it was right for Kate.' She took a small box out of her bag and put it into Jessica's bandaged hands.

'Liz, I told you not to . . .'

'Inspect it later. And give it to Tony to keep when he comes. He's still here, isn't he?' Katherine Vane had told her that she had seen him in the hospital twice.

'Yes. He's staying on at his cousin's for the moment. I like having him around.' Her shoulders drooped. Her eyes half closed. It's going to take a long time to get her well, Liz realised painfully.

'I can't stay long, Jess. I'm not allowed. And Christopher's outside with the car. He's taking me to the station. I'm flying back to New York tomorrow. You knew that, didn't you?' She spoke quietly. She wasn't quite sure how much Jessica comprehended. But she nodded and seemed to understand.

'Mother told me,' she said. Talking was an effort for her.

'And Jess, I must tell you this. Jason has come to live with us, Dick and me, permanently. Legally.'

'But what about his mother? Linda?'

'She's decided to bail out of motherhood. She's gone off to California — to find herself.' She would tell her the rest another time.

'Jason. That's nice for you. I'm glad, Liz. How's Ma bearing up under all this?'

187

'Katherine? She's fine.'

'Kate and I will have to stay for a bit. At Fontwell. Until I'm better.'

'It's the best thing, Jess.'

'Tony thinks so. I don't know. Ma gets me down, rather. All that swanning about doing the flowers, being charming . . .'

'Look, Jess. Katherine doesn't run a business or put out a monthly magazine. But she works all right at keeping Fontwell going. And hard.'

'One in the eye for me, you mean,' and she grinned, quite the old Jessica.

'Yes. That's right. She cares about you, Jess. Very much. Try and reciprocate it.'

'I will. Promise.' She seemed suddenly very tired. Liz saw the nurse hovering disapprovingly a few beds away.

'Amazing flowers,' she said to Jessica, nodding towards huge sprays beside her.

'Tony. Liz?'

'What?'

'I've decided to tell them — Mother and Dad — about Hugo. Only the facts, no inquisition, but fully. I think it's fair. It came to me, suddenly, at the christening. Do you approve?'

'I certainly do. That will please them. Very much.' The nurse had her eyebrows raised meaningfully. 'Jess, I'm going now . . .'

'Your train. I forgot.' Liz saw that she was close to tears. Her lips moved. 'I wanted it to be perfect, Liz, your trip over . . . and at Fontwell. Like it used to be . . .'

'I know you did. But we've all changed. So much has happened to us. You get well, Jess. That's the important thing. For Kate. For all of us.' She picked up one of Jessica's bandaged hands and held it against her cheek.

'Liz, what I said about you and Chris . . . I'm sorry . . . I didn't mean it . . . I do understand.'

'I know. It's called friendship. It endures. For all of us. Take care, Jess.' Her voice was shaky. She placed Jessica's hand very carefully on the folded sheet, got up and walked quickly out of the ward.

Christopher was waiting for her on the hospital steps. 'All right?' She nodded. He held her arm and steered her towards the car. He sensed that she needed time to compose herself. He eased the car into the traffic and headed towards the station. Liz cleared her throat.

'She was coherent. But very tired,' she said.

'Last night when I saw her she was pretty dopey. They're sedating her quite a lot.'

'She made sense just now. Christopher,' she turned towards him. 'Her recovery is going to take a long time.'

He looked straight ahead.

'Yes. Tony has arranged for one of the top plastic surgeons in the country to come down next week and have a look at her. Frankly, John Clark is not very optimistic. It's going to be a slow business. Apparently the fracture was more serious than they first realised.'

'I don't like leaving her like this.' Liz stared out of the window, unseeing.

'You have your own life, Liz. Responsibilities. Jason, too, now. And remember there were moments − perhaps an hour − when we thought she was dying. Both of us. As it is, she *will* recover. That's what we have to hold onto.'

'I know. And I think Tony Langdon is going to be increasingly important in her life. And Kate's.'

'I think you're right. I didn't, but I do now.'

'She respects him. He has some control over her. Jessica needs that. For all her brittle and competent exterior, she's very − vulnerable.'

'Yes.'

'She's going to tell your parents about Hugo. She told me that this morning. She sounded quite definite.'

'Really?'

'Yes.'

'I'm glad about that.'

Christopher turned the huge car into the station and parked. For just seconds, Liz watched his hands lying still on the steering wheel. All her emotions were raw. She panicked. Breath caught in her throat. She said, not looking at him,

'Please don't come in, Christopher. I hate goodbyes. Especially now. I couldn't bear it. Please.'

'Whatever you want, Liz.'

'Let's not say — anything.'

Wretched, she blundered out of the car, eyes swimming behind her dark glasses. She almost snatched her suitcase from him. ''Bye, Christopher.'

She started to walk into the station. She had only gone a few yards when she heard,

'Liz . . .' Authoritative; quite commanding. She dropped her suitcase and turned. Christopher was leaning against the Range Rover. He was tanned from these days in the country; his fair hair blown carelessly, the white tennis sweater and open-necked shirt. 'Dishy,' Jessica would have called him at that moment, 'decidedly dishy.' He was smiling, his arms held out to her.

She ran to him.

'I couldn't let you go like that,' he murmured against her hair. 'Not without a word of love or thanks.'

Moments on a hot afternoon in a room full of shifting green light; hands clasped in the ambulance, watching Jessica's torn face; his shoulders moving beside her when he cried like a child for Vanessa.

'No need,' she murmured back. 'I wanted to thank you, too.' She meant it. He held her away from him — still smiling, a bit shaky, a bit shy.

'How I'll miss your kisses, darling Liz. Always. No one will ever kiss me like you again.'

Liz thought, *Oh yes they will, my love, Oh yes they will. Dammit*. But she laughed, too, and kissed him long and hard and lovingly; crushed in those athletic arms, quite disregarding her bruised face and the stitches that pulled.

And when she walked into the station, this time, he did not call out to her and she did not once look back.

CHAPTER 23

All the way over the Atlantic, Liz stared out at the limitless blue, at heaps of white clouds piled like meringue below; caught the flash of silver wings.

She ordered a drink, changed her mind and asked for mineral water. She ate nothing. Reading hurt her eyes – and she found it hard to concentrate. Her stitches were starting to irritate; she supposed they were healing. She would call Pete that evening. The contusions on her face had subsided. Dark glasses helped.

The stateless, limbo-like tranquillity of the plane – the smooth hum of the engines – lulled her. It was not full. She had a row of seats to herself. And she could admit, now, that she was relieved to be on the plane at all. The train journey from Cheltenham yesterday, queuing for a taxi, crossing London to the hotel, had been more of an ordeal than she had anticipated. Since the accident, she had eaten practically nothing. Her hands shook and she had difficulty walking in a straight line. A kind of delayed shock, she thought.

And Jessica?

Last night, she had 'phoned Fontwell. Katherine Vane had answered.

'I spent a few minutes at the hospital earlier, Liz.' She sounded strained and worried. 'She's holding her own, of course. But very weak, I thought, didn't you? To be expected – naturally. John Clark thinks she will be there for some time yet. Then a long period of recuperation . . .' Christopher and his father were at the hospital now. Yes, she would tell them both that she had 'phoned and sent her love.

'And bring Dick and Jason next time, Liz darling.'

'I will, Katherine. Thank you for everything. And look after yourself.'

Liz glanced at her watch. Hours to go yet. 'No, thank you,' she told the enquiring steward, she wouldn't watch the movie but she would like more water. Pérrier if possible.

She thought about Jason. His mother's apparent disintegration (breakdown?) and eventual disappearing act must be handled carefully. Very carefully indeed. She thought – and hoped she was right – that there was enough understanding between them for her to rely on her instincts. To take his lead; answer questions as they arose; deal with visitation rights when she and Dick had to. Above all, to give him a secure home. What he had seen, or understood, of the Boston ménage was impossible to gauge. Perhaps they would never know.

The practical considerations engaged her interest most. Her mind stretched and clicked. Caroline would know of a summer day camp in Westchester. Jason was fascinated by the twins. (Thank Heavens I remembered to get them yet more sweaters at the Scotch House, Liz thought.) Martha knew everything to be known about schools in New York. A larger apartment? They would see about that . . . As for friends, Dick had mentioned on the 'phone that Jason had already found one, a child of his own age whose family had recently moved into the block.

How on earth were they coping with the cat? The calm, practical Lilly must have managed something.

Of *Gibsons'*, Liz hardly thought at all. Her decision had been instinctive. Now that it was definite, it seemed no more than a natural progression. Inevitable. And yet, for three years the magazine had been a large part of her life. The largest, perhaps. There would be regrets, of course, at abandoning the people who had trusted her, given her the chance in the first place. She would miss the strong team she had built up, the excitement, the power. But someone else could take over now; build on it, impose their own ideas, do with it what they wished.

She, Liz, had rescued old *Gibsons'*; blown new life into it; kept it part of the American scene – sleeker, contemporary, talked about.

She had won.

It was enough. For her own future, she had other ideas.

Of them all, her secretary, Pam, was the one she would miss the most.

Dick would be leaving for Kennedy airport to meet her soon. She closed her eyes. Wincing, she moved her shoulder slightly. She looked out onto the calm skies. They were flying down the East coast of America. Past Boston and over Cape Cod; on down to Montauk Point, the furthest tip of Long Island.

Was Dick on his way? The captain was explaining, inaudibly, New York's weather. She must have dozed. He was not bringing Jason. He had told her that quite firmly on the 'phone last night and she agreed. They needed some time by themselves.

They were starting their descent. Liz looked at herself in her compact mirror. She grimaced and dabbed on a bit of blusher. Her hair looked awful. She had been too exhausted to wash it last night; and her left arm was still sore.

Briefly, vividly, she had a vision of Christopher's hands lying still on the steering-wheel. Long wrists; hairs growing very fair, almost white.

She dismissed the memory instantly. Nervous, she gathered up her bag and her unopened newspapers. She saw a headline. Her old friend, the Senator, had officially thrown his hat in the presidential ring. That would give Jessica some sardonic amusement when she heard. The plane banked over the beaches of Long Island, slow Atlantic breakers heaved beneath them.

Already, England seemed far away, dream-like. She could feel a changing of emotional gears. She wanted to be with Dick, to hold onto him; to be reassured by him that everything was going to be all right between them. And when she finally caught sight of him, beyond customs, she realised with a rush of pleasure that she didn't mind at all that his hair was receding. And he wasn't brushing it across his head any more. He looked very distinguished in his light suit and horn-rimmed glasses. Tall, exceptionally trim for his years. Had he always stood with such assurance?

'Dick . . .'

He saw her immediately. She had just time to register the concern on his face before she half collapsed against him. Waiting to get her passport stamped, retrieving her luggage from the carousel, had exhausted her. Unaccountably, her feet still refused to walk in a straight line. His arm went round her, he kissed her cheek very gently.

'It's okay, Liz honey. Take it easy. You're back. We'll soon have you home.' A porter materialised and her luggage was whisked away. 'Jason's going mad with excitement. He had me call twice to see if your plane was late.'

'He did?' Liz felt absurdly pleased. Her nervousness vanished. Even then, in the airport maelstrom, heads turned towards Liz. Burnished hair; long, slender legs in sling-back shoes; poised, in a tailored, cream coloured suit.

Outside the glass doors, they were met by a blast of hot, New York air — soft, humid, city-smelling. Dick signalled. A black limousine edged towards them.

'I figured this would be more comfortable than the car,' Dick said, holding her arm firmly. The driver opened the door and they settled into air-conditioned comfort. The luggage stowed, they glided off towards Manhattan.

Dick turned towards her. Very carefully, he touched her face, took off the dark glasses; saw the ugly bruises, the puckering line of stitches.

'Liz, why didn't you tell me?' He looked at her with immense concentration.

'It will go,' she said quickly, turning away. 'It's the bruising coming out. But this . . .' She indicated the stitches. 'This was quite bad. It will probably scar,' she said carelessly. She felt herself starting to shake.

'Luckily, knowing you rather well I suspected something of the kind. I've pulled the alarm bell. Pete is coming over to the apartment about five. How is Jessica? Really?'

'Poorly. Badly cut. I saw her yesterday. But she'll pull through. We thought — for a while . . . Oh God, Dick, it was so ghastly . . .'

'Don't think about it, Babe. You're back. It's over.' He held her against him. They drove in silence. The air-conditioning obliterated the sounds of streaming midday traffic, the whine of jet engines. Trucks passed them noiselessly.

'I've been thinking about Jason so much,' Liz murmured, her head on Dick's shoulder, comforted already by his staunchness, his familiarity. 'Caroline can help with a camp and Martha is an authority on schools and . . .'

'Look. We're going to take it all very steadily. It will all fall into place. He's an awfully good kid. I'm afraid it's going to be a lot of extra responsibility for you, Liz. And work.'

'I don't mind.'

'There's nothing I can say − about how grateful I am you've taken it like this.'

'I love Jason. You know that.'

He kissed her forehead. His arm tightened round her. 'I've got the legal wheels turning over custody arrangements. And there'll be no visitation rights until we're satisfied the conditions are suitable. *Linda*. Can you imagine? She was always kookie, a bit fey, but this . . . drugs, a twenty-one-year-old junkie, a commune. When he heard, Pete told me he always suspected she was neurotic, unstable. Now we know.'

'We thought Jason wasn't happy. How right we were.'

'You can say that again,' Dick agreed grimly. 'I've put the Boston house on the market, just as it is. When it's sold, I suppose I'll have to go up and do some clearing. Linda was already on that goddamned commune when I got there. I guess she couldn't face me.'

They had reached a toll bridge. The East River shone like a mirror. Skyscrapers rose behind it, sombre sentinels against the cloudless blue. The limousine floated them over the massive structure, round and down labyrinthine ramps − into Manhattan − joining the streams of traffic pouring down the East River Drive.

'Nearly home,' Dick said. 'What do you bet me that Jason's waiting downstairs on the sidewalk?'

Liz smiled. It was a good thought, being waited for by Jason.

'And guess what he and I did this morning?'

'What?'

'Shopped at Gristede's. Jason picked out everything he said you liked best. Mike came along!'

195

'Mike?'

'Jason's new friend in the block. They're about the same age. He's a cute kid.'

Liz said, 'You mean you didn't go to the office?' She sounded incredulous.

'Nope. I'm a big shot now, remember? Equity partner and all that. Slowing down. Saving myself for the big stuff. Family obligations. Priorities. And I think I'm going to like it.'

Had she heard him correctly? Did he mean it?

She lifted her head and looked up at him. 'Really? Honestly?' He smiled back at her. His eyes were very steady. He wasn't kidding; he did mean it.

'Pete?' she asked.

'Pete,' he agreed. 'And some soul-searching of my own. I've been spending a lot of time on planes between Japan and Boston recently.'

The car turned off the Drive, lurching over badly potholed streets, shooting across traffic lights, past neat, faceless apartment blocks. Liz looked out of the window. They were careering up Third now. Despite her tiredness and the perpetual ache down the side of her face, something in Liz responded to the raw vitality of the place. New York City. Steamy and fast-moving. Dirty. Noisy, despite the car's air-conditioning. Not much charm. They passed a hot-dog stand on the corner, a newsagents, a stall piled high with fruits and vegetables. The gutters were littered. Puny trees were already rimed with summer dust. Two buses lumbered past, billowing fumes.

Liz closed her eyes. She had a mental picture of Fontwell, nestling in its green hollow, shrouded in mist; of Christopher in a white tennis shirt sprinting down the path from the cottage. The picture faded. 'Here we are,' Dick was saying, 'and what did I tell you? He's there all right.'

'Okay, Champ, they're here,' Liz heard Frank, the doorman, say to Jason as she emerged onto the hot sidewalk. There was a flash of brown legs above immaculate white socks and sneakers – *Lilly*, Liz thought . . .

'Liz, Liz, Liz . . .'

Jason's skinny arms were twined round her neck. She hugged him tightly.

'Take it easy, Jason,' Dick warned. 'I told you Liz hurt her face in the crash.' Jason took no notice. 'I've been waiting and waiting and waiting, Liz.'

'I know you have, Jason. I'm back now. The waiting's over. We're all home.'

She took his hand as they walked into the lobby, Jason hopping and chattering non-stop at her side. Dick saw to the luggage, took her arm, shushed Jason. The familiar elevator doors shut.

And only a week since I left, Liz thought. A week and a bit. I still feel as though, at any moment, I'll wake up — and none of this, Fontwell, the accident, Jason here, will have happened.

Lilly was waiting for them at the door. The apartment was bright and cool, the paintings vivid against white walls. Pale rugs on the dark polished floors. A mass of yellow roses, welcoming her back, on the hall table. She followed Lilly into the kitchen while Jason helped Dick with the cases.

'Why, Mrs Conrad, you poor child,' Lilly said spontaneously as Liz took off her dark glasses.

'It looks worse than it is, Lilly. Dr McEwen is coming tonight. What I really need is a cup of tea. I expect Mr Conrad told you about the crisis with Jason's mother?'

'He told me. If you ask me, he's better off here with you and Mr Conrad.' Liz watched as Lilly filled the kettle, an old and battered relic of her Greenwich Village days. Out-of-place, but oddly comforting, in this clinically perfect kitchen.

'I think so, too, Lilly. Thanks for coping while I was away. These family things always blow up at the most inconvenient times. Mr Conrad in Japan, me in England . . .'

'He's a good child, Jason. Not a bit of trouble.' Cups and saucers rattled on the tray; a jar of cookies materialised. The kettle began to whistle and sing.

'*My God*!' Liz looked down at her feet. A very handsome black cat rubbed against her legs, sniffing the hem of her skirt with exquisite fastidiousness. Mr Woo. Liz and Lilly laughed.

'Frankly, Lilly, I've been more worried how you'd manage the cat than Jason.'

'He likes you, Liz, he does, he does. Look, he's rubbing up against you.' Jason came running into the kitchen at full tilt. He grabbed the cat and held him up for Liz to inspect.

'He's very handsome,' Liz admitted, somewhat uncertainly. She had never had anything to do with cats and wasn't sure she wanted to now. He had a bib of white fur on his chest and a white line running down the centre of his face.

'You've got very fine whiskers, Mr Woo,' Liz admitted. The cat, half strangled by Jason's enthusiastic grip, blinked majestically. 'What does he eat?'

The 'phone rang. Liz heard Dick answer it in the study.

'Tins. Lots and lots. He's very particular which ones. And he's *very* clean, isn't he, Lilly? He's got a tray. In *my* bathroom,' Jason added, eyeing Liz apprehensively.

Dick joined them. 'That was Caroline,' he said putting an arm round Liz and tickling the cat under the chin. 'She wanted to make sure we got you back in one piece. She's coming in tomorrow – about eleven. You've met Mr Woo, I see. How do you think we got along all these years without this cat?'

'Rather well, actually,' Liz said. She caught the disappointment on Jason's face. 'But I expect we'll be friends, Mr Woo and I, when we get to know each other. Great, Lilly has the tea ready.'

The 'phone rang again. Dick went to get it. 'That will either be Martha or your office. They've both been 'phoning all day. I'll handle it. You're definitely incommunicado for the present.'

CHAPTER 24

'The strangest week of my life, Pete. Like being shaken up in a kaleidoscope – and all the patterns changed forever,' Liz told him, later, as he came out of the bathroom drying his hands.

'Just what I ordered,' he said. 'Now let me have a look at this embroidery.' He moved the bedside light directly onto her face. 'Hmmm . . . he did a pretty good job that guy. Nasty cut. Where did you say it was again?'

'Casualty. Cheltenham Hospital.'

Pete opened his bag. 'Dick tells me your friend, the one who was driving, is in bad shape.'

'Fractured skull. Terribly cut about the face and arms. But she will recover.'

'Seat-belt?'

'Jessica? No – no, she wasn't. Luckily, I had mine on.'

'There was someone else in the car Dick said.'

'Yes. Jessica's brother. Christopher Vane.'

'Was he hurt?'

'Not a scratch.'

'I see. Her brother, huh?' He moved the light around. 'I'm going to snip out these stitches. It should heal up nicely.' His huge, paw-like hands were amazingly gentle. 'Hurt?' he asked, looking down at her.

'No. *Ouch*. It's okay.'

'All over. But I want to look at that shoulder.'

Cleaning up, putting his instruments away after he had examined her very carefully, Pete asked, 'So how was merrie old England – apart from crashing cars, that is?'

'Magical, Pete. Warm, sunny, green. Bewitching . . .'

199

'Bewitched, were you?' Pete looked at her over the top of his glasses, a bear of a man, hair sticking out wildly. Shrewd. A sound diviner of human nature.

'A little.' How could she explain the Cotswolds on a marvellous May day; the gardens at Fontwell, the lavender and the pinks outside the drawing-room windows? Christopher. 'Yes. A little,' she repeated. 'A little bewitched.'

Pete pulled a chair up to the bed and covered both of her hands with his.

'Now, listen, Lady . . . I've got an investment in you which you may or may not know about.'

'How come?' He could always make her smile.

'Your husband and I killed a bottle of Chival Regal the other night. Strictly in your best interests. I was attempting to knock some sense into his thick head.'

'I know. He said. 'Phoned from the airport.'

'Good. Because you two have been heading in one direction — apartness. I figured someone ought to re-introduce you. And I figured it better be me.'

'Thanks, Pete. You're a pal.'

'Damn right.'

'But I still don't see the investment.'

'*Dummy*. It was my bottle.'

Liz threw back her head and laughed. Pete turned at the door. He looked sheepish.

'Orders. Bed for two or three days. Absolutely no rushing round town. I'll look in over the weekend. No work until I give the word.' Liz nodded. 'And one more thing. You've got plenty on your plate here. Forget bewitched.'

'It's all right.'

Long after he closed the door, she was still smiling.

———

Liz tucked Jason into bed.

'I think Mom will be happier in California, don't you, Liz? It made her sick when she couldn't go there to all the meetings.' He turned his head sideways on the pillow.

'I expect so, Jason.' Liz put her hand on his shoulder. 'We'll talk about it tomorrow. Maybe you could write her a card. She'd like to hear from you. You could tell her about Mike.'

'Okay. Liz? When you're all better, could we go and see the twins and the tree house?'

———————

The sky above Manhattan was slashed with vibrant colour — pink, violet, a pale wash of blue. The first lights came on in the skyscrapers; pinpoints of silver in the dusk. Wearing a comfortable old dressing-gown, Liz padded into the living-room.

'I don't feel at all tired,' she said. 'Too wound up, perhaps. And the scar feels easier now that the stitches are out.'

'How about a drink?' Dick was mixing martinis.

'Better not.' She curled up in a corner of the sofa. 'I've hardly eaten for days. And Pete has left an array of pills I'm supposed to take.'

'He really means it about you staying home and taking things easy. An accident like that is an appalling shock to the system. And no worrying about Jason.'

'I'm not. He seems all right. He mentioned his mother to me just now, when I put him to bed. About her being happier in California.'

'God, how I cursed Linda on those flights last weekend. I was wild by the time I got to Boston. But after I had collected Jason, I simmered down. I guess she felt she couldn't cope any longer. At least she had the sense to think of Jason's wellbeing. I suppose you can say that.'

'Kids are amazing. He actually used the word "sick" about her — not being able to be in California made her "sick", he said.'

'He's smart, Jason. It's kind of nice having him around all the time. He came to the park with me this morning. Jogging.'

Liz thought he looked more relaxed than she ever remembered seeing him in New York, more like he was at the Cape.

'Dick?'

'What?'

201

She paused. 'I'm glad Caroline is coming tomorrow. She's great with kids. Jason wants to go out and see the twins again, he says. Maybe I will have a drink after all.'

Handing her a glass, Dick sat on the sofa beside her, his arm along the top.

'What were you really going to say?' he asked. He looked at her gravely. The huge, light room had suddenly darkened.

'Well . . .'

'Was it something to do with *Gibsons*'?'

'Yes.'

'You're thinking of leaving, aren't you? Resigning?'

'Yes. But how on earth did you know? When?'

Dick laughed. It sounded astonishingly like relief.

'When? I'll tell you. The moment I took your glasses off in the car this afternoon. I knew it was something important. And then it came to me – *Gibsons*'. Tell me when you decided.'

A dinner table in Chelsea, moths fluttering about the candles, Jessica opposite, Tony and Christopher beside her. Her own voice speaking strange words with such assurance . . .

'When I was away,' she said finally. 'I suppose, deep down, I had been toying with the idea for months. But in England, away from it all, I saw everything more clearly. I saw what I had to do.'

'I do understand, Liz.'

'Yes?'

He leaned back. The hum of traffic far below had lowered to its evening decibel. 'I think so. You know, in lots of ways our careers haven't been so different. That merger. I pulled it together, brought it off. I proved to everyone – and particularly myself – that I could do it. Master it all. Smell out the figures. Use the lawyers and the accountants – all the flunkeys – enough but not too much. Control the power and the greed and the egos. Orchestrate it. Make it work.'

'You did all that, Dick.'

'I did. And in a different way, it's what you did at *Gibsons*'. Rescued it. Put it on its feet. It's an accomplishment. No one can take that away from you. But

202

— *the hunger goes*. I guess that's why I was in Gristede's with the kids this morning.'

Liz laughed and touched his hand.

'That's it. Exactly.'

We do understand each other, Liz thought. We always have. I was right, there.

Dick groped for his drink on the table.

'For years, ever since Vassar, even while I was married to Jake, I've been dreaming up ideas for articles, sniffing out trends. Re-writing copy. Now I'm going to try it on my own. Freelance. Why not? I've made a name. And while everyone is buzzing about Liz Conrad leaving *Gibsons'* — and they will for a few days — I want to line up a column, a couple of contributing editorships. Maybe a book. Who knows?'

Dick said nothing. It was so dark, Liz couldn't see the expression on his face. She leant towards him.

'Dick? Don't you think I can try that — make it work?'

He said, very quietly, 'Do you want to leave me?'

'Dick — why are you even asking that?'

'In the car . . .' His voice sounded hoarse. 'I knew there was something . . . I know things got bad between us last year. I'm very aware of that. I thought this afternoon, perhaps, that you had decided. I knew something in your life had altered dramatically. I hoped — Christ how I hoped — that it was *Gibsons'*.'

Only days ago, when she left for London, they had been on the brink of estrangement. So much of the good feeling between them had evaporated. Their lives were leading them in different directions — apart. Pete had known that.

Liz thought: did I have to go away, to love Christopher, to see Jessica close to death on the roadside, to be part of the Vane family again, to understand the strength of my own marriage?

It was Dick, of the two of them, who had found the wisdom to halt the drift; Dick who had made that invaluable 'phone call from Kennedy airport to her hotel room in London.

And Christopher? She had a fleeting sense of regret, of what might have been. Then, at ease with him as with

203

nobody else in the world, she leant over and kissed Dick's cheek.

'*Gibsons*' goes. You stay,' she said, smiling in the darkness. 'Jason and me. You're stuck with us for good.'

He put his arms round her — and kept them there.

CHAPTER 25

'Good morning, again, New York . . . and it sure is a hot one . . . you can expect that temperature to go soaring right up into the nineties, today, folks . . . so all of you out there who can get to a pool or the beach count yourself mighty lucky . . .'

Coming in from the bathroom, hair still damp from a shower, Liz snapped off the radio. She tied the belt of her robe. Nearly eight. The camp bus would soon be downstairs to collect Jason. Was he ready?

'Jason,' she shouted in the hall. 'It's getting late. Have you had breakfast yet?'

Ominously, there was no reply. From the direction of Dick's study, Liz could hear the high-pitched yodelling of television cartoons. She went to investigate. Jason was sitting, cross-legged, on the floor in front of the television. He was still wearing pyjamas and eating cereal out of a packet.

'Jason Conrad! Get dressed at once. Do you know what time it is? The bus will be here any minute.'

Jason went on staring at the screen. 'I'm not going to camp today.'

Hands on her hips, speaking quietly, Liz enquired, 'What did you say, Jason?'

'I said: I'm not going to camp today.' He continued to eat his cereal. This was his third week of the daycamp in Westchester which Caroline had found for him. The first week he had been deliriously happy there, the second less so. Now – this.

Liz took a deep breath. 'Look, Jason, we agreed that you

205

would go to camp for four weeks. Until we go up to the Cape. Dad and I are working and it's a lot nicer than your hanging round the apartment all day.'

'I don't mind. I like it here.'

Liz ignored him. 'So as that was what we agreed, and as you liked the camp, you will please get dressed, collect your lunch box from Lilly, and go downstairs and wait for the bus.'

'I won't. You can't make me. You're not my mother. Not like Mom. I won't. And you can't make me.'

Liz felt the heat prickling on her neck. Despite the air-conditioning which was working furiously, heat generated by the huge windows seeped in. Whether or not it was the blazing hot morning, and the thought of the day ahead, or her natural instincts, Liz did not know. But she acted with despatch.

She snapped off the television, picked Jason up and dumped him in his room telling him she wanted to see him washed and dressed in five minutes and in the kitchen to pick up his lunch-box from Lilly — to whom he would please say thank you.

She caught the look of utter amazement on his face as she shut the door firmly.

Somewhat to her surprise, Jason did just that. There were no sulks. He kissed Liz goodbye quite cheerfully and waved to his cat. When he had left the apartment, Liz collapsed in the kitchen, shell-shocked, grasping her coffee. Minutes later, Dick came in from his morning run with a very red face and sweat pouring off his forehead.

'Fabulous day — but not in New York City. Coffee ready?' He was panting hard.

'Listen. I've just had a set-to with Jason,' Liz told him, handing him a mug. 'He didn't want to go to camp. Sitting on the floor watching idiotic cartoons was more appealing. I'm afraid I showed him who was boss round here.'

Dick laughed. 'Good girl. If I wasn't in such a muck sweat, I'd give you a kiss. Presumably, you won?'

'Yes. But I feel awful about it,' Liz said faintly.

'Don't. He had it coming. It was probably exactly what he wanted. I arrived just as the bus was moving off and he looked fine. I got a very cheery wave and grin.' He gulped his coffee. 'Don't worry, honey. It's all in the days' work with kids. I'm off to shower.'

While they were getting dressed, Liz went back to her row with Jason. 'I still feel bad about it,' she said. 'I was quite rough on him.' Knotting his tie in the mirror, Dick looked over at her with a serious expression.

'I'm afraid we've got to expect these outbursts from Jason. Testing us versus Linda. He's bound to do it.'

'I can cope.' Liz took a beige linen dress out of her closet.

'Sure. But I'm sorry you have to.'

'And another thing . . .' She was searching for a matching belt.

'What?'

'I've decided to spring it on them today. *Gibsons'*.'

'Nothing to do with Jason, I hope?'

Liz shook her head. 'Me. To do with me only. I promise.'

It was four weeks since she had returned from England. Under Pete's orders, she had only gone back to the office at the beginning of last week. Her stitches had healed to a fine red line, but her arm and shoulder, deeply bruised, still gave her pain. She had agreed with Dick that she should work for at least a week before resigning, to be absolutely sure in her own mind. That time was up.

'My heart has gone out of it,' Liz said. 'It depresses me, starting projects I won't finish. Knowing. I'd rather have it out in the open at once and get on with other things.'

'Then do it.' Dick put his hands on her shoulders and kissed her cheek. 'And good luck. Call if you need any support. We'll eat out tonight. A celebration. And you swear you won't beat it to the nearest commune?'

Going through the mail as she left the apartment, Liz found a letter from Jessica. She read it on the bus as it lumbered downtown. Her eyes skimmed the densely written pages.

She, Jessica, was back at Fontwell, still feeling pretty rocky but recovering. The plastic surgeon hoped to do the first graft quite soon. (Liz suppressed a shudder.) Tony had been a brick and raced back and forth between London and

Gloucestershire. He was keeping an eye on the shop, too, and they had had their best month ever. 'Trust Tony! Mother and Dad seem quite helpful and content. No explosions, you'll be glad to hear. In fact, we're talking rather a lot these days, Mother and I. The Hugo confessional seems to have broken down some barriers − for both of us. Kate is gorgeous and about to take off and walk at any moment.' She only mentioned Christopher at the end. 'He's back here permanently, of course. Last weekend, he invited a ridiculous girl called Fiona down from London. She giggled non-stop and talked about nothing but "Lady Di". Even Dad got fed up − and she was exceedingly young and pretty . . .'

Walking the few blocks from the bus stop to the office, even then, at nine o'clock in the morning, the heat was fierce. She kept to the side of the street which was still shady.

A girl called Fiona who was exceedingly young and pretty . . .

She was pleased for him, for Christopher. It was what they all hoped would happen. Wasn't it? All the same, something ached. She shifted her bag to the other arm and began to compose, in her head, the letter she was about to write.

———

Liz entered *Gibsons'* offices with relief. It was wonderfully cool, all polished floors and trailing greenery. Already, there was an air of activity; 'phones ringing, typewriters clicking; the immaculate receptionist at her desk in the foyer.

'Good morning, Mrs Conrad,' 'Morning, Liz,' 'Hi.'

Taking off her cotton jacket, already creased by the heat, Liz looked round her handsome office. The canyons, still half shadowed, stretched down to the tip of Manhattan where the blue sky was flushed with pink. Her desk was covered in neat piles − the mail sorted and files to be attended to. A list of 'phone calls she must make that morning.

It would be so easy to change her mind at that particular moment. Call Dick and say, I've decided not today; next week, maybe; maybe not at all. Say that perhaps, after all, I was wrong. I still want it. The 'phone was there, she had only to lift the receiver, dial an outside line.

And she was, in fact, giving up a great deal. All of this — the power and the money and the prestige. Work which she often enjoyed, which often gave her deep satisfaction. Everything she had worked for all her adult life. A very considerable New York success.

And there was no guarantee that she could use it to build from. She was an editor and an administrator. Not a writer, however good her ideas, however crisp her editing. At least, not yet.

She sat and pulled a file towards her. She ran her finger along the edge of her desk. Then she pressed the bell to summon her secretary.

'Oh Pam,' she said, looking up with a quick smile. Confident and goodlooking. Liz Conrad of *Gibsons*'. Doing a great job, doing it with style and verve. Nobody could have guessed what was going through her mind at that moment. 'Come in, Pam,' she said, 'and close the door. There's a letter I want you to take for me. Now.'

Liz left the office early after working straight through the sweltering lunch hour. She needed to gather strength for tomorrow's onslaught, when her letter of resignation would hit. And she could no longer bear Pam's moist, hurt eyes. 'I can't believe it, Liz,' she had said, hearing Liz's words, pencil poised. 'I just can't believe it, that's all.'

Liz began walking uptown quite fast. It was a little like swimming through pea soup. Subway air-holes erupted in steam and the tarred street surfaces softened. Her face was damp behind the dark glasses. Bare arms helped; she had left her jacket in the office. Tempers were short and nerves frayed; horns blared. Liz watched a sweating, shirt-sleeved cab-driver bawling out of his open window at another car.

Conscious of her arms in the hot sun, Liz reflected that during these past four weeks of living with Jason, she had come in for several surprises. (Doubtless, there would be more.) One was the amount of decisions she was called upon to make on his behalf every day — yes, you can have tuna fish sandwiches; yes, you must take your sweater; no, you can't stay up to watch a horror movie on TV; yes, Mike can eat dinner with us if he asks his mother. It was endless; an aspect of parenthood she had never fully realised.

Another minor surprise had been the rate at which normal little boys like Jason dispensed with shirts. 'I put my arms up, Liz, and it broke. Right down the back, Liz. Honestly.' She pushed her way into a department store and was met by a blast of Arctic air. She took the escalator up to the children's department on the third floor.

An hour later, exhausted, she got back to the apartment. It was pale and cool and immaculate. Four o'clock. It was Lilly's afternoon off and Jason wouldn't be returning from camp for at least another hour. She dumped her packages in the bedroom and went into the kitchen to get a glass of iced tea. The 'phone rang.

Liz took it in the living-room which gleamed in the full afternoon sun. There was a pause and an echoing sound. She stood very still. She knew that it was Christopher.

'Liz . . .' His voice coming from so far away, from a different world.

'Christopher? Hullo . . .'

'I never thought you would be in. I worked out the times. But I tried anyhow. Are you busy?'

He meant, are you alone? Can we talk?

Liz said, 'Lucky. I left the office early today. There's no one else here.'

'I miss you terribly.'

Uplifted with joy; a small moment of triumph. She looked out at the vast sweep of blue sky where planes darted like silver birds.

'I know,' she said. 'I do know, Christopher. How is Jessica?'

'Improving. Quite remarkably. And Kate has taken a step or two. And what's life like with Jason?'

'Up and down. All right, I think. His mother, we hear, has left the commune. She lasted there exactly a week. But she's staying in California.'

There was a tiny silence. The line hummed. He would be

'phoning from the cottage, that long room filled with chintz and books and photographs.

'Liz, I said, I miss you terribly. It was . . .'

'Special. Extraordinary. For both of us.'

'For both?'

'Yes. And thank you for 'phoning. I'm glad you did.' It was an effort to keep her voice quite steady. 'Goodbye, Christopher, goodbye.'

Liz replaced the receiver and stood for some time looking across Manhattan, watching the sun strike those bridges which span the East River.

That night, Liz remembered it particularly, Dick said, 'Why don't we throw away those pills?'

'What pills?'

'The blue and silver packet in the bathroom with the arrow pointing to Day 1, Friday . . . which happens to be tomorrow.'

Liz laughed. 'My, but you're observant. That's fine with me. I think we may have had this conversation before . . .'

(Given time, and affection, the unsayable could, after all, be erased, Liz reflected. Cousin May had been wrong about that.)

Holding onto Dick very tightly she said, 'Dr Mattson said, when I saw him . . .'

'Why don't we see what we can do by ourselves – and then call in Mattson?'

A few days after the bombshell of her surprise resignation from *Gibsons'*, Liz appeared on a live television talk show.

'Half the time I'm in the office I feel like crying,' she said, explaining her action. 'I hate to leave the team we've built up. That hurts. But I felt, for me, it was time to move on. I've got a typewriter – and I'm going to write. Freelance. And I'm open to offers . . .'

The 'phone, at home and in the office, never stopped ringing.

Liz rated five lines – she counted – on Page 2 of *The New York Times*. Pam was continually on the verge of tears, no help at all.

———————

'You must be out of your mind. Crazy,' Martha screamed at her down the 'phone. 'Every woman in New York envied you that job. Listen, when you come out to the Island for the weekend, I really want to know *why*. Okay?'

———————

'I think you're right. You've had enough,' Caroline told her when they had a quick lunch together. 'I wish – Oh well, it doesn't matter.'

———————

'No regrets,' she told Dick later, when he asked. 'A reasonable choice all round, I think. And did Jason tell you about the award he won in camp today?'

'He sure did. And I forgot to tell you something. You know we were talking about getting a larger apartment, close to that school we're thinking of for Jason?' Liz nodded. 'I had a guy in my office this afternoon who's moving here with his family from LA. One kid in college. He knows this building and says he likes it. His wife is here, apartment-hunting. She's going to call you tomorrow and come over. Okay? You never know, it might be just what they're looking for.'

'Right.' Liz stared at a large canvas on the opposite wall, bleeding reds and oranges that had never made any sense to her at all. 'And I'll tell you something else. We could throw a couple of abstract impressionist paintings in with the deal . . .'

POSTSCRIPT

'Can we always spend New Year's Eve at the Cape, Liz? Like this. Always and always,' Jason pleaded.

They were at the cottage, sitting on the rug in front of a blazing log fire. The Parcheesi board, a Christmas present from the twins and Jason's latest enthusiasm, lay between them. A severe Atlantic gale was blowing, battering the clapboard cottage. Waves pounded against the sea wall at the bottom of the garden.

'Always? We'll try to, Jason. If the weather's not too bad – and if I can arrange it. I promise.'

'I understand, Liz.' He nodded gravely with his old man's expression. 'Come on, come on. Your shake, Liz. *I'm winning.*'

'Not so fast, young man. And no cheating, you two.' Dick put his head round the kitchen door. It was nearly midnight and he was wrestling with a bottle of champagne.

They all looked fit, their faces chafed from walks in the wind along empty beaches, watching Jason jump, spread-eagled, from the dunes. After a loud bang, Dick came in with a tray and three glasses.

'A drop for you, too, Jason. This year is special.' Settled on the floor, Dick lifted his glass. 'Happy New Year, everyone.'

They clinked glasses solemnly. Jason rubbed his eyes, trying to disguise a yawn.

'Liz.' Dick leaned over and kissed her where the scar on her forehead was gradually fading. 'Happy New Year,' he repeated.

'You, too. And Jason.' She held up crossed fingers. 'To all of us . . .'

'And you're looking very good tonight, Liz Conrad,' Dick said, leaning back on his elbows, admiring. They all wore heavy, turtle-necked sweaters. (Jason had one on over his pyjamas.) Liz's face had filled out; she was clear-eyed; her mane of hair, more grey than tawny now, was brushed back from her forehead.

'Yes?' She smiled at him, and her eyes crinkled at the corners. 'My new persona must suit me.'

'Your turn, Dad, your turn,' Jason said, watching them impatiently.

'Look,' Liz said. 'You two are winning. Battle it out between yourselves.'

'Okay. Ready, Dad?'

They faced each other, crouched over the board. So alike, Liz thought with affection. Wanting to win, both of them, even this game. Lean, tense, determined, as they shook the dice furiously, red chasing blue to home base.

Liz reached up for a cushion from the sofa, wedging it behind her back, moving her legs to a more comfortable position. She could hear the pitch of the storm grow louder. She thought back over the year that was passing.

For months, now, workmen had been tramping through their new apartment in a solid old block on the West Side. Conveniently, it was round the corner from Jason's school. Liz's study had already become her refuge: She wrote there, and several articles had already been published. She had retained a monthly column in *Gibsons'*. She was considering a book. She knew that she had been lucky in her professional transition.

Her thoughts wandered to Jessica. Silently, she wished her – and Kate – a happy new year. She knew that the facial surgery had not ended; she needed at least two more minor operations. But she had resumed her old life in London and the previous summer, she and Tony had spent a couple of weeks away in France.

Christopher had sent them a Christmas card, illegibly scrawled; The Cottage, Fontwell Manor, Gloucestershire printed along the bottom.

Liz did not want to think about Christopher. Not then.

She drank her champagne.

'I've won, I've won.' Jason jumped up, tiredness banished.

'Fair enough. Shake hands,' Dick told him crisply, getting to his feet. 'My turn to tuck you in. Say goodnight.'

'And Liz,' Jason's arms clung round her neck, postponing the inevitable. 'Dad thinks we should build a proper patio. He said so today, didn't you, Dad?'

'We're thinking about it. By the summer, Jason, maybe. Next summer.'

He took him firmly off to bed.

Next summer. Liz placed both hands on her stomach. She glanced down at her watch. A minute past midnight. This, now, was the year.

Soon, she felt definite movement beneath the folds of her corduroy smock. Her heart lurched both in excitement and terror.

Next summer, Dick had said.

But long before then, she could almost count the weeks — in the springtime of the year — their child would be born.

Judith Michael

The new bestseller by the author of *Deceptions*

Possessions

'A believable modern odyssey, a woman's search for identity unburdened by melodrama or undue gimmickry.' *Publishers Weekly*

Katherine and Craig Fraser had shared ten golden, loving years together. Then one day Craig vanished leaving Katherine with two children, no job, no money – and the discovery that her husband had been living a double life.

Severing all ties with the past, Katherine and her children flee to San Francisco. There she discovers the wealthy Hayward family – the family from which Craig had fled fifteen years ago. Swept into the whirl of Californian society, Katherine forges a life richer and more meaningful than anything she had ever had with Craig. Until she realises that it's not the future which threatens her happiness, but the past and its claim on the most valuable possession of all . . .

FICTION   0 7221 6042 9   £2.95

Also by Judith Michael in Sphere Books:
DECEPTIONS

Britain's most controversial agony aunt tells her own story

Anna

R A E B U R N

Talking to Myself

'This book is not about success. It's about learning to survive on my own terms.

It is also *the truth*. Some of it will surprise you and some of it may even shock. It would have been easier to make myself nicer than I am and to have pretended that there were no dreadful mistakes. But I tried to tell the truth rather than have some shadow from my pale purple past leap up.

For years I've been asking other people to face up to the truth about themselves and their lives.

This book is about practising what you preach.'

AUTOBIOGRAPHY   0 7221 7216 8   £1.95

A selection of bestsellers from SPHERE

FICTION

TOUGH GUYS DON'T DANCE	Norman Mailer	£2.50 ☐
FIRE IN THE ICE	Alan Scholefield	£2.25 ☐
SOUVENIR	David Kaufelt	£2.50 ☐
WHAT NIALL SAW	Brian Cullen	£1.25 ☐
POSSESSIONS	Judith Michael	£2.95 ☐

FILM & TV TIE-INS

MOG	Peter Tinniswood	£1.95 ☐
LADY JANE	A. C. H. Smith	£1.95 ☐
IF I WERE KING OF THE UNIVERSE	Danny Abelson	£1.50 ☐
BEST FRIENDS	Jocelyn Stevenson	£1.50 ☐

NON-FICTION

WEEK ENDING: THE CABINET LEAKS	Ian Brown and James Hendrie	£2.95 ☐
THE POLITICS OF CONSENT	Francis Pym	£2.95 ☐
THE SPHERE ILLUSTRATED HISTORY OF BRITAIN VOLUMES 1, 2 AND 3		£3.95 each
	Ed. Kenneth O. Morgan	☐

All Sphere books are available at your local bookshop or newsagent, or can be ordered direct from the publisher. Just tick the titles you want and fill in the form below.

Name _____

Address _____

_____

Write to Sphere Books, Cash Sales Department, P.O. Box 11, Falmouth, Cornwall TR10 9EN.

Please enclose a cheque or postal order to the value of the cover price plus:

UK: 55p for the first book, 22p for the second book and 14p for each additional book ordered to a maximum charge of £1.75.

OVERSEAS: £1.00 for the first book plus 25p per copy for each additional book.

BFPO & EIRE: 55p for the first book, 22p for the second book plus 14p per copy for the next 7 books, thereafter 8p per book.

Sphere Books reserve the right to show new retail prices on covers which may differ from those previously advertised in the text or elsewhere, and to increase postal rates in accordance with the PO.